Raves for Michael Baron's *When You Went Away*:

"Nicholas Sp—— fans will rejoice to hear there's a
new male au——
about love a——
Tears of sad——
mensely sati——
is Baron's fi——

— RT Book Reviews

"Michael Baron writes with such depth that the
emotions were tangible. It is rare that a talent like
this comes along. This will be a classic. This is one
to read and recommend."

— BookreviewsRus

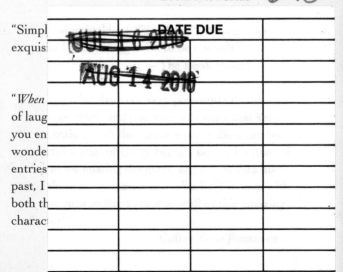

"Simpl——
exquis——

"*When*——
of laug——
you en——
wonde——
entries——
past, I——
both th——
charac——

"Touching, tender and gentle, the moments between father and son in *When You Went Away* pull at the heartstrings and the tear ducts . . . an exceptional read, and one that makes me want to watch for more works by this author in the future."

– Freelancing and Fiction

"Michael Baron creates an unforgettable tale. . . . I truly loved this story. It is so well-written that it's hard to keep yourself separate from the fictional characters. I absolutely recommend this book and plan to read every other work written by this author. Triple-A reading!"

– Fresh Fiction

"A gem. I couldn't put it down. The characters are people I'd like to know."

– Peggy Webb, author of the Southern Cousins Mystery Series

"More than a novel about grief and fatherhood; it's a novel about being lost and the journey to find the right path."

– Savvy Verse & Wit

Crossing the Bridge

a novel by

MICHAEL BARON

THE
STORY PLANT

The Story Plant
The Aronica-Miller Publishing Project, LLC
P.O. Box 4331
Stamford, CT 06907

Copyright © 2010 by The Fiction Studio

Cover and interior design by Barbara Aronica-Buck

ISBN-13: 978-0-9819568-1-7
Visit our website at
www.thestoryplant.com

First Story Plant Printing:
January 2010
Printed in the United States of America
10 9 8 7 6 5 4 3 2 1

DEDICATION

To A, for always keeping my hopes alive.

I marvel at what you're becoming.

ACKNOWLEDGEMENTS

As always, my wife and kids were a huge source of inspiration and sustenance during the writing of this novel.

I'd also like to thank the brother I never knew for putting mysteries in my head that I've only begun to explore in this novel.

Thanks to Danny Baror and the people at The Story Plant for their encouragement.

Thanks, Barb, for the beautiful design.

Thanks to Ann Pearlman for the thoughtful cover comments.

I'd like to thank the towns of Essex, CT and Lennox, MA for being sources of inspiration and endless stationery stores on Long Island for allowing me my research time.

Music is always a tremendous source of inspiration for me. As such, I'd like to thank Lucy Kaplansky, Lowell George, Richard Shindell, Fountains of Wayne, and the irreplaceable Kurt Cobain for being especially inspiring this time.

Crossing the Bridge

CHAPTER ONE
One Definite Destination

They closed the Pine River Bridge for six hours after my brother drove off it. I heard that the rush hour commute was a nightmare that day. I remember thinking that Chase, who loved to make fun of the "drones" heading to Hartford every morning in their Brooks Brothers suits, would have found it satisfying to see so many of them backed up on River Road, chafing at the maintenance crews who couldn't possibly appreciate how valuable their time was. Chase could find entertainment in practically anything. He would have found even this amusing.

By the time the police reopened the bridge for traffic, my mother was on her third Valium and my father hadn't moved from the window in hours. I wasn't sure what he thought he would find by looking out there. It wasn't Chase. Richard Penders knew his son was gone forever.

I sat in the living room with them for hours, sharing their suffering and their astonishment at the way life pivots. But other thoughts filled my mind as well, thoughts of something I couldn't ever talk about to them. Chase and I had been together only a few hours before he died. His personality changed when he was drunk, and he had a lot to drink by the time I met up with him. The alcohol had made him say things I didn't want to hear, and when I'd had enough, we'd argued and I'd left him to make his way home on his own.

I should have known not to let him drive. Before I got in my car and took off, wondering what the hell was wrong with him, I should have reminded myself that my annoyance with him was temporary. Then I should have taken him with me to sleep off his foul mood. That I didn't, that I tossed it off with the easy confidence that I had the luxury of being pissed at him and that I would always be there when Chase really needed me, was something I knew I was going to have to live with. But I knew I couldn't share it with my parents. If I ever admitted in any way that I had anything to do – even tangentially – with their son's death, I don't know where that would have left me in the family.

I couldn't move myself to try to console Chase's girlfriend Iris until the wake. They'd been together for nearly a year and I knew she needed consolation at least as much as the rest of us. But as soon as I thought of her, I convinced myself that I wasn't the person she needed to get this from, that in fact she might prefer no comfort at all to any she would receive from me.

Though at eighteen Chase was three years my junior, he'd gone on his first date before me and always had more women around him. Iris was the first one – after many had flitted in his space before her – who didn't seem like a groupie. She was centered and

soft-spoken. And it was only when he was around
Iris that Chase showed any desire to let someone take
care of him. She was the only person I'd ever seen
him willingly defer to, though even then it didn't happen often.

I found it fascinating to watch the two of them in
action. At least until the day that I realized that what
really fascinated me was watching *Iris* in action. Long
after it began, I became cognizant of how completely
she had taken residence in my thoughts. I thought
about talking to her, sharing quick snippets of conversation, a meaningful glance over my brother's es-
capades. I thought about what the two of them were
like alone together, laughing, kissing, making love.
This was very new territory for me. It wasn't simply
that I hadn't thought this way about any of my
brother's previous girlfriends. I hadn't thought this
way about any woman at all. It was simultaneously
disorienting and seductive. I considered it all harm-
less fantasizing on my part.

Until the day that it went beyond that.

On the first warm day of the early spring, when
Chase left me to await Iris' arrival while he attended
to other business – something he was doing with
greater frequency – Iris and I kissed. Before it happened and even more so afterward, I was conflicted
and unsteady. But while we were kissing, maybe
thirty seconds that redefined the act for me, I knew
that this was precisely what I should be doing, what
I needed to be doing. And in the moment, Iris' reac-
tions seemed to echo mine. At first, she seemed confused to be moving toward me, and afterward she
looked at me with embarrassment and regret. But

while it was happening, I remain certain that Iris was fully and willingly there with me.

From then until the day Chase died, I tried my best to avoid being with them. I came home from college less often on the weekends and made certain never to be alone in a room with Iris. It wasn't that I didn't think I could control myself. I just couldn't bear to see the warning in her eyes.

When I arrived with my parents at the wake, Iris was sitting alone in Chase's viewing room in the funeral parlor. Chase had been dead fifteen hours at that point and I'd spent most of that time standing guard over my mother, watching her watching the distance. While I did, I replayed my last conversation with my brother, thinking about how leaving this home – something I'd planned to do once college was over anyway – would have an entirely different meaning to me now. Chase would forevermore occupy every chair and glance out from every picture frame. These were the thoughts I'd been tape-looping since the police officer had come to the door to tell us about the accident. But still, when I saw Iris sitting by herself, the very first thing that came to my mind was, *do I touch her?*

I approached her tentatively, hoping that someone would get there before me or that she would make some movement that would give me an indication of what to do. Instead, her eyes stayed focused on the casket at the front of the room. When I was only a few feet away from her, she turned in my direction. She stood and we embraced awkwardly, our stomachs and heads touching briefly and then pulling away. Then she sat down quickly. My parents were settling into seats in the row reserved for immediate family and I knew that I should join them, but I felt compelled to sit with Iris, at least for a short while.

The first time I met Iris, I thought she was beautiful. All of my brother's girlfriends were beautiful, so this didn't surprise me in any way. What did surprise me was that she seemed more beautiful to me as I got to know her and as I got to see her from a wide variety of perspectives. She was more stunning with disheveled hair after wrestling with Chase, with a flushed face after a snowball fight, with clothes spattered electric blue after helping my brother paint his room. And she seemed nearly unearthly now, with her eyes thickly encircled in red, her cheeks ruddy. Looking at her this way, I somehow felt that her loss had been greater than mine.

"Anything I say would be inadequate," I said to her. She glanced over at me, pressed her lips together in a semblance of a smile, and reached out to give my hand a momentary squeeze.

"I'm so sorry for you," she said. "I'm so sorry for Chase." She turned from me and leaned forward to touch my mother's shoulder, and my mother held her head against Iris' for the longest time, both of them sobbing. When Iris sat back again, she didn't attempt to dab at her eyes. And she didn't try to look in my direction.

I wanted something other than that kiss to be between us at that point. I wished she and Chase had been together for years so my role for her could have been more brotherly. I wished that the age difference between us had been greater so I could have simply put her head on my shoulder and cried with her. I wished I could have said to her, "Give this time. We'll work through it together." But all I could do was sit there confused, wondering how to fit this new collection of wishes into the set of things I was already hoping had turned out differently.

"I need to go with them," I said after a while.

She nodded without turning.

When the funeral was over, I didn't see Iris again. As she left the gravesite, she brushed her lips on my cheek and said good-bye. Her parents had come with her and, as he walked past me, her father clapped his hand on my arm and gestured upward with his chin. My eyes moved from his to Iris' back, only leaving there when another friend of Chase's approached me.

For the rest of that summer, I attempted to set myself in motion. Motion of any type might have sufficed, but I found myself rooted to my room, my Discman burning dozens of batteries. I started skipping dinners when I realized that I could find no sustenance in my mother's open-throated sorrow or my father's empty resolve. I've heard that grief sometimes pulls families together. But I had no experience with that. I never felt more untethered in my life than I did in those months after the accident. It wasn't simply that I didn't know how to act or when any sense of pleasure or laughter or peace would return. It was that I also didn't know where I would be or who I would be with when they did.

The summer was ending and my senior year at Emerson College was ready to begin. But as I packed during the third week of August, I knew it wasn't for Boston. When I got in the car, I still didn't know where I would end up driving. But as I crossed the Pine River Bridge, I had one definite destination in mind.

Anywhere but here.

CHAPTER TWO
Taking Inventory

Since leaving Amber, Connecticut on that late August day, I'd never stayed anywhere for more than a year and a half and never held the same job for more than fourteen months. I still have the dress shirts and ties from the one ludicrous attempt I'd made at office work in Atlanta when I was twenty-seven. Those ten months coincided with the time I spent with Emily, and both experiments ended on the same day. Beyond that there were five months doing telephone sales in Wilmington (three of which were spent with Susan) and seven months making sandwiches in Columbus. There was a year, maybe my best, with Gillian in Richmond during which I sold real estate for ten months. I spent a couple of seasons doing data entry in Houston and a summer at a Public Radio station in Minneapolis (which turned into a sizzling fall and a very chilly winter with Kristina). In one or two of the jobs and even some of the romances, I'd given thought to what might happen if I dug deeper. But I tended to view such notions as fanciful, much in the way that some others would think about running away from it all.

I'd been in New England again, first in Concord,

New Hampshire, then in Portland, Maine, and most recently in Springfield, Massachusetts, for the past couple of years when my father got sick. I'd been home on a number of occasions since leaving, but never stayed very long. I couldn't help but get the impression that my being in the household only served to remind my parents that Chase wouldn't be coming for a visit.

When my mother called to tell me about my father's heart attack, she insisted that it was nothing to worry about. I nearly believed her until she mentioned "a little angioplasty" that he'd had done the year before. For the first time since I'd been gone, the possibility that one of them might die while I was out looking for my next thing became real to me.

"I'll come down the day after tomorrow," I said.

"I didn't call to alarm you."

"It doesn't matter why you called. And you aren't alarming me. If Dad's in the hospital, I should come to see him."

"That might be a good idea."

My father seemed devoid of color lying there in the bed. Not simply his face, but everything about him seemed washed out, diluted. My mother didn't get up to greet me, but simply reached out a hand. I leaned over to kiss her and then him.

"What are they saying?" I said.

My mother patted my father's hand. "He's going to be fine."

My father grunted. "Yeah, as long as I don't do anything strenuous – like move."

"Richard, don't say things like that."

My father cocked his eyes toward me. "I'm fine,

Hugh. The doctor is talking about certain 'lifestyle changes,' but hasn't exactly told me what those might be."

I sat down on the other chair in the room. It dawned on me that when I envisioned my parents, I always saw them as vulnerable. Still, I was surprised at how defenseless my father appeared.

"What's going on with the store?" I said.

My father looked quickly over to my mother. "Tyler's in charge while we sort this out."

"Tyler?" I didn't remember hearing the name before.

"He's my manager."

This meant that Tyler was no older than twenty. My father had always steadfastly refused to staff his stationery and gift store with anything other than high school and college kids, arguing, "What could I expect from an adult who was willing to work in a card store?" The logic made a certain amount of sense and it had essentially served him well. But his business model didn't accommodate situations such as this one.

"Have you spoken to him lately?"

"He called yesterday and gave me a complete rundown. I told him I didn't want him worrying about calling me every day. He's fine. He's been with me for two years. He knows the place."

I looked over at my mother, who was studiously avoiding eye contact.

"I can take a few days if you want me to look in on the store while you recover," I said, knowing as the words left my mouth that this was just about the last thing in the world I wanted to do.

My mother's face lifted. "You don't have to get back to Springfield?"

"I can take a little time."

"Tyler's a good kid," my father said. "I'm sure he can handle everything." He stopped, as though he wasn't sure that the doctor would approve of the effort required to keep talking to me about this. "But I would appreciate it if you checked to see that everything is okay."

• • •

I got to the store midmorning the next day. Amber Cards, Gifts, and Stationery (rumor has it that my father actually labored over the naming of his store. I could imagine him considering, "Is it Amber Gifts, Cards, and Stationery? Amber Stationery, Cards, and Gifts? If I just called it Amber Stationery, would people surmise that we also had cards and gifts?") had been a fixture on Russet Avenue since before I was born. My father spent his first few years out of college managing a warehouse for an office supply manufacturer in Hartford. When a couple of stock investments he made shot through the roof, he took one of the few risks in his life and moved to the emerging riverside town of Amber to open the shop on its main street. Thirty-four years later, my father could never claim to have had a windfall year (or, for that matter, another investment that scored the way that pair in the '70s did, even during the Internet boom). But he would boast that his "little enterprise" had given his family "everything they needed to get by."

I spent enough after-school hours and summers working in the store to know that small-time retailing was not in my DNA. I didn't have the disposition to placate customers when the supermarket inserts were missing from the local paper or when we ran out of red poster board the night before a class project was due. That required a level of patience and concern that I simply didn't have. I never once felt shortchanged.

It had probably been five years since I'd stepped foot in the store. My father had moved the card racks, and the merchandise at the front was more focused on lower-priced items than I remembered. But the vibe was very much the same. Generic instrumental versions of popular songs peeking from the speakers, a handful of people pondering Hallmark sentiments, the guy breezing in to buy a copy of *Forbes*, the woman with the three-year-old looking at the figurines as a gift for Aunt Claire.

There was a young woman dusting shelves who continued to do so even as a customer asked her a question and there was a guy behind the counter taking notes from a textbook. I walked over to him.

"Are you Tyler?" I asked.

He glanced up from his reading. "Yeah, hi."

"I'm Hugh Penders, Richard's son."

He tilted his head for a moment as though he didn't understand what I was saying. I imagined him thinking, *Richard's son? But isn't Richard's son dead?* Then his eyes brightened.

"Oh, hey, yeah." He reached out his hand. "I'm Tyler – which you already know. How's it going with your dad?"

"It depends on who you ask. According to him, he'll be in this afternoon. Seems the doctors have different ideas, though."

"I'm sure it's driving Richard crazy to sit in a hospital instead of being here. I've been meaning to get over to see him, but between the extra hours I'm putting in and studying for a bunch of tests I have coming up, it's been tough."

Tyler seemed to be the latest in a line of college kids my father occasionally happened upon who actually thought it was worth *doing* their part-time jobs as opposed to simply showing up for them. It was apparent in the way he talked about my father. I began to relax a little. I'd been dreading meeting Dad's latest "manager" from the moment I first learned about him in the hospital. Some of the people Dad had entrusted with responsibility over the years had been truly unworthy of the gift.

"I'm sure he understands," I said. "Listen, I'm in town for a few days and I told my father that I'd spend a little time giving you a hand."

Tyler looked briefly insulted, which I also took to be a good sign. "Yeah, great," he said. "Could always use a little help." He leaned in to me conspiratorially and gestured toward his dusting colleague. "Leeza's not exactly MBA material, if you know what I mean."

I nodded and looked over to see her absently straightening cards. "Mind if I come back behind the counter?"

"No, come on in. I assume you know your way around the place."

"I haven't been here in a while, actually," I said as

I surveyed the desk. "The cash register is different from when I was last here. He still has the hourly log book, I see."

"Man, does he ever. You miss a register reading and it's like you shot his dog."

For the next half hour, Tyler briefed me on the operations of the store. I rang up a couple of sales and helped a customer find graph paper. It felt precisely as it had when I was seventeen – like something that stood between waiting in line at the Department of Motor Vehicles and shoveling snow in entertainment value.

Russet Avenue is designed for foot traffic and browsers. There's parallel parking on the street and a couple of municipal lots around back. Among other things, there's an inn, a craft shop, a print gallery, a few restaurants, a jewelry designer, and a chocolatier for the tourists, and a bank, a drug store, and my father's store for the locals. I'm not sure which category of consumer I fit into at this point, though I certainly hadn't returned to Amber for its quaint New England flavor. As the morning turned into afternoon, Tyler returned to his books and I spent a lot of time watching pedestrians out the window from behind the counter. I remembered quiet afternoons such as this when I felt shackled to the store and believed that every other teenager in Amber had something more interesting going on.

It was while daydreaming that I saw Iris entering the gourmet food shop across the street. As I watched, my thoughts ranged from wondering if it was actually her, to how I would respond if she walked in here, to considering going to the stockroom until the moment passed.

When I saw Iris come out of the shop and head down the street, I decided it was foolish to pretend (or even wish) that I hadn't seen her. I told Tyler I'd be back in a few minutes and went out the door. I was crossing the street and she was about to walk into the bakery when I called out her name. She turned in my general direction, but didn't make eye contact for several seconds. When she did, she seemed stupefied by the sight, as though we were standing on a street in Bali rather than in the town where we both grew up.

"What are you doing here?" she asked as I walked up to her. I noticed her eyes scanning me from head to toe. She didn't seem to be appraising me; it was as though she was taking inventory.

"I read about this place in a guidebook and decided to check it out," I said.

"You look good. You seem – taller."

"Yeah, I get that a lot."

She looked stunning to me. I was surprised at how my memory had failed to do her justice. Her hair was shorter than I remembered, but her eyes seemed even more cobalt, her skin smoother, her posture even more approachable.

"So what *are* you doing here? Last I heard, you were off wandering the globe."

"Yeah, moving from suburb to suburb in search of thrills. I finally got tired of the fast lane and decided to stop by for a little small town calm." As I said this, I rolled my eyes to make sure that she understood I was being ironic. "Actually, my dad's sick and I'm here to check up on him."

Concern darkened her expression. "Is he okay?"

"I think so. I'm gonna watch the store for him for a few days."

"Wow, things *have* changed."

"Well I guess you can do anything for a few days, huh? So what are you doing here? You haven't moved back, have you?"

"God, no. I live in Lenox now. I come down every month or so to see my mom. My dad died a few years ago."

"I'm sorry to hear that. He seemed like a good guy."

Iris nodded and looked up the street. I couldn't tell if she was thinking about her father or feeling uncomfortable about seeing me.

"Do you want to go grab a cup of coffee?" I said.

She wrinkled her nose. "I can't. I've got a few more stops to make and I told my mother I wouldn't be gone long."

I shook my head and looked down at my shoes.

"That just sounded like I was blowing you off, didn't it?"

"No, your mom doesn't like to be alone. I get it."

"Actually, my mom is fine being alone. She just gets irrational if I tell her I'm only going to be gone a short while and then I come back a few hours later. Even if I call her." She chortled. "Mothers. You're here for a few days?"

"Yeah, three or four probably, assuming everything turns out okay with my father."

"I'm going to be here until the weekend. Do you want to get a drink sometime?"

"That would be good," I said, disproportionately cheered by the fact that she wasn't blowing me off. "Tomorrow night?"

"I'd like that. I'll meet you at the Cornwall at, say, 8:30?"

"The Cornwall. Yeah, absolutely."

"It'll be nice to catch up. You can tell me about all of your adventures." She smiled and touched me on the arm. "This was a nice surprise. I'll see you tomorrow night."

She headed into the bakery and I returned to the store. It was no more active there than when I left and I again found myself looking across the street from the window. When Iris came out of the bakery, I saw her take a quick glance in my direction before walking away.

For a reason that wasn't entirely clear to me at that moment, I found this extremely satisfying.

CHAPTER THREE

An Explanation That Works for Just about Anything

The first time I met Iris, I was serving as the brunt of one of my brother's jokes. I'd been home after my sophomore year at Emerson for a little more than a week and wondering how long I could get by with the excuse of a summer independent study class before my father penciled me into the work schedule at the store. That day, Chase hadn't come home directly after school. This wasn't unusual now that he had his driver's license. But in the late afternoon, while I was alone in the house and listening to a vintage Clash album at a volume only allowable when my parents weren't around, the phone rang. It was Chase speaking agitatedly, telling me that he needed me to pick him up from the mall in Milton. He'd left his car at school because the girl he was with had offered to drive, but when they got to the mall, her behavior became increasingly erratic. He was concerned that she was some kind of psychotic and he definitely didn't want to get back in the car with her for fear of where she would take him. He'd managed to shake her with the excuse of needing to go to the bathroom, but he was sure he was going to run into her again if I didn't come for him soon, and he had no other way of getting home.

I wasn't accustomed to this sound in Chase's voice. He was four inches taller than I was and at least thirty pounds heavier. I'm not sure that I had ever seen him intimidated. He had also been handling women deftly from the time he was preadolescent. Yet the rising pitch in his voice suggested that I should make the fifteen-minute drive to Milton without even stopping to turn off the stereo first. I told him to wait for me in The Sharper Image and that I would get there as soon as I possibly could.

When I got to the store, he was holding an electronic nose hair clipper in his hands while he scanned the room. The nervousness seemed incongruous with his broad, solid form. I imagined the girl he'd taken a ride with as a teen version of Glenn Close in *Fatal Attraction*, and my mind reeled at the notion of what she could possibly have said or done to him to make him this skittish. The very fact of his nervousness caused my heart to race.

I called out Chase's name. His head snapped quickly in my direction and then his shoulders sagged. He came up to me, clapped me on the arm, and thanked me dramatically for coming to get him. I led him out of the store as he further described his encounter with the girl. He explained that she was extremely attractive and had always seemed even-tempered in school. For most of the drive to the mall, she had appeared to be completely normal. But then, just as they were getting out of the car, she had started talking about fate and the way things were meant to be and about the two of them going far away together never to be heard from again. He had managed to distance himself from her as quickly as possible, but as we walked, his head was in constant motion and he warned me that she could be anywhere in the mall. He told me that if she found us I needed to remember not to let her fool me. She might seem sensible, but under no circumstance was I to leave him alone with her again.

I found my pace quickening as he spoke and my eyes scanned the mall, even though I had no idea what the girl looked like. Chase matched me step for accelerating step.

That's when she came out from behind a store directory.

"Oh, there you are," she said. "I thought you were going to meet me in The Limited after you went to the bathroom." She didn't look at all the way I imagined she would from Chase's description. She had inviting eyes and lustrous hair, and for some reason I immediately noticed the sculpting of her bare shoulders. I realized that I could just as easily have fallen into her trap as Chase had.

Chase stuttered (which was way over the top and in retrospect makes me feel especially foolish for buying into any of this) as he explained to her that he was in fact planning on meeting her at The Limited but then saw me and got distracted. Mention of my name caused both of them to look in my direction.

She extended her hand. "I'm Iris. Chase has said great things about you."

I shook her hand, surprised at how soft it felt even

though her grip had some real integrity. I'm not sure what I was expecting.

"Are you gonna hang with us for a while?" she said.

I glanced over at Chase, whose eyes were imploring me to make a move.

"Um, you know, something has come up and I came to get Chase because we both have to go."

Concern quickly registered on Iris' face. "Nothing bad, I hope."

"No, nothing bad," I said. "Just something that means we have to leave right now." I looked over at Chase again and he offered the faintest nod to acknowledge that I was taking the right approach. I thought I sounded like a bumbling idiot.

"Sorry to hear it," she said. Iris turned to Chase and he stiffened immediately. "You don't look okay," she said to him. "Are you sure there isn't anything wrong?"

Chase simply nodded, as though he was dumbstruck. Anyone who could move my brother to silence had the power to do much more than that to me. Genuinely concerned, even though every instinct told me that there was nothing to fear from Iris, I took Chase by the arm.

"We really have to go," I said.

"Where are you parked?" Iris asked. "I'll walk out with you."

Chase put his hand over the one I had placed on his arm. If I had been thinking at all rationally, I would have realized how absurd this performance was. Instead, I jerked myself toward the girl and

sharply said, "No, Iris. That really won't be necessary."

She looked like I had slapped her, and I felt terrible about being so abrupt. Then I heard Chase laughing. He hugged my arm before pounding me on the
shoulder. Then he walked over to Iris to kiss her
while still laughing. It took him more than a minute
to calm down enough to speak.

He told us that he wanted to introduce us and just
thought he'd have a little fun with it. I reddened,
thinking about the way I'd treated Iris and how I
should have known better, since this kind of trickery
was always a possibility with Chase. It had been happening once every few months for as long as I could
remember, and as stupid as I felt after each incident,
I nevertheless marveled at his ability to devise fresh
practical jokes that caught me completely unprepared.

"I was never really convinced that you were insane," I said to Iris.

She smiled weakly. "You looked pretty convinced."

I took a deep breath. "I might have been. He's
pretty good at this stuff."

"I'll keep that in mind."

Chase was still chuckling as he walked down the
hallway, beckoning us to follow him. We wound up
eating bad Mexican food at the mall and then going
to see a Cameron Crowe movie together. When we
parted, Chase started toward Iris' car, hesitated to
throw me a concerned glance, and then laughed
about his little hoax all over again.

"You can have him if you want," Iris said to me.

"No, that's okay. You keep him."

• • •

The morning after I saw Iris on the street, I was back in the store. Tyler was already there.

"When do you go to school?" I said.

"I was supposed to be in a marketing class this morning, but I figured I should be here instead."

"Really?"

"Yeah. You know, your dad asked me to take care of the place and you didn't say when you were coming in again."

I laughed to myself and wondered what it was about my father that inspired this behavior. I could think of at least a half dozen people he had previously employed who would have done the same thing. Tyler introduced me to Carl, a college freshman who usually shared this shift with my father. Carl shook my hand while looking over my shoulder and then retreated to the stockroom.

The foot traffic on Russet Avenue was light, as was often the case on midweek mornings in the early spring. The locals were at work or hadn't gotten around to setting out on their errands yet and the tourists were few, many perhaps returning to their rooms at one of the inns after a multicourse breakfast to prepare for the drive home. There were two people in the store, one intently scanning the relationship cards, the other looking at the magazine rack while sipping at a paper cup from Bean There, Done That, the coffee bar down the street.

I joined Tyler behind the counter and the two of us stared out at the display of ceramics. A limp instrumental version of The Beatles's "We Can Work

It Out" was just barely audible through the sound system.

"Radio always on one and always set to the 'beautiful music' station," I said, mimicking my father's oft-repeated instructions.

Tyler laughed. "Yeah, Richard likes things a certain way."

I nodded. "They were playing the same music on this station when I was in high school. Do they still do that string version of 'Where the Streets Have No Name'?"

"At least once a day."

I looked over to the shelf behind the counter to see Tyler's statistics textbook.

"Business degree?" I asked, gesturing toward the book.

"Yeah, I graduate from MCS in two months." MCS was Middle Connecticut State, a modest college that most of us frowned upon because it catered to commuters.

"Let me guess – just missed at Yale."

"Actually, I turned Yale down."

I looked at him skeptically.

"I know," he said. "I wanted to stay home, if you can believe it, and no one commutes to Yale."

When I didn't comment on this, he added, "It had to do with a girl."

I nodded. "An explanation that works for just about anything."

"My parents would have had a hard time affording it anyway." He moved over toward his textbook, as though he needed the contact. "As you might have guessed, it didn't work out with the girl. I could have tried to matriculate at Yale in my sophomore year, but I found I actually kinda liked MCS."

"Hey, it's a good school," I said, gesturing with my hands. "So what are you going to do with your degree?"

"I'll probably ultimately get my MBA, but I'd really like to try to hit Manhattan for a while. I've started talking to some recruiters. I'd love to hook up with one of the major marketing firms."

"Better not tell them that you've skipped out on class today, then, huh?"

Tyler smiled. "Yeah, I guess not."

I nodded toward the book. "Listen, if you want to go in the back to study for a while, I'm pretty sure I can hold down the fort over here."

"Nah," he said, shaking his head. "Richard doesn't pay me to do my homework in the back office."

"He doesn't pay me at all. The way I look at it, it balances out."

Tyler ran his hand over the book. "Maybe I'll just stand over here and read. This way, I can jump in if you have any questions or if things back up."

For the first few hours, it didn't seem that I was going to need any help. In fact, I probably could have left the store unattended and my father would have made nearly as much via the honor system. But then there was a flurry of activity around lunchtime and the afternoon was relatively busy. Some guy came in and bought a $200 pewter dish, which might have been the most expensive item in the store and had quite possibly been there for several years. Around 3:00 Mrs. Deltoff, the mother of one of my best friends in high school, bought some wrapping paper.

She didn't seem to recognize me and I decided not to say anything to her.

In spite of the increase in action, there were rarely more than a few dozen customers in any given hour. Standing by myself while Tyler went for coffee, I tried to think of what could possibly have held my father's imagination for more than three decades. For thirty-four years, six days a week, eight to ten hours a day, he stood someplace near where I was standing now, ringing up a newspaper, dusting a shelf, placing an order. Did the ceramic figurines come to life in his mind, regaling him with clever verbal exchanges? Did the Charleston Chews do the Charleston with Baby Ruth when no one else was looking? If not, I couldn't imagine anything about this store keeping my interest for thirty-four days, let alone thirty-four years.

Of course, I did have something nearly as fanciful as dancing candy bars to keep me entertained through the late afternoon. Seeing Iris after all of this time was an utterly unexpected – though certainly not unimagined – surprise. A day later, it seemed funny to me that I wasn't certain it was her when I first saw her on the street. Iris' image was entirely distinctive to me. I couldn't possibly confuse her with anyone else and I certainly would never have forgotten what she looked like. I'd even done a somewhat effective job of aging her in my mind.

From the point at which I watched Iris walk away from Chase's gravesite, I believed that we were meant to have more time together. I'd had unresolved relationships before and I'd certainly had well beyond my quota of them since. But unlike the others, it simply seemed wrong that this one would go *so completely* unresolved. We had so much to deal with. Our shared and separate experiences with Chase. The friendship that had emerged between us during the time the two of them were together. The abandon of those seconds when we were kissing. While I lay in my room those weeks after Chase died, listening more to his CDs than my own, I thought often about calling Iris, meeting her in the park, crying with her, slowly facing our own relationship, whatever it might be, and staying in each other's lives. But whenever I did so, I would think about Iris and Chase together. I'd think about how they were always touching, always feeling each other, and I'd shrink back into the music. I'm sure that Iris was the only woman that Chase had ever loved and the memory of that was both sad and intimidating.

And a day after seeing her on the street, I began to feel some of the same trepidation again. I even thought about calling and saying that all of my evenings in Amber had suddenly booked up. But at the same time, I couldn't help but feel a certain hopeful expectation at being with Iris again. I imparted great meaning to our brief encounter the day before. I found it encouraging that she tried so hard to assure me that she needed to get back to her mother's house. I read much into her glance back toward the store when she left the bakery. I even wondered about her choice of the Cornwall as our meeting place. Surely, she remembered the dinner we had there with my family. Chase got sick and I wound up driving her home. We spent twenty minutes on her driveway debating the upcoming presidential election and another couple jokingly castigating each other over our opinions. It was the first time I'd had the chance to speak to Iris without Chase's unremitting energy serving as counterpoint and I remember driving back home that night convinced that my brother had happened on someone who would turn into a woman of genuine power. Of course, I had no idea what Iris remembered of that night or if she even remembered it at all, but I couldn't help but think that her selection of that particular restaurant was portentous.

At the same time, as was the case in those months before we kissed, I had no clear idea of what I was expecting from our drinks date. Back then, while my feelings for Iris were undeniably romantic, there was no way to imagine doing anything with those feelings because she was involved with my brother. Now, while it was impossible to know what kind of transformation those feelings had taken, there was the very real fact that, though Chase had been dead for nearly ten years, she was still involved with him, would be eternally involved with him as far as I was concerned. Certainly, nothing momentous was on the horizon, but it was entertaining to consider the possibility that there might be some kind of charge between us, something to give us some brief hesitation before we headed back to our lives.

All of which was considerably more interesting to think about than straightening the greeting cards or restocking the magazines. Though I eventually did these tasks because I needed to do something to make the time go faster.

I truly had no idea how my father managed to get out of bed for this.

• • •

When I visited my father at the hospital that afternoon, there was more color in his complexion. He cheered noticeably when I told him that Tyler was doing a good job. I spent an hour or so with him and my mother after I left the store, but we didn't talk very much beyond that debriefing. I was preoccupied with thinking about Iris and I'm sure they were preoccupied with thinking about what the doctor was going to say when he finally got around to saying it. I couldn't convince my mother to leave my father's bedside to go to a restaurant with me, so I had a tuna melt at a local diner before heading off to meet Iris.

The Cornwall had been at the same location for more than fifty years, which meant that it had been around for a long time before Amber evolved from a fishing village to a tourist destination. When it opened, it was the only available option for a nice meal within fifteen miles and families from all over Middlesex County frequented it. While the three generations of owners made little attempt to change with the town, its popularity was a constant. Somehow the tacky nautical motif, laminated wine lists, and a menu filled with outmoded "classics" like Lobster Newburg and Seafood au Gratin worked when you were aware of the restaurant's origins.

I think the owners always meant the bar to be comical and, at this point, it was just downright silly. A huge pirate head, complete with a dagger in his teeth, dominated one wall. Sprinkled throughout were fiberglass reproductions of various ship paraphernalia. And one could choose from a special drink

list that included such original creations as The
Matey (three kinds of rum and ginger ale), The
Plankwalker (151 rum, Drambuie, and grapefruit
juice) and the ever-popular Landlubber (rum, Coke,
and maraschino cherry juice). Fortunately they also
had a huge list of bottled beers (and did even in the
'50s), which made the place very popular among my
friends when we reached fake ID age.

The restaurant was relatively busy, but there were
only two occupied tables in the bar when I arrived.
Iris wasn't there yet and I ordered a Belgian beer
while I waited. I found that I was in no hurry for her
to arrive. I considered the possibility that we might
not have much to say to each other or that the conversation might go badly and started to feel that it
wouldn't disturb me terribly much if she didn't show
up at all. It was the same push and pull I felt nearly
every time I knew I was going to see her in the
months after the kiss.

She arrived at the bar about ten minutes later. I
was facing away from the door at that point, listening
in on a conversation between the bartender and a pa-
tron, and didn't see her until she pecked me on the
cheek.

"Reconnecting with the locals?" she asked as she
sat down across from me.

"They were talking about swordfishing," I said,
nodding toward the bar. "It could be 1958."

"I love that about this place. Do you ever come
here when you're visiting?"

"I haven't been in here since – " I realized I was
about to say "since Chase died" and thought better

of it. "I have no idea when the last time was that I was here."

"So then it really is old home week for you, isn't it?"

I chuckled and repeated, "Old home week."

A waiter came over and took Iris' drink order.

"How's your dad?" Iris said after the waiter left.

"He looked better today than he did yesterday. The doctor still hasn't told him what the long-term deal is going to be, which I know has him a little worried. I think he's out of immediate danger, though."

"When my dad died, it happened all at once," she said wistfully. Then she looked up at me with a mildly startled expression. "I didn't mean to suggest that I thought your father was dying. This kind of thing just makes me think of my father, that's all."

I held up my hand. "I get it. It's not as though the thought hasn't come to mind. I think he's going to be okay, though."

Iris' beer came and she took a moment to sip it. It hadn't dawned on me that she might be nervous to see me, but she seemed to be at least a little anxious. I looked over toward the pirate head and let the moment settle.

"My friends and I had developed an entire personal profile for that guy," I said, pointing to the pirate. "His name was Phil; he had a wife and three kids at home and a real affection for macramé. He did the pirate thing to pay the bills, but what he really wanted to be was an ice dancer."

"Ice dancer?"

"It was around the time of the Olympics. And did

you ever see some of the outfits those guys wear? Phil would fit right in."

"You have a rich fantasy life."

I laughed. "Actually, that's about as rich as it gets."

"What about 'moving from suburb to suburb in search of thrills?'"

It tickled me that she quoted a line back at me.

"It might have been more exciting if I had a better imagination."

We spent most of the next hour catching each other up in a top-line kind of way. Iris had put in four years at Mount Holyoke College and spent a lot of time around theater and dance groups, though she didn't have much talent at either discipline. What she did have, she realized, was a real love of these fields, a sharp organizational mind, and an interest in helping these operations succeed. When she'd graduated, she'd handled a variety of back-office duties for local arts organizations and finally settled in the Berkshires, where she had been for the last three years. She had a dog who made all of the trips back to Amber with her and a surprising affinity for potted plants, of which she had "dozens, I don't know, probably thirty or so."

Not wanting to bore her with my entire travel itinerary over the past ten years, I told Iris only about the longer stops. She listened to my stories with a combination of amusement and disbelief. I could tell that she was having some trouble synching these details with the person I was back when she knew me, but she was too polite to acknowledge this.

Once we had boiled the last ten years of our lives down to fifty minutes, we came to the point in the conversation where we were going to have to move on to other things. The first attempts at getting something started fizzled. Three sentences on how Amber had changed in the last decade. A few exchanges on her mother's failed attempt at a spot on the City Council. She said something about the new IMAX theater that opened just across the bridge and I cringed internally. Was this really everything we had left between us?

A sudden memory caused me to laugh and to abandon caution. "I remember when I was fifteen my parents took us to a 3-D IMAX theater to see a movie about dinosaurs. At one point, a T. rex reared up on the screen and Chase was so startled that he spilled his entire soda onto his lap."

It was the first time that either of us had invoked Chase's name – although it was ludicrous to think that either of us hadn't been thinking of him nonstop since meeting on the street. I tried to gauge Iris' reaction, wondering if this was only going to make things more awkward. I saw just the briefest hesitation on her face and then she started laughing.

"The poor thing," she said. "Was he humiliated?"

"For all I know, he might have been, but of course he kept his cool. He jumped out of his seat when it happened, but then he just brushed off the ice cubes and went back to watching the movie. When we left, he kept pointing to his pants and telling the people waiting in line for the next show that the movie was *really* exciting."

Iris laughed again and nodded her head. Neither of us said anything for a minute or two, but the silence wasn't nearly as uncomfortable as the small talk had been a short time before.

"I had my first interview with the director of that dance troupe in Lexington after getting caught in a downpour," Iris said. It was hard for me to imagine that what I'd just said had caused her to think about times when she had been very wet, but I let it go. Chase's name didn't come up again for the rest of the night, but unlike the first hour, it no longer seemed to be because both of us were avoiding it. We'd both nodded toward his memory and silently acknowledged that, if we were going to get to that subject, it would be at some later point. Even the small talk seemed easier to handle after that, and when I walked Iris to her car a couple of hours later, we made plans to see each other again the next night.

"This has definitely been the highlight of 'Old Home Week' for me," I said.

"I'd take that as a compliment if I didn't know what else you'd been doing since you got here."

"Take it as a compliment anyway."

She smiled, but her eyes darted downward for an instant. Then she looked back up at me and nodded before kissing me on the cheek and getting in her car.

• • •

The bar of choice the next night was a place that Tyler had recommended. It was just over the bridge and had been open for only a few months. Given that Tyler had just turned 22, I'd half expected it to be stripped-down concrete with blaring rap metal and indifferent waiters. Instead, it was an oversized and eclectically decorated living room, filled with large couches, original art, and muted lighting. I again arrived a few minutes ahead of Iris. Shortly after she got there, a trio of acoustic musicians began playing their own earnest compositions.

"Do you think they're any good?" Iris said when she saw my attention flit to the stage.

"Not really. It sounds like the guitarist can play, though. They'd probably be better off doing other people's stuff, but you have to give them credit for trying their own."

This seemed to make Iris think, though what I'd said was hardly profound. She leaned forward and rested her chin on an up-propped hand.

"My husband was a musician."

It would have been silly for me to pretend that I wasn't surprised to hear she had been married. "Husband?"

"Yeah, we met right after I got to Lexington. He was doing a composition for the dancers and we sort of connected." She laughed. "Yeah, sort of. We were practically living together a week after I met him. One weekend a couple of months later, we just decided to get married. It was very exciting and insane and I was madly in love with him. It was something of a whirlwind."

"Sounds intense," I said, still trying to grapple with this information. "How long did it last?"

"All together a little more than a year." She looked at me knowingly. "Like I said, it was a whirlwind."

"The road called?"

"Nah, nothing so romantic. The passion just disappeared. It went from tearing each other's clothes off to picking dirty underwear off the floor, if you know what I mean. It turned out that I didn't get much of a charge from the domestic thing."

"So you were the one who left?"

Iris smiled and her expression became wistful. "I'm always the one who leaves. Seems to be the way it goes. At least it was with Roger and Pete as well."

"You've been married three times?"

Iris' eyes opened widely. "No, not married. God, could you imagine? Well, I guess you could imagine, since you just asked. No, I only *lived* with Roger and Pete. Sixteen and thirteen months, respectively. Roger when I was still in college, Pete a couple of years ago."

"Same story?"

"No, not really. With Roger, we were coming up on graduation and doing a lot of thinking about the future and it became obvious to me that we had different futures in mind. With Pete, it just sort of sizzled then fizzled. You know, that story."

"Yeah, I've had a fleeting association with *that story.*"

Iris smiled and seemed pleased at the opportunity to redirect the conversation. "Details, please."

"Nah, the details aren't interesting enough. I never actually lived with anyone. You know, stuff at each other's apartments, that kind of thing, but never any official cohabitation."

"Yeah, that's smart of you. It avoids the hassle of sorting through the CDs when it's over."

"Exactly. I've never even seriously thought about living with someone."

The conversation moved on. We didn't talk about Chase this night, either. I was aware that I was avoiding mentioning him and I felt a little self-conscious about this, but I wasn't doing it because I thought it would make Iris sad or uncomfortable. I just wanted to have some time when I was talking to her alone, rather than to her and my brother. I have no idea why she was avoiding it.

Fortunately, we also weren't talking about movie theaters and shopping centers.

"So what was the story with you and this job in Springfield?" she asked. The night before, I had told her what I still hadn't told my parents: that I'd quit my latest job a couple of weeks earlier.

"Nothing that hasn't been 'the story' with other jobs. It just played itself out. I mean, I never really thought I was going to have a long-term future in the career counseling business. It would have been ironic if I had, wouldn't it? If the firm wasn't so laid back, I probably never would have applied for the position at all. But, you know, as it went on, they wanted me to attend seminars and association meetings and that kind of thing. And then when they invited me to a retreat to 'contribute to the direction of the enterprise,' I just got the sense that they were expecting a lot more out of me than I was out of them. It seemed like the right time to give them notice."

"Do you have something lined up for when you get back?"

"Lined up? Gee, that sounds like a plan. I'm rather plan-averse, if you want to know the truth. Something has always come up. It probably won't be in Springfield, but who knows? I've been thinking about a few other places."

"So many strip malls, so little time."

"It sounds so exotic when you put it that way."

She tilted her head. "I actually think there is something exotic about it. I mean it's not as though you're exploring the Himalayas or anything like that, but you really are sort of casting yourself out there. It's anybody's guess what you'll discover, but the potential for discovery is always available."

I smiled at her and took a long drink of my beer. When I finished, I looked at Iris again and our eyes met in a way that they hadn't in more than a decade.

"I literally couldn't put it better myself," I said.

There was something especially fulfilling about being "seen" by Iris. Other women had given me their impressions of what they thought went on inside of my head, and a few had even been moderately accurate. But in all of those cases, their observations had felt like an invasion. With Iris, all attention was welcome and the thought that she would expend the effort to consider my perspective on things was flattering.

I realized that Iris and I had a unique kind of history together. We had not spent very much time as friends. And yet because of the intensity of her relationship with my brother and the fate of that relationship – not to mention the "moment" we had together – our own connection went considerably deeper. Iris was almost certainly the most significant living person from my Amber days, and as such qualified as my most reliable personal historian. More so than someone I might have known since elementary school.

Late in the evening, the acoustic band on the stage began a medley of Joni Mitchell songs. As I suspected, they played them well and even with a bit of inspiration. I began to think about Iris' husband. I'm not entirely sure why it was such a surprise to me that she had gotten married. Certainly, a decent percentage of people got married by the time they were in their late twenties. I suppose what surprised me was that Iris would have gotten married on a whim and then split in the same way. I suppose because I was still thinking of her with Chase, I saw her as the kind of person who would make a lifelong commitment to everything she did. I imagined that when she married, it would be to someone she knew she could stay with for the long run. She never struck me as casual about anything, especially her affections.

Through the entire Joni Mitchell set, neither of us spoke. When the band went back to playing an original composition that they announced as their last song, Iris turned toward me again.

"When are you heading back?"

"I'll probably stick it out through the weekend."

"I'm going back to Lenox tomorrow afternoon. A lot of stuff seems to happen with the Ensemble on the weekends and I need to be there just in case."

"Wow. I've never had a job that I would build my nonworking hours around."

Iris finished her beer, turned to look for our waitress, and then seemed to think better of it.

"There are a lot of talented people in the group and they do good work. I've gotten caught up in the whole thing."

"In other words you actually care about the fate of the people you work for."

"Yeah, of course."

I shook my head. "That's like Sanskrit to me."

She laughed. "Gotta care about something."

"That much I understand. That this something would be a job is the part that's hard for me to connect with. Do you want some coffee or something?"

Iris looked at her watch. "I should probably get going pretty soon. My mother gets up at a ridiculously early hour, and even though she 'tries to let me sleep,' she's not exactly light on her feet."

I took a final swallow of my beer and we left the bar. The early spring warmth had taken its predictable turn toward late evening chill while we were in there and Iris rubbed her arms as we walked to her car. I wished I had worn a jacket so I could put it over her shoulders.

"This was really good," she said as she got to her car door and then turned to face me.

"Really good," I said. "I've missed you."

She smiled and cocked her head. "Yeah, I've missed you, too. I didn't even realize it until I saw you last night. But I have."

I knew she was cold and I knew I should let her get into her car, but I wanted to prolong the moment.

"You're going back to Lenox tomorrow afternoon?"

"Gotta."

I nodded. "Let's not lose touch, okay?"

"Hey, you're the one who'll be heading off to Ixtapa or Duluth or something," she said, laughing.

"I know, but I really don't want to lose touch. Is that okay?"

"Yeah, it's okay."

And then she moved toward me. At first, I thought she was going to hug me, so I wasn't prepared when her lips came up to join mine. Just as I wasn't prepared for how the kiss made me feel – undeniably grounded, riveted in the moment. It was a very different kiss from our first one. Then, there was something illicit to it, something that needed to be said, if only in a whisper. This kiss carried with it no such qualifications. This was a kiss with an undetermined result, a kiss with unknowable consequences.

All of these thoughts passed through my mind in milliseconds and then were replaced by an unyielding need to feel this moment. I pulled Iris toward me and returned the kiss hungrily as she molded herself to me naturally. I stroked her hair gently as we continued and I realized that there was very little in my romantic history to compare to what was happening just now. It was no longer cold outside. It was no longer *Connecticut* outside. I could very easily have stayed in this space, doing precisely this, indefinitely.

But then Iris pulled back slowly. Caught in the ardor of the moment, I moved with her, but relented when it became clear that she wanted to stop. Even in the spotty streetlight, I could tell that her face was flushed. She brushed her hair back from her face and smiled at me with an expression that I interpreted as amazement.

"Gotta get my wits about me," she said, which wasn't what I would have scripted for her. Her car keys had been in her hand the entire time and now she quickly snapped the remote behind her to unlock her door. Before getting in the car, she looked up at me. For a moment, I thought she was going to kiss me again. Then she just said, "It's late . . . my mother," and started the car.

"I'll be in the store the entire day," I said to her behind her closed window. "Call me before you go."

"I will," she said, backing her car out of the space and leaving the parking lot.

I stood in the same place, as though planted there by that kiss, until she drove away. Then, instead of getting into my own car, I went back into the bar and ordered some coffee. I wasn't ready to drive just yet.

CHAPTER FOUR

Everything That's Between Us and All

I slept later than I intended the next morning, and when I went down to make myself something for breakfast, my mother had already gone to the hospital. An unopened box of Honey Nut Cheerios – which I ate practically every morning while I was still living at home – sat on the counter. I hadn't eaten them in years, but my mother couldn't have known that. I threw a couple of slices of bread in the toaster and poured myself a cup of coffee while I waited.

I hadn't been completely alone in the house in nearly ten years. For some reason, I felt that I should take the opportunity to examine things more closely, the whole-place equivalent of checking out the medicine cabinet. I walked into the den, sat in my father's recliner, and looked around the room. There was a book on the coffee table that they'd brought back from a trip to the Grand Canyon a few years before. There was a photo of my mother standing uncomfortably (the only way she ever posed for pictures) next to her goddaughter Lisa on the weekend of Lisa's wedding. The Raku vase I'd given them for their thirtieth anniversary sat on a shelf next to the television, at complete odds with all of the other adornments in the room. And the old tapestry throw pillows had been replaced by a set of navy velour ones. Other than that, the room looked exactly as it did before I moved out. They still had Chase's lacrosse trophies lined up on one bookshelf. The set of ceramic candlesticks he'd made in seventh grade and given to my mother for Christmas sat next to my vase. My parents' wedding picture was on one side of the fireplace and the photograph of them renewing their vows twenty years later was on the other. The frames with our high school photos hung on another wall. I suppose when you've been living in the same house for as long as my parents have, you stop thinking about making changes.

I heard the bread pop up in the toaster and returned to the kitchen. The local daily paper, the *Amber Advisor*, sat on the kitchen table and I absently perused the front page while I ate. There might have been unrest all over the globe, a crippling political scandal in Washington, or a life altering scientific breakthrough commanding the headlines of the *New York Times* or the *Boston Globe*. But the *Advisor* reserved the space above the fold for matters of traffic lights, Amber High's SAT scores, and the visit of a Lithuanian folk musician to the Community Center.

Just as they'd reserved it ten years earlier for the report of an accident on the Pine River Bridge that had claimed the life of the eighteen-year-old son of a prominent Amber shopkeeper. I hadn't read the paper that morning, in fact didn't remember seeing any newspaper in the house for several days after the accident. But just before I'd left town, I'd found the issue with the story sitting on top of a pile of other "commemorative newspapers" on my aunt's bookshelf. I'd frozen at the sight and then walked away without reading more than the headline.

After I finished eating, I headed to the store. A college-age woman stood behind the counter reading a copy of *Entertainment Weekly*. She didn't look up when I entered and I think I could have taken the entire front display of stuffed toys out the door without her noticing. Only when I walked behind the counter did she pay me any attention.

"You the son?" she said.

"Yeah, hi. You're . . ."

"Tab." She moved her head back and forth quickly as though she was shaking off excess water. "Tabitha. I hate that name, so I make it as short as I can. No one calls me Tabitha."

"I'll keep that in mind."

"Yeah, thanks." She looked back down at the magazine and turned a page. Clearly, this was all the information she thought it was important for us to exchange.

"Where's Tyler?" I asked.

She kept her eyes on the magazine while she answered. "He doesn't come in on Fridays. Some independent study thing or something."

"So he's not going to be here at all today?"

"Not unless he's planning to surprise us."

She turned another page. I wondered if I should apologize for breaking her concentration. A customer walked up to the register and Tab moved over so I could ring him up. For the first time since I had been back in the store, I felt an urge to flash the authority that was my birthright. I got over it and helped the customer. A few minutes later, I suggested to Tab that there might be shelves that needed restocking or merchandise that needed straightening and she laboriously closed the magazine and walked to the back of the store.

The stock guy, Carl, was working again, but as was the case the day before, I saw him only on the occasions when he wandered up from the back room. With Tab tinkering at whatever she was tinkering at, I was alone behind the counter to register a few sales and answer a couple of customer questions. None of it was particularly taxing and, while I was slightly irritated at Tab's laxity, it was hard to fault her. The closest thing to a challenge came just before lunchtime when the candy vendor showed up – the same man who had sold my father candy ten years earlier – to take an order for the next week. To keep myself entertained, I reviewed every item available on the vendor's stock list and ordered a box of BlisterSnax.

"You sure about this?" the salesman said. "Your dad doesn't usually carry these."

"We're gonna take a walk on the wild side."

That marketing experiment addressed, I navigated my way through what stood for a lunchtime rush and then settled into the long lull that typified the early afternoon. Without Tyler there to talk to, and with very few customers to deal with, I had no choice but to think about the way the night before had ended. I hadn't been conscious of how much I wanted to kiss Iris again until I was actually kissing her. I was certainly aware of how much I enjoyed talking to her,

how beautiful she seemed to me, and how I felt –
especially that second night – that I was beginning
to get to know her in a new way. And of course, I
was aware that I simply saw her differently than I
saw most other women. But it wasn't until she
reached for me, until we were actually kissing, that I
realized how much I wanted her physically. It was
like exiting the highway expecting to eat at Denny's
and finding The French Laundry instead.

And at the same time as I was buckling under the
sensual weight of the kiss, I was sucker punched by
the emotional impact. I hadn't been smitten for a long
time, but when Iris kissed me, there was so much
possibility to the act that I allowed my mind to race.
I began to calculate the distance from Springfield to
Lenox, to think that New Mexico (one of the desti-
nations I'd been considering) could wait for a while,
all immediately in the seconds after our lips first
touched. And when we continued to kiss, I swear I
had actual visions of Iris and me walking together
and holding hands. It wasn't simply a kiss; it was a
time altering act transporting my sensibility back to
my junior year of college.

And then she pulled away. And there was that shake
of her head, that muttering about "gathering her wits,"
that look in her eyes. It was a different look from the
one Iris had given me when we kissed ten years before but, like that look, it suggested that she had experienced our moment differently than I had. And I
didn't know what to make of it. After all, she had
reached for me. But in the end, something about kissing me, something about an act that had sent my imagination whirling, had caused her to retreat into herself.

It felt a little strange to me that while I had been kissing Iris this time, I hadn't thought about Chase at all. In fact, I hadn't thought about Chase until I was back in the bar with a double espresso. I'd played a medley of guilt and frustration before settling into the slow jam of confusion that I was still working on while I stood in the store.

As Amber High let out, the place got a little busier, allowing me to move on to other things, at least occasionally. Tab's shift ended and a high school senior named Merry came on. Merry didn't seem to take the store any more seriously than Tab had, but she was at least willing to make the effort to ring up a greeting card or show a customer where the all-occasion wrapping paper was.

Merry had been in the store about fifteen minutes when Iris walked in. I went over to her as soon as I saw her and then pulled up short when I got within five feet, suddenly remembering that her personal space was decidedly not mine.

"Do you have a couple of minutes?" she asked. I nodded and we started walking down the street.

"I'm getting ready to head back home," she said, and then added, pointing back in the other direction, "the dog's already in the car."

"I'm glad you stopped by. It was really good seeing you the last few days."

"Yeah, it was great seeing you." She looked over at me quickly and then looked back ahead. "I didn't want to leave without talking to you a little about what happened last night."

I assumed that anything I said at that point would

either be inappropriate or make me feel foolish, so I simply kept listening.

"I was a little surprised when that happened," she said. "I mean, I know it was me who started it, but I was just a little surprised that I did it. It had just been so good talking to you and it was kind of fun seeing you after all this time. And it just brought up a lot of stuff – good stuff. You said that thing about missing me and I just got . . . inspired, I guess. Then when we kissed, it was a lot more intense than I was expecting it to be."

"I felt that, too," I said, still not entirely sure where this was going and hoping that letting her know that I shared the experience might help.

She pursed her lips and didn't make eye contact. "That's why it would be a really big mistake to do anything with it."

Even though only a few minutes before I hadn't been sure that I was ever going to see her again and was positive that if I did she would say something like this, I felt deflated. "What do you mean?"

"You know, with everything that's between us and all." I could see out of the corner of my eye that she glanced over at me. "You aren't going to tell me that it wouldn't feel very weird if we actually went after this, are you?"

"I'm not sure what I'm thinking about it, to tell you the truth."

"Yeah, well, there's a major difference between the two of us. I've been thinking about it constantly since last night."

I could have – in fact should have – clarified

myself, but there didn't seem to be much point to it. By the time I was out of college, I had decided that no relationship was worth pursuing if the pursuit required convincing the other party. The fact that Iris had come to the store – with the dog waiting to go home – with the express purpose of clearing up any romantic misinterpretations I might have had was enough to make me just wish the entire encounter was over. I simply laughed, turned, and took a couple of steps in the direction of her car.

"Can I meet your dog?" I said.

Iris' expression relaxed. She was clearly unsure of how I was going to react to what she had to say and was relieved that I was letting her off the hook. We walked toward the car. When the dog saw her, it pressed its nose against the side window, fogging it with its breath.

"Big guy," I said. "What is it?"

"It's a Wheaton Terrier. And a gal."

"This huge thing is a terrier?"

"Yeah, I know. She's really friendly." Iris opened the passenger door and the dog came bounding out, jumping up on Iris and then doing the same to me. She calmed when I pet her, but then left our side and jumped back into the car.

"She kinda likes road trips," Iris said.

"Maybe I should get one of these to come with me to the southwest. Do they like the Dave Matthews Band?"

Iris took her car keys out of her jacket and walked toward her side of the car.

"When do you think you're going to go?" she said.

"I'm not sure yet. I need to find out what's going on

with my father and then I have to take care of some
stuff in Springfield. I have to do a little more research
on the place, too. I'm not *that* spontaneous. I'm thinking New Mexico. Maybe by the end of the month."

She nodded and I thought she was going to say
something else. But again she seemed to fix on something in the distance. After a moment, she looked into
my eyes.

"Let's stay in touch, okay?" she said.

"Yeah, sure."

"I mean it. It was *really* good seeing you. And I really liked talking to you the last couple of nights. I always did. You were a good friend, Hugh, not just
Chase's brother. Don't let what happened last night
get in the way. I don't want to completely lose touch
with you again."

I closed the dog's door. "I'll write you when I get
out to wherever I'm going. Maybe you can visit
sometime. And I'm sure I'll be back here every now
and then to check on my parents. Maybe our trips
will coincide again."

"That would be good." She came over and kissed me
on the cheek. Then she opened her car door. "I've
gotta get on the road. Stay in touch, though. I mean it."

I nodded and she got into the car. I said good-bye
to the dog and then watched as Iris drove off.

Before going back into the store, I took a side trip
to the chocolate shop. I bought a hazelnut truffle and
a dark chocolate toffee, and then went to Bean There,
Done That for a triple espresso. I planned to take
them back to the store with me, but changed my
mind and sat on one of the sidewalk benches until I
finished.

Russet Avenue pedestrians had begun the annual
process of slowing their pace for the upcoming season. The winter's brisk and purposeful headlong
charge began to relax in early March. By the beginning of April, you could see walkers stopping to talk
with one another on the street, examining shop win-
dows, and simply getting from here to there with less
velocity. As a kid, I'd loved getting a couple of quar-
ters from my father for ice cream from Layton's
Fountain Shop (now replaced by The Cone Connection) on days like this one. I would sit on a bench,
peripherally watching the passersby, but essentially
taking as long as possible to enjoy whatever flavor
I'd chosen that day, all the while forestalling my favorite part, which was eating the melted ice cream
that gathered at the bottom of the very last bite of
cone. Early April days were especially appealing, because it was warm enough to sit outside comfortably,
but not so warm as to make the ice cream get soft too
fast. A few months later, I would need to lick much
more deliberately and it simply wasn't as much fun.

Sitting with my two pieces of chocolate and my
coffee wasn't as idyllic. Still, there was the feeling I
remembered with absolute precision of being completely unmoved to action. Then as now, being on a
bench on a warm spring day in Amber seemed the
best possible alternative to whatever else was going
on in my life.

A teenaged couple walked by with a small dog
bouncing at their heels. I wondered what Iris thought
about when she was "constantly" thinking about our
latest kiss. Was there ever a point during this when
she thought that perhaps we should see what would

happen between us? Or did she spend all of this time thinking about how she was going to tell me that nothing was possible? As much as I wanted to shrug aside her dismissal the way I had with other women over the years, I knew that this was unrealistic. It would be pointless for me to write off what had happened the night before. Even before we'd kissed, I'd known that I was being drawn to her all over again.

And yet it would be equally pointless for me to go after it. There was nothing about the way Iris had approached me this afternoon that suggested equivocation. She hadn't said what she'd said because she wanted me to protest or because she was unsure of her feelings. Iris had made one thing abundantly clear: no matter what we were like when we were together, we could never take that to another level because of what I represented.

That was a wall I felt utterly incapable of scaling. And as I bit into the second chocolate, I realized that I was at least somewhat relieved. There was no way that a romantic relationship wasn't going to be fraught with the kind of emotional gymnastics I'd been doing for the past fifteen hours. She was and would forever be Chase's last girlfriend.

I finished the chocolate and took the rest of the espresso back with me into the store.

CHAPTER FIVE

Strenuous Activity

Chase had been dating Iris for a little less than a month when he told me that he was going to be "re-newing her contract." We were sitting on the grass on the banks of the Pine River drinking beers and wasting as much time as possible before we got back to town. We'd actually done surprisingly little of this that summer. Chase had Iris and a new group of friends from this year's lacrosse team. I had made a couple of trips back to Boston to visit my friends there and to try to work a spark into something warmer with a woman from the CD shop near the school. I also got the impression that the novelty of doing this with me had lessened from the previous summer now that Chase looked old enough to buy his own beer.

"Should I alert the media?" I said in response to his news.

Chase laughed and pulled on his beer and then smiled at me in a uniquely goofy way.

"She's getting to you a little, huh?" I said.

I was surprised at the way Chase spoke about Iris. At first, I had misinterpreted the sober tone he used as suggesting that he wasn't that excited about being with her. But then I realized that it was something else entirely. That sound in his voice was respect. Chase didn't talk about Iris with the wildly colorful language he had used for some of his other girlfriends because to do so would have been disrespectful of her. When the message finally got through to me, I felt a little taken aback by it. If Chase was going to take this woman this seriously – so seriously that he would circumvent certain hardwired attitudes about dating – then this had to have an impact on other parts of his life. I wasn't sure I was prepared for that and I wasn't sure I wanted it.

But by this day, as we sat by the banks of the Pine, I had spent some more time with Iris myself and I saw that she wasn't bending Chase or forcing him into a different mold. She was like the proper seasoning on a well-prepared meal – she was bringing out his optimum flavor. And so I approved of the news that he was planning to continue seeing her. Chase, of course, first needed to use a string of profanity to explain how he felt about my "approval" before clapping me on the shoulder and telling me he was glad that I liked her. I responded by pushing his hand off my shoulder in playful defiance, to which he responded by knocking me over. Before long, we were rolling down toward the river, laughing and cursing at each other the entire time. I managed to stand up and, when Chase lunged for me, I actually moved deftly enough to parry his approach and land on top of him, a technique I'd learned during an intramural wrestling program I had been in the fall before. I pinned Chase down and, for a moment, he couldn't pull himself free. It had probably been ten years since I'd been able to exert that much control over him.

"Shit, man, you *are* getting soft," I said.

And then I was temporarily airborne before plunging into the river. The water wasn't particularly deep, no more than four or five feet at the banks, but I was so disoriented that I couldn't immediately get myself out of it. I flailed a bit and then finally found my footing. When my vision cleared, I saw Chase laughing and then suddenly pulling himself up short. My instinct was to charge him, assuming if nothing else that I could get him wet, but I wasn't feeling particularly steady on my feet. When I saw Chase put his hand up to his right temple, I did the same, and that's when I discovered that I was bleeding. I must have hit a rock when I fell into the water.

I'm not sure what my expression said to him, but Chase moved very quickly to action. He lifted me out of the water and laid me down on the shore. I knew enough about these kinds of wounds to know that if I was conscious, I was probably okay, but I still found the amount of blood that I could see very upsetting. Chase pulled off his shirt and tore it into strips to wrap my head, telling me the entire time that I was going to be okay and that he would take care of things. It was the second time that afternoon that his voice seemed out of character, though, since I was shaken up myself, I might not be remembering it accurately.

An hour later, a doctor at the emergency room had stitched and properly bandaged me. A still-shirtless Chase was pretending not to preen for the nurses.

"This is great," I said to him when they released me. "I look like one of those Revolutionary War musicians and you're taking phone numbers."

Chase pretended not to know what I was talking about and reminded me that he wasn't in the market for phone numbers any longer. I insisted on buying him a T-shirt from the hospital gift shop before we left anyway. While we were there, he picked up a silk rose for Iris, telling me, laughing, that I had screwed up and made him late for his date with her.

• • •

The night after Iris left, I stayed with my parents until the end of visiting hours. My father looked tired, but I was guessing that it was largely from being immobile for so long. When my mother and I got back to the house, she made us tea and we sat in the sunroom.

"We really appreciate you looking after the store the last few days," she said as she opened a package of Oreos. "I guess you have to get back home soon, don't you?"

"In a couple of days, yeah."

"This was a lot of time for you to be taking off from work. Will that be okay?"

"I don't really have to worry about work right now, Mom. I quit a couple of weeks ago."

My mother looked down at her mug and then took a slow sip. "What was wrong with this one?"

I shrugged. "They just wanted more from me than it made sense for me to give. This place wasn't meant to be a career."

"Any prospects?"

"Not really. I haven't actually been looking. I'm not sure I want to stay in Springfield. There isn't a lot going on there."

She studied her tea for several seconds. I wondered if she was looking for a message. Something that would tell Anna Penders how to deal with her perpetually wayward son.

"This isn't a good time for me to be worrying about you," is what she said.

"You don't need to worry about me. When have you ever needed to worry about me? I've never once been concerned about finding a way to make money or a place to live. You shouldn't, either."

"Of course you haven't. You're smart, you're talented, and you know how to talk to people. Someone like you can always get by." She sipped again. "Don't you think you might be underachieving a little, though?"

"Mom, I'm fine. Don't waste any energy wondering about whether I'm underachieving."

We'd had this conversation before. It was always an easy one to brush aside. This time was no different.

"Ben Rice from the Chamber of Commerce came to visit your father today."

I nodded. I had never heard Ben Rice's name before.

"He said that a Banana Republic was trying to lease the space that Miriam Wallace's boutique used to be in."

"Did the Chamber of Commerce call out the militia?" This had been an ongoing tug-of-war since

Amber had grown to its current size. National chains would occasionally try to take space on Russet Avenue and the town would vehemently oppose it, believing that one of the primary reasons why tourists came to Amber was because of shops you couldn't find on any Main Street in America. In fact, only one store in the entire downtown area had an additional location elsewhere.

"I guess they had more trouble this time than usual. Ben said it was touch and go for a while. Your father was getting more riled up than he should until Ben told him that the landlord was nearly certain he was going to lease the space to a pottery gallery instead."

"Better that they bring in another craft store than another stationery store, huh?"

"Don't even joke about that."

I took another Oreo from the package and stood to go to bed.

"You're okay for money, right?" my mother said.

"I'm fine, Mom."

She nodded and turned back to her tea. I kissed her forehead and walked up the stairs.

Somewhere around 5:00 that morning, the phone rang. I couldn't hear what my mother was saying, but after she hung up, she started to rustle around in her room. I threw on a pair of jeans and went to see her.

"What's going on?" I said.

My mother was dressing and pulled a sweater up in front of her to cover her bra. "He's had another heart attack."

"Is he okay?"

"They've brought him to the ICU and are monitoring him."

I turned to head back to my room. "Let me get dressed and I'll drive you."

"You don't need to come. He's going to be fine."

"I'll drive you. Then we'll see that he's fine together."

By the time we got to the hospital, the doctors had stabilized my father and he was sleeping in Intensive Care. They weren't sure yet what had caused the second heart attack and they were going to watch him closely over the next few hours. One doctor told my mother that my father was out of immediate danger and suggested that we go home to get some more sleep. This wasn't a realistic option for my mother and she wouldn't even go down to the cafeteria until she was certain that the ICU staff had her cell phone number.

"If they don't know what caused it, it can happen again," she said as she picked at a bran muffin, pulling it to little pieces.

For whatever reason, I was very hungry, although I wouldn't normally have had breakfast for several hours. I took the muffin away from her and ate it. "If you're going to have a heart attack, this is probably the best place to have one."

"Yes, but no place is the best place to have two."

"We'll have to wait to see what the doctor says. You like these guys, right?"

"I like his other doctor. I don't know the one we just talked to."

"He seemed to know what he was doing. I'm sure he'll be very careful with Dad."

This didn't reassure her in any way. She seemed

much more rattled than I had seen her at any time since I'd been back. For a moment, her eyes seemed to mist over and then she blinked the tears back.

"I have nothing if I don't have your father," she said. I reached out and squeezed her hand, but she didn't seem to notice.

We went back up to the ICU waiting room and didn't talk much over the next few hours. I tried a few conversation starters just to get her mind on something else, but I was useless.

We checked in on my father occasionally and she must have felt some sense of relief that he was resting comfortably. She relaxed enough to ask me about the time I spent with Iris and then she inexplicably asked if I had retained contact with someone I dated in my senior year in high school. She had never met any of the women I saw in college and the one time I brought Gillian home, my mother was in bed with the flu for most of the weekend. Therefore, this high school girl was as real to her as anyone I'd ever spent time with.

By 10:30, my father was awake and there had been no further incidents. At my mother's suggestion – "he doesn't need both of us standing over him like this" – I headed off to the store. Tyler was working the counter and Tab was busying herself around the wrapping paper.

"Hey, what's happening?" Tyler asked when he saw me.

"My dad had another heart attack this morning."

Tyler's eyes opened wide and he was temporarily speechless. "Is he okay?"

"I think so. The doctor seemed pretty even tempered about it, though he doesn't know how it happened."

Tyler shook his head and he had a dazed expression. I began to wonder if I should have delivered the news to him more carefully.

"I don't know what I would do if I were in your shoes," he said.

Until that moment, I hadn't particularly considered how this was affecting me. I was concerned for my father and worried that my mother was borderline unstable, but I didn't think of myself as part of the dilemma.

"You just go through it and hope for the best," I said.

"Man, if my father was having multiple heart attacks, you'd have to peel me off the walls."

I shrugged. "I think it's different when you're actually in the middle of it."

The store was especially quiet on this morning, as though people had heard that Richard Penders had had another heart attack and just assumed that his stationery store wouldn't be open for business. A Muzak version of a song I ultimately recognized as Led Zeppelin's "Communication Breakdown" played ever so softly on the radio. In the first hour I was there, we couldn't have had more than half a dozen customers. I gave some thought to leaving, but I really didn't have anywhere to go. Things picked up around lunchtime and actually got busy for a while. When a new shipment of cards arrived, Tyler and I reassigned Tab to the cash register so we could restock the displays.

We had been at it for a couple of minutes when Tyler laughed and handed me a card that showed a couple caressing while a huge gorilla loomed behind them. The inside of the card read, "It's never as easy as you think." I chuckled and handed it back to him.

"There are a bunch in this line that are pretty clever," he said.

"That's an improvement. For years, the only humorous – and I use the term loosely – cards my father stocked either had pictures of wrinkled fat men or fart jokes."

"Wow, sorry I missed that era."

Until that point, I hadn't been bothering to read the insides of the cards while I put them up. Now I opened another that showed a post-apocalyptic landscape and read, "Sorry about last night." I laughed, shared it with Tyler, and then checked the back of the card for the name of the line.

"What kinds of cards do you like to buy?" Tyler asked me.

"I don't really buy a lot of cards."

"Really? You mean it's not in your blood?"

"Must skip a generation. If I ever need a card, I tend to go with blank ones on nice paper. Sometimes I leave them blank."

"Yeah, well if there's a picture on it, you've got a thousand words right there anyway, right?" He pulled the plastic wrap off another package, glanced at the sentiment, and then put them up on the rack. "I used to buy cards all the time when Elizabeth and I were together. Hopefully she didn't keep them. Some of the stuff I wrote to her was pretty embarrassing."

"Yeah, you only make that mistake once, I would imagine."

"That one anyway. I can't believe how convinced I was. I guess it happens to everybody."

"Just about everybody, anyway."

Tyler nodded. "I think my parents kind of spoiled me. They started dating when they were high school seniors and they're still kinda sickeningly affectionate with each other thirty-something years later. As much as it made me feel weird sometimes to have my parents nuzzling in front of my friends, I sorta just assumed that that was the way things would go for me."

"Until Elizabeth tore your heart out."

He snickered and pulled the wrappers off several packages at the same time.

"Actually, I tore her heart out. I went on this trip during spring break and wound up sleeping with some girl from Duke. I figured it meant that I wasn't as totally in love with Elizabeth as I thought I was. I couldn't even tell her why I was doing it, but I just started backing away from her. It took me something like a month to break up with her. Now that I think about it, I can be pretty sure that she didn't keep my cards after that."

"Well at least something good came out of it."

He smiled at me and we focused on the card display. A few minutes later, I looked up to see that a line had formed at the cash register.

"I better go help Tab before she sprains something," I said to him.

He gave me a little salute and went back to work.

• • •

When I got to the hospital that night, they'd moved my father back to a semiprivate room. He was awake and had a bit of color in his face. He even seemed somewhat relaxed, though my mother didn't appear any less uneasy than she had looked when I left her that morning.

I leaned over to kiss him on the forehead. This was something I had never done before this trip. When we lived under the same roof, we rarely touched at all, and after I moved out, I would shake his hand in greeting. When I'd seen him lying in bed in the hospital that first day, it hadn't seemed right to reach out for his hand and so I simply leaned over and kissed him. I assumed I would stop doing this when he returned home.

"This room looks better on you, Dad," I said.

"Fluorescent lighting flatters me."

"I guess you must be doing all right if they moved you back in here."

My father shrugged. I looked over at my mother, who was in the process of squeezing my father's hand tighter.

"I have okay news and lousy news," my father said. I didn't respond in any way other than moving to sit down next to my mother. She looked at me briefly with a thin-lipped smile.

"The doctors say the second heart attack came from a blockage that they'll be able to clear up with a procedure tomorrow morning. After that, they think I'll be in decent shape for a while. That's the okay news. The lousy news is that once I get out of the hospital, I'm going to have to curtail strenuous activity. The bottom line is that I'm not going to be able to work in the store any longer."

For some reason I took this harder than I might have taken more dire news about his condition. If he had said, "the doctors tell me I have six months to live," I wouldn't have been easily able to fix that prognosis in my mind with the ultimate outcome. But I had literally associated my father with the store for as long as I had known him. And as stultifying as I found the place to be personally, I knew that he thrived there, that in many ways he identified himself through it.

"Wow."

"I'm having some trouble believing it myself."

My mother rubbed my father's hand. Her expression was grim. If she had at any point during the day tried to keep his spirits up, perhaps suggesting the things they would be able to do together in their retirement, that time had passed.

"What are you going to do?" I said.

My father tried to sit up a bit more in his bed, but even that seemed to take a lot out of him. I stood up to help him rearrange his pillows, but he waved me off.

"Your mother tells me that you're between jobs."

"We can talk about that some other time, Dad."

"She also said that you were thinking about leaving Springfield."

"Yeah, I am."

Still holding my father's hand, my mother turned to

face me. Her expression was less grim, but not less serious.

My father continued. "The two of us were talking and we wanted to know if you would be interested in taking over the store for me."

I couldn't have been more surprised if he'd asked me to play a round of tennis with him. I couldn't possibly have been equivocal in any way about my feelings for that kind of employment and surely both of them had to know that what I'd been doing for them in the store over the past few days was out of a sense of responsibility and not out of any level of interest.

"You want me to take over the store?"

"You know your way around; you know the way I like to do things."

"That's true, Dad."

"And coming home to Amber would be good for you. Give you some roots."

It didn't seem appropriate to tell him that I wasn't particularly concerned with roots and that even if I had been, the last place I would want to be rooted was Amber. For the first time, it occurred to me that they might have absolutely no idea what had been running through my head for the past ten years.

But beyond that, I couldn't possibly imagine spending any length of time at the helm of Amber Cards, Gifts, and Stationery. I tried to envision myself after twenty years of such unrelenting tedium. It wasn't difficult with my father sitting in a hospital bed.

"I'm not sure that would be a good idea, Dad."

His expression tightened. "I would be a silent partner. Give it a little thought."

"I really don't need to. I know how much the store means to you, but I don't have the same feelings about the place and I can't imagine that I ever would. I'm not cut out for that kind of work."

He stiffened. "What kind of work are you cut out for?"

I put my head down and laughed humorlessly. "That's a good question. I don't have a good answer for you on that. But I know what I'm not cut out for and, if anything, the last few days in the store have proven it to me. I'd go postal there."

My father leaned his head back in his pillow. For a few minutes, none of us spoke. Then my father turned to my mother.

"You have to call Howard Crest tomorrow. We've got to get the store on the market."

"Not tomorrow, Richard. Your operation."

"The next day, then."

"Don't rush anything," I said. "I can't do this for the long run, but I'll take care of the store while you sell it. I don't want you just taking the first offer that comes in. This is your nest egg."

"You won't go *postal*?" my father asked. I wondered if sarcasm qualified as strenuous activity.

"I'll be all right for a while," I said, forcing myself not to react to his disapproval. "It's not like this is going to take six months to do, right?"

"It could take a couple of months."

"I'll be all right for a while." I stood up and looked at my mother. "Shouldn't we be letting Dad rest up for tomorrow's procedure?"

She looked in my direction only for a second before turning back to my father.

"You go ahead if you want. I'm going to stay here until visiting hours are over."

CHAPTER SIX
In the Neighborhood

I remained diligent about watching the store for my father for a couple of weeks after that. One day, though, I stopped by only long enough to tell Tyler that I was not going to stay. I needed to get in my car and get away for the day – it was either that or stick around for another week or so and let things get to me to the point where I just drove off permanently.

My father came home from the hospital three days after a successful procedure opened the blockage. He spent his time adjusting to lean meats and dramatically reduced sodium and working up his courage to ascend the stairs. I wouldn't have thought his infirmity would have intimidated him so badly, but he slept several nights on the couch rather than making the climb, and on the nights when he did sleep in his own bed, he would stay there until close to noon the next day. His doctors told him that he needed to step up his level of exercise gradually, and at their suggestion, my mother purchased a stationary bicycle and a treadmill. But even though she placed them in the den where he was spending the vast majority of his time, my father hadn't been on either. He said he wasn't ready.

I wondered how much of my father's response to recovery related to my refusal to take over the store. It hadn't even dawned on me that my father making this proposition to me was as much a commitment of trust on his part as it was a convenient way to keep the business in the household. By turning him down, I suppose in some very real way I had announced to him that his trust didn't mean much to me.

If I had felt out of place in my parents' house earlier, I now felt flat-out repressed. Anything I did (or, for that matter and much to my surprise, my mother did) could be interpreted as a disturbance and therefore a hindrance to my father's convalescence. I could read or listen to my iPod in my room, which made me feel like I was still in high school, or I could watch television with the two of them. I chose as often as possible to do neither.

But spending evenings out of the house was equally unfulfilling. None of my old friends lived here anymore. Amber wasn't the kind of place that one moved back to. You could grow up here or you could discover the town later in life and choose to settle down, but once you left, you only ever returned for a visit. I reacquainted myself with several of my friends' parents only to learn that all of those friends had moved to Boston, New York, or out of the Northeast entirely.

And so I took to going out at night by myself, something I was never fond of but which I had grown accustomed to doing over the past decade. I went back to the bar that Tyler introduced me to and outside of which Iris and I kissed. The music was listenable, the bartender was funny, and I didn't feel particularly conspicuous if I found no one else to talk to. I also spent a fair amount of time at The Muse, a bookstore/café just off Russet Avenue. The espresso was good and, while it was clearly a place where locals got together to meet, there were always several people sitting by themselves with magazines or novels. After my third visit there, I decided to find out if it would take me longer to read all of John Updike's fiction than it would take Howard Crest to sell my father's store.

My progress over the first couple of weeks was considerably greater than Howard's was. He'd come into the store a few times to ask questions or meet with the store's accountant, but he had yet to bring any potential buyers. When I asked Howard how long he thought the process would take, he was noncommittal, saying that, while small retailers were always interested in Amber, they weren't necessarily interested in the kind of store my father had. This was a burdensome observation. An extended sale process meant that I had committed to spending much more time in Amber than I had intended. And all of it in a mind-numbing work environment, a frustrating home situation, and a social circle where I was on a first name basis with only the woman who made my coffee and the guy who poured my drinks.

I needed an escape of at least a temporary kind. It was a Monday, I knew things would be quiet in the store, and I knew that Tyler was more than capable of dealing with anything that came up. I got in my car and headed over the Pine River Bridge. From there, I simply drove. North on Route 9 and then north again on 91. I had no idea where I was going and I was convinced that it didn't matter. In fact, I thought that the simple unpredictability of the day would prove to be refreshing in and of itself. I had an R.E.M. album on the iPod and when "Everybody Hurts" came on, I was nearly giddy to hear the original version and not the version that played regularly on the store radio.

After about an hour, I exited to get some coffee and to go to the bathroom at a diner just off the road. While there, I decided to pull out my atlas to see what lay ahead in this direction. As I followed the map up into Massachusetts, my eyes shifted to the left and landed on Lenox. I could get there in a little more than an hour by switching over to the Massachusetts Turnpike. Iris had said she wanted to stay in touch. This seemed like an excellent way to find out if she meant it. I switched my iPod to The Bravery and jumped back onto the highway, taking the surprisingly good coffee and a homemade cranberry muffin along with me.

Lenox was in many ways what Amber wanted to be when it grew up. One of the largest towns in the Berkshire Hills, it was the home to dozens of craft shops, boutiques, restaurants, specialty stores, and inns, and drew a huge summertime tourist business from numerous superior performing arts venues, the most famous of which was the Tanglewood Amphitheater. It combined urban sensibility vacationing at its country home with Colonial history. And while it thrived during the summer, it was now very much alive twelve months a year. I'd made a late fall trip there just six months earlier with a woman I dated for a short while. I wonder what I would have done if I'd run into Iris then.

A Broadway character actor and one of her former professors at Yale founded the Lenox Ensemble in 1987. In their early years, they did repertory versions of the works of Williams, Albee, and Wilson, among others, and in recent years had concentrated on staging younger playwrights who they believed were doing important work. Last summer they had produced their first commissioned play and were committed to doing two of these every year in the future. I learned all of this from a flyer I found at an inn where I stopped to get some information. I knew how to get to Lenox, but I had no idea how to find where Iris worked.

The Ensemble's offices were located in a modest farmhouse about two miles from downtown. The theater itself was in a converted barn a couple hundred yards away. Inside the house was a series of desks where a handful of people in their early twenties made phone calls, typed on computers, and sorted through papers. There were offices to the left and to the back of this. As I entered, Iris came out of one of these talking heatedly with a man who was easily nine inches taller and twenty years older than she was. It had something to do with a problem with scenery and it wasn't clear whether they were on opposite sides of the argument or at various stages of extreme on the same side. At one point, Iris looked over and threw me a surprised glance before going back to her discussion.

A guy at a computer asked if he could help me and

I sat in a chair to wait things out. When Iris finished her exchange, she went back into her office and, for a moment, I thought she was either going to ignore me or had forgotten I was there. But then she walked out in my direction, looking considerably more relaxed than she had only moments before.

"You might be the last person I expected to see here," she said, kissing me on the cheek.

"I was in the neighborhood."

"Do you define the entirety of New England as your neighborhood?"

"I needed to get the hell out of Amber."

She looked at me, confused. "What were you doing in Amber?"

"A question I ask myself several times a day, starting from the moment I wake up. Some stuff has happened. Want to hear about it?"

"Yes, I think I would," she said, smiling. She looked at her watch. "I have a nightmare day. I don't know how much you heard of that conversation, but one of the set designers has had a creative crisis. We think it has something to do with the woman he started dating last month. Our first performance is in three weeks and we're just this side of royally screwed."

"In other words, I should have called first."

"Something like that. But I'd really like to talk to you. Can you hang around until dinnertime? I can suggest some things to do."

"I think I can take care of myself. What time should I come back?"

She looked at her watch and then back toward her office. "7:00?"

I wondered if I should simply get in my car and head back toward Connecticut. She was obviously very busy. But having made this move, I didn't want to get just three distracted minutes with her.

"I'll meet you back here then."

"Great." She kissed me on the cheek again. "I'm sorry, but I really have to run."

Using up five hours was not in any way difficult. I had my copy of *Rabbit Is Rich* and settled in to read for a while at a downtown café. Afterward, I browsed through the various shops, spending more than an hour at a used-and-rare CD store. I came away with a replacement copy of a Richard Shindell album I'd lost in one of my moves and bootlegs of Dave Matthews, Phish, and Umprhey's McGee. A little later, I walked into a store called Paperworks. It was a stationery, card, and gift store, but unlike my father's in so many ways. You could buy a spiral notebook there if you wanted, but you could also buy hand-marbled paper. You could get a Hallmark card if that's where your head was, but many of the cards were from much smaller suppliers, including an entire four-foot display from a local artist who printed them himself. And the gift items included kaleidoscopes from San Francisco, pottery from Tuscany, and maplewood cooking utensils from Vermont. There was plenty of mass-produced stuff here, but also many things for sale that I hadn't seen anywhere else. I wondered if the new owner of Amber Cards, Gifts, and Stationery would be this creative, and even thought for a second about asking the owner of Paperworks if he had any interest in a Connecticut location.

As the afternoon continued, I decided to take a walk away from downtown. The houses started modestly and then grew larger with more spacious lawns as I got farther from the commercial area. For some time now, I'd enjoyed wandering through unfamiliar neighborhoods. I usually drove, but I actually preferred to walk. I liked to imagine what life was like inside these houses, and when I was walking, the stray overheard voice or barking of a dog would take my imagination in unexpected directions. I passed one house where a preadolescent boy wearing a Boston Red Sox T-shirt was tossing pitches to a backstop, narrating the game action as he did so. Of course it was the World Series and of course he was winning. In my mind, the boy would go in to dinner in an hour or so and, while his parents discussed zoning issues, the day's business, or perhaps an upcoming performance from the Lenox Ensemble, he would eat his pasta quietly, reveling in that day's accomplishments.

I walked for nearly an hour and then went back to my car. On the way, I picked up a bottle of water at a convenience store and I sat in the car, sipping, listening to Richard Shindell, and wondering what I would do with the time that remained before I could see Iris again. Completely unbidden, I leaned my head against the side window and dozed off.

I got back to the farmhouse a little after 7:00. It was considerably quieter now and dimly lit. The guy who had greeted me when I arrived earlier that day was still seated at his computer.

"You're looking for Iris, right?"

"Yes, I am."

"She said you'd get here around now. The latest in our never-ending series of crises came up but she said she'd try to get back as close to seven as she could. Said you could wait in her office."

I thanked him and went to Iris' office, which was lit only by a table lamp. She had a poster of B.B. King on one wall and of Twyla Tharp on another. Just to the right of her desk was a photograph of an abandoned country road in a handmade frame. In spite of first Iris and now the guy at the computer telling me that her day – in fact, all of her days – had been hectic, there was little sign of commotion on her desk. There were probably hundreds of pieces of paper there, but they were all neatly arranged and seemed eminently accessible. A bookshelf against the far wall held a wide array of titles from a history of the Berkshires to one with local codes and ordinances to several business and accounting books to the collected works of Tennessee Williams to novels by Janet Evanovich, Barbara Kingsolver, and Saul Bellow.

As it got close to 7:30, I thought once again about heading back toward Amber. I was going to get home very late and I was sure that Iris would appreciate not having to entertain me after all these difficult hours at work. I decided to give it another fifteen minutes and then, when that passed, decided to give it fifteen minutes more.

I was flipping through the book of ordinances when she came in a little before 8:00.

"Thinking about running for city council?" she said.

"Nah, purely pleasure. This book is un-put-down-able."

She kissed me on the cheek and then walked behind her desk, looking through a stack of messages as she spoke.

"I'm really sorry I'm so late. I thought I'd be back here before you returned, but my hand-holding mission turned into a full-blown therapy session."

"If you want to call tonight off, I'm totally okay with that."

"No, jeez, after making you wait all this time? To tell you the truth, I'm looking forward to the diversion. If you hadn't shown up, I'd have just wound up staying here all night obsessing about everything that's going to go wrong in the next two weeks."

She walked behind her office door, retrieved a sweater, and put it on.

"Let's go," she said.

"You're positive?"

"Extremely positive."

We drove in separate cars to Stockbridge for sushi. As I looked at the menu, it dawned on me that these kinds of Japanese restaurants had become as comforting and familiar to my generation as roadside diners had been to previous ones. You could travel all over the country and find the same dishes as you found in The Plum Tree in Stockbridge, Massachusetts. The quality might vary, the preparations might even range slightly, but you could essentially order before you walked in the door.

"So did you have fun playing hooky today?" Iris said.

"More than I even thought I would. To tell you the truth, I had sort of forgotten that I was playing hooky."

"You'll have to show me how to do that. Now explain to me what the hell you're still doing in Amber. You haven't decided to move back there, have you?"

"Are you kidding? I think that's grounds for institutionalization in certain states. No, the thing with my father turned out to be worse than expected. He had another heart attack. He's got a good chance of being okay, but he can't work in the store anymore."

She wrinkled her nose. "That must be tough for him."

"As indicated by his expression, his demeanor, and the way the belt of his robe drags behind him if he ever decides to get up and walk."

Iris shook her head. "I would think it would be hard. I mean he's gotta be worrying about his health and he's definitely gotta be upset about losing his career."

"I know. And I do feel for him when I'm not annoyed at how defeated he seems and how much of a crimp he's put in my plans."

"You mean the reason you're still in Amber?"

"Yeah, that. He asked me to take over the store for him."

Iris' eyes doubled in size. "You didn't – "

"No! Please. But I told him I'd take care of things until he found a buyer. The way commercial real estate flips around on Russet Avenue, I figured I wasn't committing to very much. But the market for stationery stores seems a little depressed at the moment."

"So you're feeling just a tiny bit tied down?"

"Just a tiny bit."

Iris sipped some green tea and seemed to give my plight serious consideration. After a moment, she looked back up at me and held my eyes for a beat. As she did, I realized that I didn't want to spend our time together complaining. I hadn't made the long drive to bitch.

"I can handle it," I said.

She took another sip and put the tea mug down. "Of course you can."

While we ate, we talked about the production that the Ensemble was working on and the various ways in which Iris contributed to it. As always seemed to be the case with small creative groups, Iris' functions varied on an almost daily basis. While her primary responsibilities were managing staff, freelancers, and finances, at any given moment she could find herself giving an interview to a local paper, running lines with one of the actors, or offering the artistic director an opinion on productions under consideration. Though she did a fair amount of eye rolling and sarcastic muttering while she talked about the Ensemble, it was abundantly clear that she was engaged in her work. She didn't hold hands, perform counseling sessions, and stay in the office until midnight because someone had to. She did it because she knew it would help.

We talked about what she did when she wasn't working and she mentioned that the café where I'd stopped during the afternoon was one of her favorite places to go for lunch. She also told me that she spent a lot of time in Paperworks and that the greeting card artist I'd noticed lived down the street from the house she rented.

"Do you think there is anyone in Amber who considers my father's store to be one of their favorite places to hang out?" I asked rhetorically.

"Your father's store has a different function. He provides a service and the community appreciates it. Where the hell else would I have gotten my protractors when I was growing up?"

"You probably only came into the store because you were hoping to get a chance to talk to Chase."

Iris chuckled, but didn't say anything for a moment. Then she smiled and said, "That's only because his cute older brother was always hanging out in the back room."

I smiled, though I knew that none of what she said was true. If anything, I spent more time behind the cash register than Chase because he would get too distracted talking to customers, and there was no chance that Iris would ever have come into the store looking for Chase's "cute older brother." Like every other female of a certain age, Iris thought of Chase as The Boy.

When our meal was over, I asked Iris if she wanted to stop by the coffee bar a few storefronts down.

"I'm okay with it if you are," she said. "I'm not the one who has to drive for a couple of hours."

While my day in Lenox had been a pleasant diversion and while I was cheered that there wasn't any lingering awkwardness from the last conversation we'd had, this encounter was feeling too much like an interlude to me: friend stops in from out of town and you go out for a quick dinner together to catch up. I hadn't driven to the Berkshires with any agenda in mind. In fact, I hadn't even started driving that morning with the intention of going to the Berkshires. But now that I had seen Iris, I needed to know what we were currently doing.

I got us both coffee and we sat down. She took the lid off her coffee, allowing steam to waft up around her chin.

"Always ridiculously hot," she said.

I looked down at my cup, but kept the lid on it. "Listen, I have to admit that I understood only about every third word of what you were saying that last time I saw you."

She held the cup to her lips and her eyes shifted focus for a moment. I'm sure she would have been much happier if we had simply pretended that the kiss and the subsequent discussion about it had never happened. She took a small sip and recoiled from the temperature.

"Way too hot," she said and put the cup back down. "You really didn't understand what I was saying?"

"I got the message. I just didn't get the meaning behind the message."

"It's not that deep a message, Hugh. Our history is just a little too complicated."

"I understand that. But, you know, we always had a good time talking and it seems that we've had a really good time talking lately."

"That only makes it more complicated."

I held up my hands. "I'm not looking for it to be complicated. I just want to clarify something: when you were saying 'hey, maybe we can get together every now and then,' were you defining that as once every four years or so?"

"We're friends, Hugh. I don't think about parameters."

"And neither do I, usually. But to be honest with you, for as long as I'm stuck with this thing with my father's store, you might be the only real friend I have for hundreds of miles. I just wanted to make sure that we could do this again in the relatively near future."

She laughed. "I'll be happy to come out and play whenever I can. And you know, I'll be down to see my mother every month or so and we'll set things up then, too. If you remember, the last time we spoke, you were heading for New Mexico."

"I'm still heading for New Mexico. Just very slowly."

"That might make these casual get-togethers a little tougher." She reached out for my hand, squeezed it, and then put hers back on her coffee cup. "But until then, stop by whenever you're 'in the neighborhood.'"

I nodded and burned my tongue on the coffee. This wasn't what I wanted to talk about or even how I wanted to talk about it.

But it was something.

CHAPTER SEVEN
Willin'

I'd been in school during my junior year for a little more than a month when Chase and Iris showed up unexpectedly at my apartment door. After two years living on campus, I'd moved to a creaky one bedroom about a fifteen minute walk from the school. I'd had a difficult time with my roommate the previous semester and decided I really wanted to live by myself. At the same time, I didn't want to live alone, so I moved into a building that housed six other people I knew from Emerson. To me it was a nearly perfect arrangement: I got to have things exactly the way I wanted them in my living space while also having people to go to classes with, drink with, and crawl home much too late with.

Though one wall of the living room had flaking paint and the refrigerator considered its function to be optional, I loved the place. I bragged about it endlessly during my phone conversations with Chase and, for one of the few times in our lives, he actually seemed jealous. He kept telling me that he was going to come up to visit – something he had only done once the two previous years I was away – and I told him that he was always welcome, never expecting him to take me up on it.

I certainly didn't expect him to arrive at 11:00 on a Thursday night without calling ahead first. He stood in the doorway grinning, as though he had just performed some huge trick. I looked over at Iris and she simply waved.

After hugging Chase, I told him that he was lucky I was home, that I might have been out at a party, leaving them sitting outside the door for hours. He reminded me that he knew that I always spent Thursday nights alone studying because only then would I be comfortable playing all weekend. I'd had that studying habit since I was ten. I had, in fact, been reading an essay by Camus when he knocked on the door. I then reminded him that he was supposed to be at school the next day and he told me that it was a half day and that as a senior he was morally obligated to take those off. My parents would of course accept this kind of thing, though I wondered if they knew that Iris was with Chase. I had no idea what Iris had told her parents and thought it wouldn't be cool to ask.

While I had seven more pages of the Camus to read and Chase promised to be quiet, I decided I could finish my work Sunday night. We went to a bar a few blocks from the school and screamed conversation at one another while Nirvana, Pearl Jam, and other Seattle imports played in the foreground. Chase was much more enamored of this angst-riddled music than I was. I simply liked how the songs went from a whimper to a bang without notice and how there was a discernable melody even at the highest decibel levels. After a while, we let the music and the beer take over, assuming that we would have plenty of time to talk the next day when I finished my only Friday class. Chase and Iris held hands and occasionally said something into the other's ear, but they seemed content simply to live in that moment. This was yet another sign that Chase had found something with Iris. When I'd been with him on dates previously, he'd always been doing something, always keeping the conversation rolling, and always moving the evening along.

When we left the bar, Chase announced that he was ravenous for something with local flavor, insisting we find some Boston baked beans. When I told him that I had no idea how to find these other than in a supermarket and that I wasn't sure that this version of baked beans even came from Boston, he decided instead that he wanted tea. I assumed this was a reference to the Boston Tea Party and didn't bother to ask for an explanation. I tried to convince him that he might want to try other Boston specialties, suggesting a trip over to Little Italy, but he'd decided that he wouldn't be able to get to bed that night without some real Boston tea. I took him to the nearest diner.

I let Chase and Iris sleep in my bed while I spent the night on the couch. I was nearly asleep when the sounds of their lovemaking came through the door. This was not the first time I had been in the next room while someone else was having sex, but this was markedly different. My roommate the previous year had taken several women back to his room, filling the air with rhythmic pounding and exclamation and the concussion of bodies flipping athletically. But the sounds that Chase and Iris made were more serene and exponentially more erotic. Iris' subtle hum of satisfaction, the whisper of a hand moving softly underneath the sheets, a warm chuckle, an intake of breath, the quiet reverence in Chase's voice the few times he spoke. I found it a little disturbing to be listening to my brother this way (and I truly had little choice) but I also found it somewhat satisfying. I was glad that the two of them had this sexual connection together and I appreciated anew the effect that Iris had on Chase. I think they were still making love when I fell asleep.

The next morning, Chase walked into the living room in his boxer shorts, waking me up as he continued into the kitchen. He rummaged around for a minute and then came back to tell me that I had nothing to eat for breakfast. He walked back into my bedroom and came out fully dressed, telling me that he was going out to "forage."

As soon as he closed the door to the apartment, I heard the shower go on. A few minutes later, Iris came into the living room with a towel wrapped around her head and wearing the Emerson sweatshirt I'd bought Chase for his last birthday.

"It was really nice of you to let us sleep in your bed last night," she said, sitting down in a chair.

"I don't think the two of you would have been very comfortable on the couch. I guess I never thought much about having guests over."

"Well it was really nice of you anyway." She smiled and looked around the room.

I'd gotten out from under the sheets, had put my

pants on, and had been folding a blanket when she walked in. Now I sat back on the couch and watched her glancing around. I couldn't help but think about the sounds she had made while she was making love to my brother the night before. That soft hum was a slightly lower register than her speaking voice and it spoke of feeling something on a deep level. I'd never heard a woman make that sound before and I wondered if it was something distinctive to Iris or if it was something my brother regularly generated from his partners.

Iris' eyes continued to scan the room and I continued to look at her. I had of course realized that she was beautiful the very first time I saw her (even though at that point I thought she was beautiful and insane), but this was the first time that I realized how sexy she was. Almost certainly, it had much to do with what I had heard the night before, but it also had to do with how she looked just out of a shower. The towel didn't capture all of the strands of her hair and a few tickled her neck. The sweatshirt was considerably too large for her and led me to think about the lithe body that it covered. I stopped myself from continuing this line of thought. In the past, it had been fine for me to appraise my brother's girlfriends in this way because I had known they wouldn't be his girlfriends for very long. But things were different with Iris and I had to consider her in a different way.

Iris rose and picked up the book I'd been reading the night before.

"I don't get Camus," she said.

"I didn't get him in high school, either. I tried

reading *The Fall* in my sophomore year and it gave me a headache."

"Yeah, exactly."

"But my philosophy professor this year has really helped me to connect with him. I'm kinda becoming a closet existentialist."

She smiled. "Your secret's safe with me. I don't think I could ever be an existentialist, though. I prefer to have a little more meaning with my worldviews."

I promise you that a sentence like that had never come from the mouth of any of my brother's other girlfriends.

"Well the last great philosopher I embraced was Bullwinkle, so I'm likely to move on again."

She laughed and said, "When Chase and I first started dating he tried to convince me that he was a Marxist. I tried to explain to him that he really didn't sound like a Marxist at all. Then he told me he was talking about Harpo Marx."

"And he is a strict Harpo Marxist."

"Yeah, I guess he is."

A few minutes later, Chase returned with a bag of doughnuts and took over the room again. I left for my class around 10:00, but they stayed until after dinner. We talked about many things, mostly inconsequential. At various times during the day, though, completely unbidden, I would remember hearing them together the night before. And for at least a moment, I would have to look away.

• • •

I went into the store the next day feeling good. Iris had confirmed her interest in my staying in touch before we parted, the Phish double-CD bootleg had propelled my drive home from Lenox, and I even found Tyler's greeting of "Morning, Captain" when I arrived cheering.

The idyll didn't last very long.

Tuesdays in the store were always quiet. Even during the height of the summer and fall, when the inns were full most of the time and it took ten minutes to find a parking space anywhere near Russet Avenue, Tuesdays and Wednesdays remained relatively still. During the first hour I was in the store, as Tyler took notes for his accounting final and Carl put up a new shipment of Father's Day mugs, it came to mind that I could easily take these two days off for as long as it took to sell the store.

It was about this time when Carl came running up from the stockroom.

"We have a problem," he said, looking at Tyler.

"What's wrong?" I asked.

"The back room is getting flooded."

The three of us moved quickly to the stockroom, where water was gushing out of a burst pipe at an absurd rate. There was already an inch of water on the floor and the wall that butted up against the back display of the store was getting soaked.

"How the hell did this happen?" I said.

Carl shook his head. "I'm not sure how it started. I came back here to get a box and there was water all over the place. I tried to close the valve over there with a wrench and the valve broke."

I threw my head back and cursed. The vision of an

enormous flood in the back of the store doing untold damage – damage that would take months to repair, thereby extending my stay in Amber – loomed in front of me as the water continued to stream out. My cursing seemed to intimidate Carl, who started muttering apologies. I wasn't interested in an apology. What I wanted was for the flood never to have happened in the first place.

While I was seething, Tyler was actually doing something. He went first to a valve that he thought controlled the water in the store, but nothing happened. As he continued to search, I continued to rant. Several minutes went by while Tyler tried to figure out how to turn off the water. During this time, the flood got worse. Nearly the entire back wall of the store was soaked now.

"Of course, it's outside," Tyler said and headed out the back door. Shortly thereafter, the water stopped streaming and Tyler returned.

"I've probably seen that valve five hundred times coming into the store," he said. "I just never paid any attention to it."

"This is a disaster," I said, looking around the room. Most of our backup stock had been drenched. Since this was essentially cards and stationery items, that meant that all of it was ruined. I walked out of the stockroom to look at the back of the store. As I suspected, the plasterboard was soaked. What I stupidly hadn't anticipated was that the carpet was spongy. Rivulets of water formed around my shoes.

"Can someone help me up here?" came a voice from the front of the store. I turned to see a man holding a magazine, looking exasperated. I turned my back to him and cursed again.

"I'll get him," Tyler said, walking to the cash register. I went back to examining the display and Tyler returned after making the transaction.

"This whole wall is going to have to be replaced," I said. "Is this a load-bearing wall? Is the entire back of the store going to collapse?"

"What do you want me to do with these boxes," Carl said from the stockroom. I stood up, opened the back door, and pointed outside.

"See that dumpster?" I said. "That's the only thing you can do with those boxes now."

Tyler put his arm around my shoulder. "You might want to wait until we talk to the insurance company."

"I don't even know who the insurance company is."

Tyler took a deep breath. I think he was doing it to try to convince me to do the same. I didn't take his suggestion.

"I'll find out," he said. He led me toward the door of the stockroom. "Listen, why don't you take the register for a while? I'll call the landlord and cordon off the back of the store and then I'll get the number of the insurance company from the files."

"This is a total disaster," I said.

"It's actually only a partial disaster. Let me take care of some stuff back here. You handle the front."

While Tyler worked, I stood behind the counter, helping the occasional customer and stealing regular glances toward the back. I knew I'd been overreacting, but this complication was one of the few distressing scenarios I hadn't considered before. We weren't likely to find a buyer for the store while it was under repair. I castigated myself for having cavalierly offered to stay until my father sold the store. If I'd thought about it at all ahead of time, I would have put an outside date on my commitment. A date that would be rapidly approaching instead of receding increasingly into the distance.

I allowed myself to be furious about this for a while longer. Eventually, the simple act of needing to be pleasant to customers calmed me down. By the time Tyler returned to the front, I'd begun to feel somewhat chastened by the way he had taken charge while I ranted. Certainly if Tyler hadn't been there, I would have eventually done all of the things that he did instead, but I wouldn't have done them with his composure.

"Thanks," I said to him when he got behind the counter.

"It's fine. It's a mess back there, but at least the customers won't get wet. The landlord's going to be here in a half hour or so. The insurance agent is Philip Watson. I'll call him if you want."

"No, I'll call him." He handed me a piece of paper that listed the broker's contact information and the policy number. "You've done way more than your share already."

By the time the afternoon came along, the landlord and Watson himself (an old friend of my father's) had been by to examine the damage and I'd spoken to a contractor about getting to work on the repairs as quickly as possible. The activity made me feel like something was happening, even though it was really only conversation about something happening. Feeling guilty, I even sent Tyler home early once I was sure that things were under control. I kept Carl around, though there was very little for him to do.

As I stayed in the store, my sense of frustration returned. I walked to the back to examine everything again. I wondered if I had missed some sign that would have told me that this was coming, and I wondered if I could have done something to prevent it. I wondered what my father would have done differently. And then I wondered what Chase would have done differently. That I knew that both of them would have acted more efficiently and might have even minimized the damage did nothing to salve my mood.

• • •

That weekend, my mother went out of town with her sister for a couple of days. They'd been planning the trip for quite some time, some kind of annual spring retreat, and my mother intended to cancel it to tend to my father until I told her that I would do that job instead. It seemed that she could use the break and, sadly, taking care of my father didn't require much.

On my mother's recommendation, I hadn't told him about the water damage in the store because I didn't want to depress him more than he already was. This had the effect of making the weekend feel even more stilted than it was already going to be. Not only was he largely uncommunicative, but I couldn't even come up with a conversation starter without thinking about the mess in the store. On Friday night, he sat staring at the television, picking at the roasted chicken I'd brought home, and only talking to me when I asked him a question. Between my stint at the store and the duty I was pulling here, I felt like a full-time babysitter.

I knew I couldn't leave my father alone (a neighbor was staying with him while I was in the store), but I certainly didn't need to be in the same room with him. Still, for some reason, I felt obligated to sit with him, even though he was at best tangentially aware of my presence. And so I lay on the couch, gazing at the trophies and photographs and shop projects, while he sat in his chair watching a sitcom (two kids frolicking and causing their parents to roll their eyes a lot), a mawkish drama (a dysfunctional family that still manages to love one another), and then a cop show (some kind of mystery emerging from deep in the past). At some point, I fell asleep. The first time in my adult life that I did that in front of a television. When I awoke, it was a little after eleven and Dad was giving the news the same hypnotic attention he'd given the other shows.

"Dad, it's late," I said. "Let's go to bed."

"I just want to finish watching this."

"All right, but we're going to bed after the news is over. I'm getting tired and I want to help you upstairs before I go to sleep."

He didn't say anything until a segment on a parade in Hartford finished.

"I'm not going upstairs tonight. I'll sleep here."

For the past three nights, he'd slept on the sofa bed in the den, unwilling to climb the steps to his bedroom. The doctors had told us that there was no reason to believe that the stress of going up a flight of stairs would do any damage to his heart, but he didn't want to hear this. If he was going to sleep downstairs a fourth night in a row, there was a good chance he was simply going to continue to do it. In his mid-fifties, my father was acting like an elderly man.

"The bed upstairs is much more comfortable, Dad. We always put the guests we didn't like very much on the sofa bed."

"This is fine. I'm not up for climbing the stairs. If you could just pull the bed out for me, I'll be okay."

I wondered what would happen if I refused to pull the bed out for him. Would this force him to come upstairs with me? I guessed that he would probably just sleep in the chair. I set things up and then tried one more time to convince him to go up to his room.

"I'm fine here, Hugh. Go to bed if you're tired."

"Do you want me to help you to the bathroom?"

He scowled at me. "I can make it to the bathroom myself," he said. At least I had some sense of the parameters now.

When I came back from the store on Saturday, we repeated the ritual. By 8:45, I was burning up with cabin fever. He was watching a rerun of a Super Bowl game on ESPN Classic. He didn't even like football. He'd always said that the only games he could watch were the games Chase participated in when he was in middle school. I tried to pass the time reading *The Witches of Eastwick*, but the play-by-play on the television was too distracting. Finally, I decided to leave the den. I'm not even sure Dad noticed I was gone.

As I approached the stairs to my room, I passed the study and noticed the computer's screen saver, a

time-lapse video image of a lily blossoming. My
mother was a dedicated e-mail correspondent with
dozens of friends and relatives. In fact, this was the
primary way I had communicated with her over the
past several years.

Rather than reading, I decided to spend a little time
online. I went to Google and typed "New Mexico."
Of course, there were nearly three million items returned, but I managed to find some truly informative
sites on the first several screens. One site even allowed me to match my temperament with my ideal
New Mexico location. While I would have expected
to be directed to Albuquerque or Santa Fe (admit-
tedly among the only places I knew in New Mexico),
the program directed me toward Tucumcari, a tiny
frontier town out on the old Route 66. The only previous reference I'd had to Tucumcari was in Lowell
George's song, "Willin'" and George had hardly provided much information. I followed a link to the
town's Chamber of Commerce site and spent a good
half hour surfing the place's history, attractions, and
community development plans. I even found a
restaurant that I would surely visit once I got out
there. Before leaving the site, I requested a booklet
about the town and several brochures.

When I got off, I felt better than I'd felt in a few
days. Spending the time exploring New Mexico reminded me that my stasis in Connecticut was only
temporary, that the store would eventually sell, and
that I would be free to make my way West. To get
my kicks out on Route 66.

I picked up my Updike book where I'd left it on
the stairs and decided to check in on my father before

going to my room. A Denver Broncos drive against the Green Bay Packers had my father's absolute attention. I wondered if he would notice if I changed the channel.

"Dad, do you need anything before I head upstairs?" The sofa bed was already open, since I hadn't bothered to fold it in in the morning. He didn't say a word as John Elway completed another pass to Ed McCaffrey. It dawned on me that it was entirely possible that he didn't know who won this game – if he was even actually paying attention.

"You sure you don't need anything, Dad?"

As the Broncos huddled up, he turned to me. "Yeah, a new body," he said.

"I'll see if I can order you one online in the morning. I'm going to read in my room. If you need me, give me a call."

He turned back toward the game. I watched him for another minute, stupefied at the way he'd decided to kill the clock.

On Sunday, the store was busier than I expected it to be and I stayed behind to give the late shift a hand. When I got back to my parents' house in the late afternoon, my mother had returned from her trip. I hadn't been expecting her until after dinner, but was relieved to see her there. We talked for a couple of minutes about her weekend and then I told her I was going out again.

"You aren't staying for supper?" she asked.

"I'll get something wherever. I'd kind of like a little free time."

She looked toward the den. "Was this too much for you?" she asked crisply.

"Not too much, Mom. But definitely enough."

"I'll see you later, then."

· · ·

I called Iris the next day and she invited me up for the following Wednesday. As had been the case the first time I drove to see her, I felt a little looser and a little more liberated with every mile that passed. It was as though the enervating frequencies sent out from Amber began to fade as I put more distance between them and myself. Though the trip was nearly two hours long, it energized me.

I met Iris at her office a little after seven. As soon as she saw me, she grabbed her sweater, kissed me on the cheek, and we were out the door.

"That was surprisingly easy," I said.

"Calm before the storm. Opening night is next Wednesday. By Friday, there will be all kinds of crises – real and imagined. But right now everything is on track and everyone is happy."

"Lucky me."

"Yeah, you wouldn't want to be here Friday night."

We went to a restaurant in town where Iris was hoping to get us a table on the porch. Unfortunately, every one of them was occupied and we were parked in a cramped spot in the bustling main dining room. We could just barely hear '60s R&B above the chattering of nearly a hundred patrons and the clattering of dishes being speedily bussed.

"Cozy little spot, huh?" she said as we were seated.

"Is it always this busy?"

"I didn't think it would be on a Wednesday night,

but yeah, it's really popular. You should see it in the summer. At least if we were outside we'd be able to talk."

A couple got up from the table across from ours and a busboy was there as they took their first step away, throwing plates into a bin.

"This is fine," I said. "They really do like to turn those tables, don't they?"

As if in response, a waiter was at our side, asking if we'd decided what we wanted to order. We hadn't even looked at the menus and I laughed, though he didn't seem to think anything he'd said was funny. Feeling pressured, I opened my menu and the waiter said he'd be back in a minute. In most restaurants, this would mean that he would be back sometime in the next hour, but no more than a hundred seconds later, he was standing at our side again.

"My heart is pounding," I said to Iris after the waiter left.

"You never let him see you sweat, though."

I caught her up on the water disaster in the store and the glacial pace at which the contractor had begun to deal with the repairs. The person I'd hired had convinced me that he would need to replace the back wall and then informed me that he needed to do this in a very slow, very deliberate fashion. I didn't know enough to know whether he was playing me or not, but since he was yet another friend of my father's, I felt that I had to trust him. After he dealt with the wall, he would need to do considerable work to the stockroom and replace a huge piece of the carpeting. The fact that he refused to be governed by a schedule was flat-out depressing.

Iris told me about the resolution to the tempest with the set designer – it turned out to be less about his romantic entanglements than it was about an adjustment to his antidepressant – and then about an actor they needed to replace on very short notice because he broke his contract to take a gig out in Utah. She related both of these stories matter-of-factly and I could imagine that she dealt with the actual situations in much the same way. I admired her for this. Either one might have been enough to send me packing.

The meal came promptly and I felt a bit compelled to eat it as quickly. As we tended to our food, we didn't say much to each other. I could just barely make out the harmonies of "Ain't Too Proud to Beg" over the din. At another table, a man animatedly explained a painful breakup to a friend.

"So what's happening with your father?" Iris asked as our coffee arrived.

"He's managed to confine his entire existence to the den."

"Well, from what I remember, it's a nice room."

"I guess I should consider it a good thing that he's not sitting in the garage."

"Are you worried?"

I shook my head. "Worried is the wrong word. Confounded would be a better word. Flummoxed maybe. He's fifty-five."

"You have a right to be flummoxed, though I don't think I've ever heard someone say that word out loud before. He's gonna come out of it, though, right? If he's relatively okay physically, he'd have to, wouldn't he?"

"He should. I'm guessing he will. It's just so bizarre seeing him this way. I mean, he was never a Type A guy, but at least he was always motivated."

Iris sipped her coffee and seemed a little hesitant before she spoke again.

"Was this what he was like after Chase died?"

Of course she wouldn't have known. I recalled my father's thousand-yard stare out the window and the stoicism that followed until the day I left. "That's definitely the last time I've seen him this resigned. But at least then he had a better reason."

"If it's any consolation, my mother's been driving me a little crazy lately, too," she said.

"What's going on?"

"She went out on a date last Friday."

"Wow. First one since your dad?"

"First one that 'counts' as my mother puts it. About a year ago, some friends invited this widower over to some dinner parties. She assumed they were trying to set her up with him, but she wouldn't give the guy the time of day. This time it was someone she met at a craft fair. He took her to dinner and it sounds like they had a very good time."

"Great."

"Except that she's feeling insanely guilty about it. I mean can't-get-out-of-bed kind of guilt. She thinks it diminishes my father's memory if she likes another man."

"That's silly."

"Try finding a half dozen delicate ways to say that and you'll understand what my phone conversations with her have been like lately."

"So is she going to go out with him again?"

"She's screening her calls. She can't decide what to do."

I shook my head and just said, "Families."

The check arrived and, seeing that there were others waiting for our table, we dutifully paid it. We'd been in the restaurant less than an hour.

"That was kind of brisk, wasn't it?" Iris said when we got outside.

"I'll never complain about slow service again." We walked toward the parking lot. I certainly didn't want to drive back to Amber yet.

"It's kind of early," Iris said. "Do you want to go to a movie?"

It was nice to have her suggest that we extend our time together. We drove to the local theater and bought tickets for the movie with the nearest start time. It didn't matter that the movie wasn't particularly interesting and it didn't matter that we couldn't talk during the show. It was just good to be in the same place with her and to bump fingers with her on occasion as we reached for the popcorn.

On the way back to Connecticut that night, I played some Temptations songs on my iPod as a reminder of the music I could barely hear in the restaurant. I sang high harmonies and pounded out the syncopated rhythms on the steering wheel.

Iris and I had set the time machine on "now" tonight.

CHAPTER EIGHT
Plaster in the Air

During the winter break of my junior year at Emerson, I helped in the store, as I had every holiday season since I was ten. This was one of the few times of year when it actually made sense to me that my father carried porcelain figurines and pen-and-pencil sets. While I would never have gone to a card store for these kinds of things (though honestly, I wouldn't have gone anywhere for these kinds of things), the citizens of Amber buzzed in here to buy every trivial knickknack we could offer. From mid-December until the twenty-fourth (Christmas Day being the one day of the year when my father closed Amber Cards, Gifts, and Stationery) there would be customers in the store at all moments. Sometimes there would be dozens at a time. My father seemed incredibly happy during these periods, less I think because of the money that this activity generated than because it reminded him that the community wanted and needed him.

This didn't mean that I actually liked working in the store during these times. The rushes kept me occupied and there was always something to do, which made the hours go faster. And it was charming to see my otherwise understated father exchanging pleasantries with the customers. But it still seemed like a chore to me, something I was doing to be a dutiful son rather than anything I would have ever chosen to do. And now that these sessions took place during my winter break, I found myself thinking about all the friends who were back in town from college and what I could be doing with them instead of being here.

I would have assumed that Chase would be feeling this way even more than I did this season. It was his first Christmas with Iris and Amber could be a romantic place during the holidays. Surely, he would have preferred a sleigh ride with her out on Pearson's Farm. Or perhaps Mexican hot chocolate and pumpkin bread at the lavishly decorated Tavern on Russet. Or browsing with her through the thousands of handmade ornaments on display at Celebrations. Or cuddling under a blanket to stay warm while listening to the carolers in the park. I know that if I had a girlfriend like Iris to spend this time with, I would resent my dad tying me down.

But if Chase minded, he gave no indication of it. A huge rush had ended a few minutes before, and while I stood behind the counter with my head propped up on my arm, he was at a display good-naturedly haranguing my father because he felt the toy selection had gone stale. He pointed to a grouping of stuffed animals and called them "stuffy animals," suggesting that they weren't at all what kids wanted as gifts. My father listened carefully to what Chase said and gave it the careful consideration that he always did, while at the same time mentioning that we'd just sold a "stuffy animal" in the last flurry of activity. Chase laughed and said that this actually proved his point, as the animal had gone to an older man who probably had no idea what his grandchild really preferred.

The debate continued for a few more minutes, Chase teasing my father for "fossilizing" while my father jokingly suggested that he should bow to Chase's "decades of experience." I had just rung up a sale and was counting out change when Chase came behind the counter, grabbed fifty dollars from the cash register, and continued out the door.

"I think you've just been robbed, Dad," I said.

My father laughed. "Assaulted maybe, but not robbed. He'll be back, though God knows what he'll be back with."

Without the sideshow of Chase and my father sparring, the next couple of hours dragged. Business ebbed and flowed, but it didn't seem as crisp or stimulating as it did when Chase was there chatting up people in line, running madly to find some piece of merchandise, making incongruous gift suggestions to those who were naive enough to ask him for one. My father asked me to straighten a display and to rearrange the copper candlesticks to make them appear less picked over (for some reason we'd had a run on these earlier in the day) and I took to the tasks, only once slipping away to the phone to set up a drinks date with some friends that night.

About an hour after Chase left, Tricia, that era's manager, arrived for her shift. She was a sophomore at MCS and had been working for my father the past couple of years. I'd gone out with her and her boyfriend a couple of times when I was in town.

"What's it been like here today?" she asked.

"The usual," I answered.

"Where's Chase?"

"One of the mysteries of the moment. He gave my father a dissertation on the marketplace, then grabbed fifty bucks from the cash register and disappeared. My father seems to think he'll be back. I think he's buying chocolates for Iris."

Tricia laughed. "What was he telling Richard he was doing wrong this time?"

"Kid's stuff."

She nodded knowingly. With Tricia there, I'd at least be able to catch up on gossip and find out if anything interesting was happening while I was in town. I couldn't have these conversations with Chase while we were in the store because he was always in the middle of something else. Tricia did a good job for my father, but she also understood that what we were doing required minimal concentration.

An hour later, Chase returned with a large plastic bag from the Toys "R" Us in the mall. He called my father over and produced a couple of handheld electronic games, a plastic velociraptor that made "authentic" dinosaur noises from a sound chip, and three stuffed animals: one round yellow thing that bleated and stuck out its tongue when squeezed, one purple and green alien with spikes on its arms, and a bald guy with a hatchet in his head. He proceeded to pull the Toys "R" Us tags off of the merchandise and remark the pieces with our price tags. My father pointed out that it was difficult to make a profit when you bought something retail and charged the same amount for it. Chase countered that buying these

things wasn't about making a profit, but rather showing that the store was on top of the market enough to
carry them in the first place.

"I'm with Chase on this one, Richard," Tricia said.
"Love the raptor, by the way." To punctuate this, she
pressed the button to activate the sound chip and the
raptor squealed. This drew the attention of a young
boy who had just entered the store with his mother.
I just shook my head as the kid told the woman that
this was the dinosaur he wanted and as she asked Tricia to hold it aside for her while she finished her
shopping. As they walked to the back of the store,
Tricia and Chase high-fived while my father took the
other items and put them on display.

"That was purely coincidental," he said, grinning.
He stopped and looked accusingly at Chase. "You set
that up, didn't you?"

Chase held up his hands to express his innocence.

"I'll talk to the distributor about getting some of
this stuff in January," my father said, grinning.

• • •

The process of taking the back wall of the store
down to replace it was even more excruciatingly
slow than described in advance. Since it was a load-
bearing wall, the contractor couldn't simply knock
it down and put up a new one. Instead, he had to
strip it down to its beams. This meant days of plaster in the air, footprints on the carpet, and dust on
the cards in spite of the plastic we'd put up to seg-
regate the work area. Given that the tourist season
wasn't yet in full swing, it was just about as good a

time as any for the store to go through this.

It was not, however, a good time for Howard Crest to bring a potential buyer to visit.

I was standing in the back of the store surveying the work the carpenter was doing when I heard Howard's halting voice.

"Oh, there you are, Hugh. Can I have a bit of your time?"

I turned around to see him approaching me with his hand outstretched. He was a fragile-looking man who seemed to vibrate slightly as he talked. My father knew him from the Chamber of Commerce and was certain of his competence, even though I'd seen little evidence of this in my first few meetings with him. I knew Howard was well aware of the repairs we were doing at the store, as I had called him about them myself. I shook his hand and then eyed him warily when I saw that someone was with him.

"Hugh, this is Mitch Ricks. He'd like to take look at the store. Can you give us some time?"

"Sure," I said, casting another glance at Howard. He clearly wasn't as concerned about doing this under these circumstances as I was. The man walked past me and up to the plastic covering behind which the carpenters worked.

"What's going on here?" he asked.

"We had a pipe explode on us. It did a lot of damage, but we're doing the repairs now." I looked over at Howard again. "All of it will be finished before any new buyer comes in."

The man looked down at the floor and scuffed up a streak of plaster dust.

"Carpet, too?"

"We're replacing the entire back portion," I said.

The tour was off to a rousing start. I took Ricks through the store, telling him as much as I knew about traffic, turns, and the strongest revenue streams. Howard said nothing the entire time other than mentioning that he'd bought his granddaughter one of the kites we had on sale. Since the back office was unavailable, we settled behind the counter and I answered some more of Ricks' questions. They weren't particularly probing and he seemed preoccupied with the sounds coming from the other end of the store. Fifteen minutes after he'd arrived, he was gone. I was relatively certain I wouldn't see him again. When Howard shook my hand as he was leaving, I still wasn't sure that he understood that he should have at least given me some advance warning.

For the rest of the morning and into the early afternoon, I remained miffed at the broker. My situation was frustrating enough without being complicated by the bungling of this man.

By 3:00, I was still peeved. Even Tyler's buying me a caramel brownie at the bakery across the street (a place I'd come to think of as Iris' bakery) didn't make me feel better. I finally decided that I needed to go see Crest.

Howard's office was on River Road, the other major commercial street in town, and the one that led directly to the Pine River Bridge. This was a funkier spot, with a number of bars and ethnic restaurants scattered between office buildings. The company Howard worked for dealt in both commercial and residential real estate, and Howard was the head of the commercial division. I'd never been in this office before, and as I drove over to it, I half expected to find it disheveled and uninviting, with cigarette-burned desktops, coffee-stained floors, and a couple of distracted brokers ineffectually shuffling through piles of papers. Instead, the place was crisply appointed, with each broker's work area partitioned by glass bricks, and original local art on the walls. I think the biggest discrepancy between my image of the business and reality came when I arrived at Howard's mahogany-accented office off the main floor. He sat in a high-backed leather chair, speaking on the phone in his clipped manner when I entered his doorway. He gestured me in and then held up a finger to indicate that he would be finished shortly.

"I had a feeling I might see you today," he said after he hung up. "I was planning to give you a call, but things got crazy." Even in this environment that attested to his success, he seemed unusually skittish.

The setting threw me off for a minute, but now that I had Howard in front of me, my irritation returned.

"I assume your client wasn't interested," I said.

"I don't think so, no."

"Howard, you knew about the work going on in the store. What made you think you should just drop in like that?"

He reached for a can of Diet Coke, took a sip, and then shook his head.

"I know," he said. "You told me about all of the water damage and I should have come in to see it myself before I brought anyone with me."

"Or at least called to let me know you were coming so we could clean things up a little."

"You're right. It was stupid. But when this man came in and told me what he was looking for, he seemed so right for your father's store. I have to admit that I leaped at the opportunity and did it without even thinking." He looked down and then took another sip from his can. "There hasn't been much activity on this."

"All the more reason to be careful about how we present it when we get some."

He held up his hands. "You're right. Completely. I just really want to do this for your dad."

It was difficult to continue to be angry with Howard when he was being this contrite. I simply shook my head. "*Why* has there been so little activity. Is the market slow right now?"

"No, the market isn't slow at all. Like I said, things have been crazy around here. It usually is. But when people think of buying a business on Russet Avenue, they think of galleries or jewelry stores or gourmet shops."

"But the store has been doing okay, hasn't it?"

"It's been fine by all indications. Not sensational, but fine. But if I can be honest with you, Hugh, stationery stores aren't exactly what people dream about owning."

"Tell me about it." Howard Crest was perhaps the last person on the planet I wanted underscoring this point for me. I'd come into his office charged with annoyance. Now I felt as drained as a Duracell that had been sitting in a child's toy for ten years. "Are there any other prospects?"

"Nothing at the moment. You never know, though. That's one of the good things about this business."

I nodded. I didn't want to take up any more of Howard's time. But I also really didn't want to go back to the store after this soul-sapping conversation. When it was clear that Howard didn't have anything more to say to me, I stood up, shook his hand, and left. Before I got back into my car, I took a walk down River Road, looking into the shops. So few of the storefronts were the same as they were when I was last there. A restaurant menu seemed interesting and one of the bars had live blues on the weekend. At some point, it might be worth going to one or both of them.

Considering how long it might take Howard to sell the store, it seemed wise to re-familiarize myself with the area.

• • •

I didn't say anything about the episode with Howard to my father that night. We ate dinner on tray tables in the den, as my parents did every night now, while *The NewsHour with Jim Lehrer* played. My mother didn't even suggest eating in the dining room any longer, and the sofa bed was open all the time.

When we finished eating, I helped my mother bring the dishes into the kitchen.

"We struck out with a potential buyer for the store today," I said while she loaded the dishwasher.

"Too bad," she said, concentrating on her task.

"Howard brought the guy into the store while the carpenters were banging away and there was plaster dust everywhere. He picked the worst possible time."

"Howard knows what he's doing."

She moved over to the stove to get a pot. My mother had been stiff and disengaged since I'd come back to town. I assumed that this had something to do with my father's illness. But she had rarely made eye contact with me since his return from the hospital and I was starting to take it personally. I'd begun to wonder if this was a response to my refusal to take over the store. In this context, she would of course have little sympathy for how Howard's error scuttled my day.

"He might know what he's doing most of the time, but he certainly didn't know what he was doing today. The store is a mess. If he had given me some warning, I could have at least made the place look reasonably presentable."

She continued to wash the dishes without saying a word. I brought a mixing spoon and another pan over to the sink for her. When she was finished washing these, she shut the water off and turned in my direction.

"You know," she said, looking past me rather than at me, "I don't think we've ever had a pipe burst in that store before."

I understood the implication and decided not to get into it with her. If she was angry with me for making the only appropriate decision I could make, she was going to have to work this out for herself. I left the kitchen and went up to my room, planning to go out for a drink. I picked up the copy of *Couples* I was reading. It was now obvious to me that I would indeed finish all of Updike's novels before the store sold. Perhaps months before the store sold. Maybe I'd move to the Faulkner canon next.

I put the book back on my dresser and headed out the door.

CHAPTER NINE
A Difficult Set to Light

The next Wednesday was the opening night of the new production by the Lenox Ensemble. I'd spoken with Iris once since the last time I saw her, and the days leading up to the premiere had been predictably chaotic for her. We were probably on the phone for ten minutes, though I don't think I actually spoke with her for more than two of those. About halfway in, I could almost guess when the next midsentence interruption was going to occur.

Other than the sound of the carpenters, the store was very quiet. In addition to the usual midweek slump, there had been a perceptible decline in sales since the water damage occurred. Since my father didn't keep detailed reports of his revenue stream, it was difficult to know whether this was because of the merchandise that wasn't available in the back of the store or because of the environment created by the contractor. Though I usually stayed until the early evening and sometimes even closed the store, it had become clear to me that my presence wasn't necessary during the trough of the week. Faced with the option of another catatonic dinner in front of the television with my parents or a drive to surprise Iris, I chose the latter.

I had dinner in downtown Lenox before going over to the barn. While I ate, I read a copy of the local paper, the *Berkshire Eagle*, skipping through the national news to get a better sense of the community. There was so much going on here, and there was a brimming sense of anticipation for the approaching summer season and the performances, festivals, and fairs that would accompany it. I found a small article about the premiere by the Ensemble. The artistic director had several quotes in the piece, and though I'd never met the man, his voice came into my head with the intonation that Iris gave to her own voice when she spoke about him.

I hadn't wanted to risk Iris seeing me at the box office, so I waited until just before the curtain to get a ticket. This nearly backfired on me, as I bought one of the last three seats and would have missed out entirely if I'd had that second cup of coffee. While this left me sitting in the very back of the theater and I chided myself for the folly of committing to four hours of driving without securing a seat first, I was impressed that the Ensemble could fill the place with a midweek opening before the official start of the season.

The production was the world premiere of the latest work from Miller Citron, a New Hampshire playwright who'd begun to generate regional attention for his earlier dramas. His previous play had in fact gotten excellent notices for a version staged in downtown Manhattan. Iris had told me that she expected it wouldn't be long before Citron opened a play off-Broadway, and there was even talk of taking this work there.

The play, titled *The Last Week in October*, was about a couple in Martha's Vineyard closing down their small inn for the season. As the play progressed, however, it became clear that what they were actually in the process of closing down was their marriage. The writing reminded me of Edward Albee. It was acerbic with a deep core of cynicism, yet occasional flashes of romance and charm elevated it and made me care about the people on the stage. The two lead actors gave nuanced performances, balancing anger, disappointment, sadness, and longing without ever allowing any one emotion to dominate. The small handful of other players was less accomplished. The best friend was too consciously sympathetic, the lawyer too openly flirtatious. Having heard so much about the set designer, I was especially interested in seeing how he dressed the stage. It was spare, offering the suggestion of a country inn rather than the depiction of one, using muted colors with the occasional touch of a vibrant red.

The play was very powerful. It moved me and caught me up in its complexities. At the same time, I remained aware that Iris had helped bring this play to the stage and I felt a strong surge of pride at her involvement. When the audience applauded appreciatively at the end, I couldn't help but think of how Iris received that appreciation.

One of the guys I'd seen at Iris' office on my visits recognized me and let me backstage afterward. The entire area was a swirl of motion. A couple dozen people either milled or darted and others made their way in behind me. I saw Iris moving quickly from one end of the room to the other and I called to her. She stopped and turned in my direction. For a moment, her eyes opened widely in obvious (and, I hoped, pleasant) surprise, but then her brow furrowed and she put up one finger to indicate that she was in the middle of doing something else. She headed toward the far corner of the room. I didn't want to crowd her, but I took a few steps in that direction. Doing so allowed me to see what she was dealing with. The male lead and the man who played the best friend were exchanging heated words. I couldn't make out all of it, especially when others in front of me began to comment on the proceedings, but it appeared that the lead felt this was the appropriate time to question some of his fellow actor's choices. His subordinate took exception to this. Their verbal sparring quickly descended to profanity and name-calling. An actor I'd admired just minutes earlier now seemed petty. I wondered if there was a history between the two or if perhaps the lead had a reputation for belittling his fellows.

There seemed an excellent chance that things were going to come to blows, especially when one actor put his hand on the shoulder of the other. But then Iris intervened. She said something sharp but *sotto voce* to the lead actor and he responded to the comment by briskly turning his back to her and walking off in the other direction. Iris then put her arm around the other actor's shoulder. The man was obviously having trouble regaining his composure and he gesticulated harshly for a minute or two before Iris turned him toward her, patted him on the chest, and calmed him down.

This fire doused, Iris started walking in my direction. Since she hadn't made eye contact, though, it wasn't clear whether she was actually coming to see me or not. She didn't get particularly far. The director intercepted her about fifteen feet from me.

"Can you believe the incompetence of those lighting people," he said.

"It wasn't that bad, Art," Iris said in response.

"Not bad if this were dinner theater. The audience must have been cringing from all the gaffes."

"Most people probably didn't even notice. I only saw a couple mistakes myself."

The director drew back from this comment. His body language suggested that Iris' statement had diminished his estimation of her.

"Don't give me that crap, Art," Iris said. "You knew it was a difficult set to light and you knew that we were going to have to make certain compromises. Did they do a great job tonight? No. Did they do it appreciatively differently from what you agreed to in the last rehearsal? No."

"Pardon me, Iris, I thought you cared about excellence as much as I do. It seems I was wrong about this."

"Art, is there any chance you might consider the possibility that you're a little too close to this?"

"A director can never be too close to his work."

Iris glanced off in the other direction and waited a beat. She was obviously trying to avoid saying something that would escalate the situation. "We'll do a run-through of the scenes that you think need to be corrected tomorrow afternoon. I'll set it up."

The director sighed theatrically (which I suppose was appropriate) and said, "See what you can do. Right now, I need a scotch."

He walked away and Iris stood in her place for a moment, staring off toward the back wall. I was about to approach her when she started walking away. Someone stopped her and congratulated her on the production and she smiled and offered thanks. While she was doing so, she glanced up at me and I could tell from her expression that she had forgotten I was there. She said a few additional words and the man walked away. Her face dropped as she turned to me and took a few weary steps.

"Congratulations?" I said warily.

She shook her head. "What a disaster this was tonight."

"I've gotta tell you, it didn't seem like a disaster from out there."

"Trust me; I know a disaster when I see one. This was a classic. Theo delivered his lines like he was on Seconal – and Walt nearly punched him out because of it. Art thinks the lighting director should never work in this town again. The reviewer for one of the local papers had to beg for his tickets because there was a screwup at the box office, and even the ushers botched their jobs. Sounds like the definition of the word 'disaster' to me. Do you have a better one?"

"Under the radar?"

She dropped her head and took a deep breath. "Did you like the show?"

"I loved it. I really did. That guy can write. And Walt might be an asshole, but he's an excellent actor."

Iris' face relaxed a little more. I'd never seen her

this tense before. "Yeah, he is. And yeah, he's definitely an asshole. I don't know how someone who is that much of a jerk can show so much tenderness on-stage."

"That's why they call it acting, isn't it?"

"I guess it is." She looked toward the back of the room and I could see her shoulders stiffen. When she turned back to me, though, she smiled. "I had no idea you were going to be here tonight."

"Spur-of-the-moment thing. I wanted to see what your opening nights were like."

She gestured toward the rest of the room. "Now you know. It's a glamour profession."

"Hey, not everyone gets to have their chains yanked by artists. Some of us only get carpenters and real estate brokers."

"I feel so much better now." Whatever had concerned her in the back of the room was continuing to bother her. She looked in that direction again and her eyes remained there for several moments. She turned back to me and said, "Listen, I've gotta get over there. Art is talking to the *Eagle*, and considering his state of mind, he could wind up saying anything. You're going to stick around for a while, right?"

"Yeah, I'll be here."

Iris moved as if snapped from a bungee cord. I went to get something from the buffet table. This scene didn't exactly mesh with the one I had in my mind while I was driving to Lenox. I'd envisioned a small cast party with champagne and erudite banter and me standing by Iris' side as she celebrated. Most specifically, I'd envisioned Iris seeing me backstage and hugging me close as she thanked me profusely for sharing this important moment with her. I'd imagined that I might even get a chance to toast her privately at a bar later in the evening.

Instead, I hadn't even gotten a kiss on the cheek.

The crowd thinned over the next twenty minutes. I milled around, eating a pastry, listening in on some conversations. I didn't know anyone here other than Iris and I was beginning to feel a little awkward about being in the room. Iris had disappeared with Art a few minutes after she walked away from me and hadn't been back since. I wondered if all opening nights were like this for her. I probably should have asked at some point. Regardless, she very obviously didn't have time for me.

I was getting another cup of coffee when I saw her come back to the room. But as she did, Art called her back in the direction she came. He was with a woman I hadn't seen before. The three gathered by the doorway, standing very close to one another and speaking intently. I figured this was my cue to leave. As I passed Iris, I caught her eye and waved to her. She tilted her head and mouthed the word "sorry," to which I responded by raising my hands in a gesture that I intended to mean, "No problem."

I drove through town and onto the highway without music. I couldn't help but feel disappointed with the way the evening had turned out. Clearly, Iris was besieged and at least some of this seemed unexpected to her. But at the same time, she hadn't given me any indication at all that she was glad I'd made the gesture. I concluded that this meant one only thing: that what I saw as a growing friendship between us meant far less to her than it did to me. I felt stupid for having let my guard down.

I didn't want to be in that position, especially with Iris. To me, it was far better to scale back my perception of our relationship – perhaps completely – than to feel like a footnote in her life. I decided to give myself some time before I called on her again.

The road was open and dark. I reached for the iPod. I wanted something loud. I scrolled down to a Korn album and let the thudding rap metal lead me back to Amber.

• • •

The next night, Tyler and I closed the store together. Thursdays were always considerably busier than Wednesdays and this one was much more so. Though it would be a month before the real peak season began in town, the days had been clear and warm for the past couple of weeks, and this meant people started coming to Amber earlier for long weekends. Progress on the repairs continued to slog along, but even this didn't seem to deter the customers. I was thankful for the activity and its ability to take my mind off the night before in Lenox.

As we walked toward our cars, I asked Tyler if he wanted to get a drink and we drove over to the Cornwall. He ordered a Danish pilsner and I got a deep red Irish.

"Home stretch at school, huh?" I said after the drinks arrived.

"Yeah, if I survive. I thought I was coasting with

this independent study project, but it's turning into something like a Master's thesis for me."

"You gonna make it?"

"I'll definitely make it. I'm thinking that next Monday might be the last night of sleep I get for the next couple of weeks, though. You'll be okay if I pass out on top of the cash register every now and then, right?"

"No problem as long as we can reach around you."

"Thanks." He took a drink of his beer. "I had a great trip into the City a couple of days ago."

When people in Amber talked about "the City," they could as easily be talking about Boston as Manhattan. New Yorkers found this hilarious. In Tyler's case, though, I knew that the only city that mattered was Manhattan.

"Job interview?"

"Exploratory stuff. I talked to someone at Pfizer, though I can't really imagine working there. I had another conversation with that nonprofit organization I told you about, which was actually interesting. I never considered myself an NPO kind of guy, but a woman I saw there got me a little intrigued. My best meeting, though, was with the president of an independent marketing firm. Relatively small shop but with some decent-sized clients. I think I'd like something like that. Not getting lost in a huge corporation but still getting to work on some big stuff. I told the guy that I would be going back to school for my MBA in about two years and he couldn't have responded better. He told me that he had set things up with other employees so they could go to school mostly full-time and still keep their hands in the business. I could definitely see myself working for someone like him. Not that he had any job openings."

"Never know, though."

"No, you never know. But you know what the best part of the trip was for me? The same thing that happens every time I go there. I just totally get into the feel of the City. I mean the second I get into Grand Central Station I just know that I'm in the right place. It's funny because a lot of people I know around here feel kind of intimidated by the size of it all. But I just love it. I can't wait to move in."

I'd never really had that feeling about Manhattan. We didn't go there very often when I was growing up and my visits since had been enjoyable, often even exciting. But I never once thought that I'd want to live there. It just had too much of everything. I could understand how some would see this as a huge opportunity, but to me it just suggested chaos.

"How have things been with Richard this week?" Tyler asked.

"Nothing new. Lots of sitting around in his robe. Gotta get him some new ones. He stopped wearing slippers this week, though. I'm not sure whether this is progress or not."

Tyler winced. "God, I hope he gets past this. I really miss him."

I shook my head. "This heart thing has really thrown him. Way beyond what I thought."

"This is such a shitty thing for him to be going through. He's such a good guy. And he was a great boss. To tell you the truth, I've been comparing all of the people I'm meeting to your dad. I'd really like to avoid going from working for someone as smart and inspiring as Richard to working for someone really lame."

I laughed. "You think my father's inspiring?"

"Yeah, of course. You don't see that?"

"Well, I know he's a nice guy."

"A great guy. But inspiring, too. He's been a real mentor to me. Shown me all kinds of things about how to make decisions, how to analyze information, about caring about what you do. I had a much more jaundiced view of the public – and about working with the public – before I started working for him."

I nodded. "That's nice to know, I guess."

It was so interesting to hear Tyler talk about my father this way. I don't know if it was just a wave of sentimentality lapping up against me because he was sick now, but I found myself warmed a little to think that my dad had an impact on someone as together as Tyler. I'd never seen him this way. I knew my mother was totally dedicated to him and that Chase was always "on" around him. And I knew that he had that incongruous track record of finding conscientious college-age kids. But I never considered him the catalyst for any of it.

"Do you two not get along?" Tyler asked.

"No, nothing like that. We've always gotten along fine. You know, playing ball, going swimming, that sort of thing. I just never considered him to be my mentor, so it's a little funny hearing someone else refer to him that way."

"Well, you've kinda made it obvious that the store isn't exactly your thing."

"I just never really got it, you know? I could never understand how this would be enough for a grown

CROSSING THE BRIDGE 129

human being. You stand behind a cash register while a customer tries to decide whether 'to my dearest husband' or 'to my darling husband' sends the right message and some orchestra plays embarrassing renditions of rock classics."

Tyler chuckled and took another drink. I wasn't sure whether he was laughing because he agreed with me or because it had become evident to him how little I understood what my father did.

"It just wasn't where I was going," I said. "By the time I was old enough to be obligated to work in the store, I had much bigger things in mind. Even before I knew the term 'multimedia,' I was envisioning a future in that world. Television, radio, computers, movies, I was going to work in all of those platforms. I was going to assimilate serious intellectual thought into material for the masses. A stationery store seemed like ridiculously small potatoes by comparison. I was majoring in communications with a minor in philosophy at Emerson."

"So how come you didn't do anything with it?"

I looked around the room. Phil the pirate was attempting to intimidate some guys at a table on the other side of the bar while they laughed loudly and ignored him.

"I don't know; the thing with Chase sorta threw me, I guess. By the time I got myself back together, I'd lost a lot of credits and I couldn't get the energy up to start in the middle again."

"It's too bad. It sounds like you had some cool ideas. But life is long, right?"

"Something like that. Anyway, that was all a roundabout way of saying that I always thought my father was a good guy. Just not particularly relevant, if you know what I mean."

"I guess I do, sort of. Most families are complicated, though."

"Yeah, complicated pretty much describes it."

"Must be tough losing a brother."

"Killed me."

"I can imagine. It sounds like Chase was a cool guy, too. I've heard a lot of stories. I'm not sure there were two days in a row that went by when Richard didn't at least mention his name."

"He took it pretty badly."

Tyler gestured for another beer. "Sounds like you took it pretty badly, too."

I nodded. "Yeah, having that car accident was a pretty shitty thing for him to do to all of us." I turned to get the waiter's attention for another beer of my own.

Once the second round came, we switched subjects. We discussed our joint befuddlement with women for a while and then spent nearly an hour talking about music. Tyler had varied and mostly sophisticated tastes and we agreed on enough that when he recommended an artist I didn't know, I wrote the name down on my napkin. He had some holes, though. He truly believed that Robert Cray was in the same league as Jimi Hendrix and completely missed the significance of the No Depression movement. I made a note to myself to show him the error in his ways while we were still working together.

Another beer later, we headed out the door. It was good having Tyler around. It was nice to know that

I'd at least have one interesting colleague to help pass the hours during my incarceration at Amber Cards, Gifts, and Stationery.

• • •

Two days later, Iris called me at the store.

"It's good to hear you survived opening night," I said. "It seemed in doubt for a while there."

"You're not kidding. They're always bad, but this one was worse than most. The reviews, of course, were great and ticket sales are strong, so I think we've managed to fool everyone again."

"I genuinely thought it was a good show."

"It probably is a good show. I usually can't appreciate them until six months later. Anyway, I wanted to thank you again for coming up." She hadn't thanked me a first time, but I let it pass. "I got a little bit of a funny feeling when you left the other night and I just wanted to make sure that everything was okay."

I wondered if I should be impressed with Iris' sensitivity or embarrassed that I'd shown my irritation so easily. My feelings that night were all very complicated and I certainly didn't want Iris to think that I was angry with her for not paying attention to me when her world was boiling over. At the same time, I was touched that, regardless of the reason, Iris had taken note and thought to call me about it. I'd been irrationally upset with her for the past couple of days because she hadn't leaped into my arms when she saw me there. But I didn't want her to know this.

"Yeah, everything is fine," I said. "I'm not sure what you were picking up. Probably just that I don't like hanging out at parties."

"So you're okay?"

"Completely."

"It really was incredibly nice of you to drive all that way for the opening."

"You made it sound too good to pass up."

"Well, I'm really glad you came – even if I didn't do a very good job of showing that to you."

"Don't be silly. You were crazed. I just wanted to see the show and then use my connections to sneak backstage afterward. I just love throwing my weight around. You're probably a little jaded at this point because these productions have become old hat, but you should be very happy with what you put on there. The entire organization should be."

"Thanks. It means a lot to hear you say that and it meant a lot to see you the other night."

A customer came to the counter and I gestured for Carl to take care of him.

"I loved doing it. And I really don't need a major excuse to get the hell out of here."

"No luck on the sale yet?"

"Does bad luck count?"

"Sorry. And you're really stuck there until the place sells?"

"If I ever want to set foot in my parents' home again. I didn't think this through well enough at all. I was certain I'd be gone by now."

"Well listen, if you think you're still going to be around in a couple of weeks, I'm coming down for a few days starting on the fourth. Do you want to get together then?"

"Yeah, that would be great. Maybe we can do something during the day. The weather's been amazing here."

"I'd like that. Can we plan on the fifth? My mother would collapse if I went out for the day right after driving down."

"You got it. I'm sure they'll get by without me here. They can close the freaking store for the day if they want to."

CHAPTER TEN
Working toward Something

A little more than a week later, Tyler graduated from MCS. The Monday after, I was in the store with the relentless Tab and a guy named Craig who didn't work a lot of hours but who we'd pressed into duty to take Tyler's shift and help with some shipments. A little before 11:00, Tyler walked through the door.

"What are you doing here?" I said.

"I'm on today, right?" he said, looking a little confused.

"You're on, yes, but I wasn't expecting to see you today."

"Did we talk about this?"

"No, we didn't talk about this, but I'm assuming you did some major partying last night."

Tyler rolled his eyes. "Man, you have no idea."

"Then what the hell are you doing here?"

"I'm on today, right?"

"Never mind."

"Hey, I've got other stuff I can do if you don't need us all here," Tab said.

I turned to Tab and smirked. "That's really selfless of you." I looked back to Tyler. "You sure you're okay to work? I have Craig here. I sort of assumed you weren't going to answer the bell."

Tyler did a quick bit of shadowboxing and said, "Yep. I got three hours of sleep. I'm ready to rumble."

He walked behind the counter and I sent Tab off to reorganize the stationery section. With the school year over and the summer coming on, my father always reduced the space he gave to notebooks and three-ring binders and increased the space dedicated to water guns (new shipment arriving Wednesday), Frisbees, and other plastic toys. Tab responded to this merchandising task with the same ennui she afforded all other responsibilities in the store. While I could hardly blame her for expressing boredom at her job, I wondered if anything ever excited her.

When Tab skulked off, I shook Tyler's hand. "So, congratulations."

"Thanks," he said, smiling. "You know, it's not like I won some big championship or something. I mean, it was inevitable. I knew I was going to graduate. But yesterday still felt really good."

"It should."

"Yeah, I guess it should. I just didn't expect the little jolt I got when I went up to get my diploma. It's only MCS and everything, but it *was* summa cum laude and, I don't know, the whole thing just got to me a little bit."

I patted him on the shoulder. I knew that he took his schoolwork much more seriously than he needed to in order to get by and I was glad that he wasn't taking this accomplishment nonchalantly. "That's good. You should be proud of yourself."

"Yeah, I am."

A customer came to the counter and I rang up the sale before turning back to Tyler. "And then you had a killer party?"

"Killer *parties*. My parents held this bash for me right after the ceremony. Lots of relatives and a bunch of friends and my father running all over the kitchen."

"Your father cooks?"

"Only special occasion stuff. It's a thing with him. And yesterday, he made all of his classics. I think he was excited about the event."

"Yeah, I know what you're talking about. Before his heart attack, my father was an artist with a box of Raisin Bran."

"Then my mother made this insane speech that might have been the single most sentimental five minutes ever experienced in human history. It was like she edited together all of the gloppy messages in all of our cards. I kept waiting for 'Sunrise, Sunset' to blast out of the CD player. She started crying and that made me start to cry and, oh . . ." He waved his hand to shoo away the memory. "It was pretty cool, actually, though it convinced me that if I ever get married, I'm going to elope."

Tyler leaned against the wall behind the counter and looked off for a moment. The speech obviously meant a lot to him, as did his father's frantic efforts to make him several of his favorite dishes. I could only imagine that it would.

"Anyway," he said, looking back at me, "this went on until the early evening. I'd been planning on hanging around until everyone left, but when it became clear that my Uncle Richie wasn't going until all of the food and all of the scotch was gone, I decided to make my exit. That's when things got a little crazy. I hooked up with a bunch of other people who graduated with me and we went to Blum's. You ever been there?"

I shook my head.

"It's right on the water and they have this back porch on the dock. The guy who owns the place is the father of one of the guys I graduated with. He closed off the porch for us and gave us total access to the bar for as long as we wanted. Once the restaurant closed, the music got extremely loud, the drinks came a lot faster, and the rest was kind of a blur. There was something that went on with whipped cream and I had this really profound walk down the beach with this woman I've been trying to talk to since my sophomore year. I think she's leaving for Seattle this afternoon, but at least I got to talk to her. Mr. Blum paid his staff to stick around and drive everyone home and I think I crawled into bed around a quarter to seven. I remembered to set my alarm, though."

"Which wins you Employee of the Month for the sixth time in a row."

"Nah, give it to Tab." He nodded toward the stationery aisle, where she was piling the notebooks on the floor one at a time.

"So now it's back on the interview trail?"

"I'm going into the City on Friday. I have some stuff lined up and I'm hoping to get a few more things going before then."

"What's the market like right now?"

"Hey, when you're a summa cum laude graduate from MCS, you can write your own ticket," he said, smiling. "It's okay. Nobody's getting their doors beaten down – even the people who graduated from Yale yesterday. It might take me a little time to find something good, but I'll find something."

"I'm sure you will." There was no question in my mind that someone would respond to Tyler's passion and determination and give him a decent entry-level position. Tyler would be pleased and consider himself fortunate, but it would be the employer who received the big break.

"Hey, I got you something," I said, reaching under the counter and pulling out a box. Though I seriously wasn't expecting Tyler to be in the store, I also knew that there was the very real possibility he'd show up, since he hadn't asked for the time off. I handed him the package.

"Hey, you didn't have to do that," he said.

"It isn't a car or anything. By the way, my mother and father wanted me to tell you that they're getting you something, too, but that they still haven't found the right thing."

"That's really nice of them." Tyler tore at the wrapping. Inside was a box of four CDs I'd recorded for him of live performances from many of the bands we'd talked about when we'd gone out for drinks.

"Wow, this is incredible," he said.

"I've been doing a lot of downloading, ripping, and burning since our night at the Cornwall."

"A seventeen-minute version of 'Dear Mr. Fantasy?'"

"I hadn't even heard that one myself until I searched for some vintage Traffic."

"This is really good stuff. I can't wait to listen to some of it in my car during my lunch break."

"Yeah, maybe I'll sneak off with you then. I'd let you put it on through the store's system, but I'm pretty sure my father has attack dogs at the ready in case we try to change his station."

• • •

Since she moved to the other side of Amber about twenty years ago, my mother's younger sister Rita has held a Memorial Day party. As the two oldest cousins on this side of the family, Chase and I would get the other kids to do all kinds of precarious and sometimes dangerous things involving rowboat oars, bug zappers, and, as we got older, purloined cans of beer and bottles of rum. As May dawned, we would begin to strategize that year's stunt, even planning escape routes if things went badly. I hadn't been to one of these gatherings since Chase died and I hadn't intended to go this year, either. Unfortunately, I couldn't find a good enough excuse for staying away and my mother was surprisingly insistent.

Before moving to Amber, my Aunt Rita was a First Wave corporate executive at a public relations firm in Manhattan. By the time she was thirty, she'd used a combination of talent, guile, and utter determination to earn a partnership. The same year, her husband, an even more avid corporate climber than she, received a senior vice president's position at a Hartford insurance company. From what I hear (since I understood virtually none of this at the time), a rather tense standoff ensued. Uncle Chad saw this offer as one he couldn't refuse while Aunt Rita considered it a violation of their pact to think that she would give up her career for his. In the end, Aunt Rita's cleverness prevented their marriage from being an innocent victim in this war of ambitions. She found a way to retain her partnership while handling most of her duties from her spectacular new home office in her spectacular new home with three acres on the water in Amber, Connecticut, less than ten minutes from her beloved sister Anna. As time went by, Chad ultimately became president of that insurance company and Rita found that she could make as much money with far fewer hassles by striking out on her own. These days she doesn't work nearly as hard as she once did, but she "keeps her hand in the business" and still handles some high-powered clients.

All of which is reflected in Chad and Rita's living space. The three-car garage (one for the roadster, none for the kids who had moved on to careers of their own), hand-carved dining table that expanded to seat eighteen, and professional kitchen were nearly obligatory. But the freeform, oxygen-filtered swimming pool, the multilevel fieldstone patio, and the hydroponic garden were all nice touches. They'd put in all of these since the last time I'd walked the grounds, and I examined each with a mixture of admiration and consternation as the party got underway.

It had been considerably less difficult to get my father out of the house for this event than I'd expected. With the exception of doctor's visits, he hadn't been in the car since coming home from the hospital. He made a huge display of getting dressed. He sent my mother up the stairs four times for different shirts and it took him an absurd amount of time to descend the three stairs on the house's front stoop. But he was otherwise compliant.

Only when we got to my aunt and uncle's house did I realize why he had agreed to come along. Chad's brother, Thomas, had suffered a heart attack a couple of years earlier. After perfunctory conversation with a few of the other guests, my father and Thomas settled into chaise lounges on the patio for the rest of the day, trading coronary stories like war veterans. It was hard to believe that they had that much to say (and several times I looked over to find both of them glancing off at the party silently) and it was even harder to believe that my father had been storing these observations until he could commiserate with one of his fellows. He'd said more in those hours than he'd said since returning from the hospital.

My mother was Rita's only sibling. In addition to Thomas, though, Chad had three other brothers – Marlon, Henry, and Preston – all of whom had children at various ages in proximity to mine. Since Rita and Chad held regular family functions while I was growing up, these children became unofficial "cousins" with whom Chase and I would entertain ourselves. A few even became friends, though I'd done little more than exchange e-mail with any of them in the last ten years.

I was standing by myself over near the garden when Liz walked up to me. She was Preston's oldest child, around four years younger than me. I remember when I was sixteen and she was twelve, she followed me all over the house during Aunt Rita's Christmas party. I found this – and her – terribly annoying. When I was twenty and she was sixteen, however, I no longer found her annoying and in fact considered her polished, intriguing, and sexy. Sadly, she was toting around a boyfriend who was a freshman at Amherst. We hadn't seen each other at all since Chase's funeral.

"There was a rumor that you were going to be here," she said as she approached.

"Rumor? Don't you mean warning?"

"Oh yes, that must have been it." She kissed me on the cheek and held my hand for a minute, smiling.

"You look great," I said. "What have you been up to?"

"A few things," she said, still smiling. "You know, things. You look good, too. More rugged or something."

"Thanks. So what have you been doing? You're allowed to tell me, aren't you? It doesn't involve the CIA or anything like that, does it?"

Liz laughed. "Hardly. I'm not the high adventure type. Just a bunch of stuff. I'm living in Boston now, doing arbitrage work. The usual MBA thing. Sixty hours a week, dating people from the office because they're the only guys I ever get to meet, share in a summer place on Cape Cod, the usual."

"You like it?"

Liz laughed again and brushed her straight black hair away from her face. "Yeah, I really do. I mean, there are days, you know? And of course, they don't pay me nearly as much as I think they should pay me and my bonuses aren't nearly as high as I think they should be. But it's exciting. And my boss is a genius. And I'm learning something every day. And I'm on a partnership track, so that's pretty good, too."

I nodded. Somewhere along the line, someone had directed Liz to loosen up a little and it served her well. Where she was once more dignified than any teenager should be, she seemed to be living in the world now.

"So what have you been up to?" she said. "Where are you living?"

"At the moment, if you can believe it, I'm living here in Amber with my parents. But it is a very temporary thing."

"I heard that your dad was sick. Are you helping to take care of him?"

"He doesn't need nearly as much care as he seems to think he needs." I looked across to the patio where he and Thomas were once again telling tales to each other. "I actually got steamrollered into taking care of his stationery store while it's on the market. You don't happen to know a buyer, do you?"

"Sorry. That's really nice of you. How can you afford to take the time off work? I'd never be able to do something like that."

"I just finished up a thing in Springfield, so I was actually available."

"'Finished up a thing?' You mean like an independent contractor thing?"

"No, like a job I hated thing."

She nodded her head slowly. I wasn't sure whether this meant that she sympathized or that she was having trouble processing the information.

"You were planning to work in the media, weren't you?" she asked.

"That was a long time ago. I've since found that there are all kinds of things you can do with three-quarters of a communications degree."

"You never finished college?"

"Some things came up. So do you have a town-house in Back Bay?"

"High-rise. The only way I can get myself to the gym is if it's in my building. And with the hours I work, I kind of like having a doorman. Are you working toward something now?"

"I'm working toward the Southwest, ever so slowly. Do you know anything about Tucumcari?"

"Is that a company?"

"It's a town. According to a Web site, it's my ideal place to live in New Mexico."

She nodded a little faster this time (only a little, though) and glanced over toward the patio. "What are you going to do there?"

I shook my head. "I'll find out when I get there. Hey, maybe it'll be something with the media and I'll fulfill my destiny."

She smiled thinly. "They're putting out the buffet. I think I'm going to get some food."

"Yeah, I'll see you later." I watched her walk away until two little boys and a little girl kicking a ball and laughing diverted my attention. I looked out on the wide expanse of open lawn that led down to the water to see people talking, a man tossing a giggling baby in the air, two older teens running toward the river, a woman and her daughter playing catch, and various others making their way toward the patio and the food.

I grabbed a beer and walked around the house to the street. The conversation with Liz had unnerved me a little. Not as much because she seemed so casually dismissive about what I was doing with my life as that it yanked a period in my past from suspended animation. During that period when Chase and I saw Liz and the other "cousins" frequently, we were nothing but potential. Smart kids for the most part, raised in material comfort, believing that we only had to choose a future in order for that future to arise. When I lost contact with these people, I fixed them at that stage in my mind. Occasionally, my mother would mention one or the other, but the update didn't mean anything to me. Seeing Liz made palpable what I of course understood at some level: that all of these people had moved on to what they were doing with their lives. Including me.

The houses were very far apart in this neighborhood and most were set well back from the street. It was unnaturally quiet here. I'd hear the occasional splash, a lawn mower in the distance, a car passing. But all I could imagine when I looked at these houses was that every one of them held families just like Rita and Chad's: an Ivy League educated daughter and son visiting from Manhattan and Philadelphia respectively, where they were stepping up their own ladders with an alacrity that astounded their parents.

I hadn't paid enough attention to my instincts to stay away from this party. As my mother was trying to convince me to come, I'd known that I should explain to her that it didn't feel right. But I'd been more reluctant to turn her down about anything lately, feeling like I'd done a little too much of that since I got back to Amber. I should have been more insistent. I didn't need more frustration at this stage.

When I got back to the house, I thought about getting in my car and driving off. I'd at least had the presence of mind to drive here in my own car rather than going with my parents. But I knew that disappearing from the party would be more insulting to them than not going in the first place.

In the backyard, some of the partygoers were organizing a game of volleyball. Rita and Chad's son, Marshall, called out to me to join them. I wanted to play volleyball about as much as I wanted to monitor my father's conversations with Thomas, but again I didn't feel I could refuse. I took a place in the middle row and hoped things would be over quickly.

Our team was awful. It included my aunt, someone's six-year-old son, and Chad's lumbering brother Marlon, among others. The only athletic-looking person on the team was a girl I imagined to be somewhere in her mid-teens.

None of this mattered when we were just batting the ball around and none of it should have mattered at all. But when we started playing a game and we started losing badly, I became very agitated. Several people were watching and laughing over our ineptitude and I found myself taking this personally. When the score reached 15–4, I decided to do something about it. I ran from the back row to spike a ball over the net. I stopped passing to anyone other than the teen girl. I exhorted my teammates like Michael Jordan in the NBA finals, even as I did everything I could to prevent them from touching the ball. Marshall was drinking a beer while setting up shots on the other side, but I was prowling the court, pent on ramming the ball back at him. We scored nine consecutive points until a shot ricocheted off Marlon's considerable belly. We took back the serve immediately, though, and won every point after that even as most of my teammates moved toward the boundaries. On the game-winning point, the teen girl set me up with a great pass and I spiked it right into Preston's face. His sunglasses came flying off and he sat down on the grass.

"Jeez, Hugh, did you have money on this game?" Marshall said angrily, while going to his uncle's side. Liz knelt down next to her father and then she and Marshall helped him up. As she did so, she turned to me with an expression that read, "This is what you're doing with your life?"

I stood on the other side of the net as everyone left the volleyball court. I wanted to leave, but I didn't want anyone to see me leave. As the action swirled around me, my aunt walked over and took me by the arm.

"Had those competitive juices really flowing, huh?" she said.

My embarrassment inched up. "I guess so."

"Preston's fine. His idea of physical exertion is pressing the intercom button for his secretary. I think you just caught him by surprise."

We started walking away from the patio and toward a bench overlooking the river. When we sat down, my aunt released my arm and patted me on the leg.

"I haven't seen much of you since you've been back," she said. In fact, I'd only seen her once, when she visited my father after he came home.

"I've been pretty busy," I said, though I hardly ever felt busy.

"It's good of you to help your father out."

"It came at the right time."

She patted my leg again. "It's still good of you to do it. I feel so badly for Richard."

I nodded and looked around. There wasn't anyone within fifty yards of us.

"So what are you doing with yourself these days?" she said.

"I've been spending a lot of time in the store. Other than that, I don't know, some time with Mom and Dad, some time with John Updike, a couple of long drives."

"I meant what are you *doing*? Anna told me that you aren't going back to Springfield. What are you going to do once they sell the store?"

I'm sure it had something to do with the setting, that my aunt was a financially successful woman married to a financially successful man who had four financially successful brothers, but the afternoon's preoccupation with what one (and more specifically, what I) did had worn me ragged. "I haven't really focused on that yet," I said dismissively.

"When will it be time to focus?"

I turned my body to face her, which also moved her hand from my leg. "It'll be time to focus when it's time. I've managed to get by so far."

"The firm would have had my ass if I'd ever approached my work that way," she said, looking out toward the water.

"That's one of the reasons I don't work for a firm."

"I didn't realize that had to do with 'reasons.'"

I could have continued to defend myself, though I was certain I could never convinced her to see the world from my perspective. Instead, I decided to turn my attention to a sailboat out on the river.

"I was thinking this morning about all of the mischief your brother used to cause at this function," she said. "He was such a ball of fire. Chad and I would actually try to guess what kind of prank he was going to pull. He was such an electric soul. Both of you were back then."

A pair of geese flew across the river and I looked up at them.

"Do you think Chase would have figured out what to focus on by now?" she said.

I watched the geese recede into the distance. "I'm sure he would have, Aunt Rita."

She stood up. "I'm sure he would have, too."

She walked away while I continued to look out on the river. I was as alien to this environment as a komodo dragon. The lizard, however, would be regarded as a curiosity and at least generate some fascination. I seemed only to generate contempt, disappointment, and a modicum of unwanted pity.

A ball came toward my bench and a young boy raced after it. When I looked at him, he offered me a nervous smile and then ran back to his playmates. A short while later, without saying good-bye to my parents or my aunt, or any of the cousins, I left the party.

CHAPTER ELEVEN
Still Alive

The New Year's Eve after Chase and Iris started dating, the three of us went to Jim Krieger's house for a party. Jim went to high school with me, and his brother was a classmate of Chase's. About forty of our peers were there as well. Jim's parents were in the Caribbean until January third and it was his intention to keep the party rolling in some fashion or other until the evening of the second. The three of us had committed to hanging on until New Year's morning, but we wouldn't agree to anything more than that in advance. While Jim had a great reputation for his taste in exotic beers and unusual spirits, and while his parents' huge home was an expensively appointed playground, the notion of spending nearly three days in this high-ticket frat house felt a great deal like overkill.

I had expected to be there with Thalia Merritt. We'd gone to high school together and hooked up again at the beginning of the winter break. But by our fourth date, we were straining for conversation and I was beginning to lose interest. Which was just as well, because the day after Christmas she told me that she was heading down to Florida with some of her friends for the New Year and that she didn't think it was a good idea for us to get together again when she got back.

I was surprised that I didn't mind being at this party without a date. Most of the other people there were paired off (with a notable exception being Jim himself, who "didn't do the couples thing") and when I'd been in situations like this before I'd felt conspicuous. But with Chase and Iris as companions, I was fine. I'd spent a great deal of time with them since returning from Boston and, as we drove to the party, I felt a little like I would be "sharing" Iris with Chase, at least until the point when they went off to bed, if any of us were going to get much sleep during this bacchanal.

When we arrived, there were fewer than a dozen people there, though you wouldn't know from the volume. The house was a center hall Colonial and Jim informed us that the living room was the "alternative rock room" while the den was the "punk room." Stone Temple Pilots was bursting from the speakers in the former while the Sex Pistols blared from the latter, and they converged in a three-chord train wreck in the foyer. We chose the living room, where there was an enormous buffet of alcohol along with a bowl of Doritos. As soon as he got into the room and before he'd even poured himself a drink, Chase started slam dancing with some guy he knew.

"I don't suppose you want to . . ." I said to Iris, nodding in their direction.

"Hmm, maybe later," she said as we walked over to the bar.

"If he's going to do that, he really should be in the punk room, you know."

"Oh, you know Chase, always spitting in the face of convention."

I watched my brother in action. Even throwing his muscular body against the doughy shape of his friend, there was a certain grace to his actions. I couldn't recall a single time when Chase looked clumsy to me, even when he was at his most incautious. I found some pride in the fact that when the two slammed together, the friend bounced backward even though he had to be forty pounds heavier than Chase.

Within the hour, partiers filled both the alt-rock room and the punk room and were spreading to the kitchen, the sunroom, and the screened in porch. Some were outside building an anatomically correct snowman while others were wandering off to one of the bedrooms. I'd decided to make ouzo my drink of choice, and by the third I felt like a bit of slam-dancing myself, though I managed to resist the temptation. I spent some time talking with a woman named Christine who told me that she was "with Steve, but not *with* Steve." Since I didn't know who Steve was, this hardly mattered to me and it registered that there might be some advantages to coming to this party unattached.

Chase had been drinking with abandon and he was quite obviously feeling the effects. He ping-ponged around the room, doing his Harpo Marx imitation, singing – for reasons known only to him – a ludicrously dramatic version of "Don't Cry for Me, Argentina" during a break in the music, and dropping into the conversations of others, only to leave in mid-sentence. Iris watched this amusedly, making laughing side-comments, inaudible to me, to a pair of female friends.

Around 10:30, there was a roar from the foyer and Chase broke away from what he was doing to see what was happening. Intrigued to see what could cause him to shift gears so quickly, I walked out after him. He was performing an elaborate hand-shaking routine (complete with the bellowing of nonsense syllables) with four guys I recognized as lacrosse teammates. The five blasted into the living room and a palpable shock wave accompanied them. They descended upon the bar and, as they did, one of the group shouted yet another nonsense syllable. This caused all five to reach for various bottles and carry them to a corner of the room.

I watched Chase curiously. In the past couple of years, he had become fond of drinking whenever he found the opportunity, but I'd never before seen him take to alcohol with this much fervor. With his four teammates, he embarked on some elaborate drinking game, the rules of which eluded me. It seemed to entail the performance of a variety of stunts (saying things backward, balancing in awkward positions, lifting things) and the seemingly random mixing of the various forms of liquor in one glass. One of the contestants regularly drained this glass, though it wasn't clear to me whether this person had won or lost the previous competition.

"Do you know what this is?" I asked Iris, who had come to stand next to me to watch.

"Pahzoo," she said.

I'd heard that word exclaimed as the group approached the bar, though it meant nothing to me at the time (which is not to say that it meant much to me now).

"Pahzoo?"

"Don't ask me to explain the rules. I'm not sure there are any. The object seems to be to get totally wasted in record time."

"You've seen Chase play this game before?"

"With those guys at the end-of-season party. I drove home. He moaned."

The boys were babbling even more incoherently now, which suggested that they were reaching their goal. After one last trick, which none of them could perform, they collapsed on the floor laughing. Slowly, Chase got up, searched aimlessly around the room, and then stumbled in our direction. When I asked him if he had won, he looked at me as though he didn't understand the question. He then put his hands on both my shoulder and Iris' and, without another word, turned back to lie down with his buddies. After a while, it became clear that he wasn't going to move.

I'd never seen Chase quite like this before and was in fact a little disappointed that he'd succumbed to drink like a mere mortal. I didn't care whether we left the other guys passed out on the floor, but I wasn't going to have people stepping around my brother for the rest of the night. With Jim's help, I carried him to one of the bedrooms and threw a blanket over him.

"I don't think we'll be seeing Chase for the rest of the year," I said to Iris when I returned to the living room.

"I'm sure he'll be okay," she said.

"Yeah, he'll wake up in the morning wanting a dozen eggs for breakfast. Chase doesn't get hung over. He gets ravenous."

I expected Iris to go back to her friends, but she stayed by my side. I liked having her there and the entire party took on a more human scale when she was next to me. About a half hour after I put him to bed, Iris asked me to check on Chase "just to make sure he's breathing." He hadn't moved, but he looked utterly comfortable.

Ultimately, Iris and I left the living room for the relative quiet of the sunroom. When it was nearly midnight, we counted down the final seconds together, and then she hugged me and kissed me on the cheek, the first time she had done either. It caught me by surprise and I'm sure I looked as dumbfounded as I did at the end of ninth grade when Ellen Aspen did a similar thing on the last day of school.

The party started to thin out not long after this. Some people went home. Several others found sleeping arrangements on the second floor. I never found out if anyone shared a room with Chase. By 3:00, the music was off and Iris and I sat on a couch talking with Jim, a girl he had his arm around, and a couple of other people. Both of us had continued to drink, though hardly with the avidity of the early evening. I was definitely drunk, but it was the kind of six-inches-off-the-ground drunk one gets from maintaining a steady high.

"The new year is off to an interesting start," Iris said to me as things quieted down further. Jim and the girl said good night and two of the other three people curled up on pillows on the floor. "Chase dropped before the ball in Times Square did."

"Not likely to happen often," I said.

"True. He'll make it his mission to outlast it next time."

I nodded and Iris leaned back farther, listing in my direction. A couple of minutes later, she leaned a bit more and put her head on my shoulder. I craned my neck to find that she was asleep. A short while after this, I rested my head on hers and fell asleep as well.

• • •

The vision of Iris in a sleeveless top and shorts was as arresting as it was transporting. I wondered if she remembered the first time I saw her wearing clothes similar to these and even if she might have worn them now in honor of that moment. It was difficult to stop thinking that way, even as I warned myself against it.

I'd asked her to meet me at the store because I had a few things to discuss with the carpenters before I could disappear. As a result, I gave Tyler the opportunity to whisper upon her arrival, "*This* is the friend you're spending the day with?" which also meant that I was going to have to deflect questions about her from him later. I wasn't sure how I was going to react to that interrogation, as I hadn't spoken with anyone about Iris ever.

"Gee, love what you've done with the place," she said as she gestured toward the back.

"If you like that, wait till you see what I have planned if we don't sell it in another month."

She walked over and kissed me on the cheek. This had become such a casual gesture between us, not at all like the first time on that New Year's Eve more than ten years ago. When I kissed her, I put my hand on her shoulder as I always did, but this time that shoulder was bare and I almost pulled back, not wanting her to think I was crossing a line.

Iris looked around at the slumbering store and asked, "Are you sure they can spare you today?"

"The A-team is on duty. They'll persevere."

We walked around the block to my car. It was a radiant day. One of those ideal early June days when you could enjoy the increasing warmth without the oppressive humidity that usually accompanied it by the solstice. I'd been feeling off my game since Aunt Rita's party, but the combination of the weather and the promise of a full day with Iris encouraged me.

"What are we doing, anyway?" I said when we settled into the car. We'd made no plans.

"Let's just go," Iris said.

"Just go?"

"Just go. Something will come to us."

"Care to pick a direction?"

"Northwest," Iris said without a moment's hesitation. I was certain that if I'd asked her four seconds later, she would have offered a different answer.

We drove out of town and onto Highway 9. As we did, Iris reached for the iPod. Hendrix was in the middle of a seven-minute solo on "Red House."

"Wrong music," she said. "Okay if I change it?"

"Be my guest. There are more than five thousand songs on there."

Iris studiously scanned as I drove. "You don't really listen to Enrique Iglesias, do you?" she asked.

"I was curious. My curiosity lasted until the third cut."

"Good thing. I almost asked you to drop me off by the side of the road. Ooh, Fountains of Wayne," she said, switching from Hendrix. "Great summer drive music."

For most of the next half hour, we did little talking. An update about the play. A modified description of what I did on Memorial Day. Other than that, some singing and a great deal of wind in our hair. As we drove down the highway, Iris pointed to a sign for Asa's Berry Farm and shouted, "That's it."

I shrugged.

"Berry picking at the next exit," she said.

"This is what you want to do?"

"Of course, don't you?"

"Of course."

Asa's was a mile or so off the highway, a large shed set on dozens of acres. Asa himself wasn't available (Iris asked), but a middle-aged guy told us that we could pick all the strawberries we wanted for a dollar a pint. Iris seemed to find this exciting and grabbed two oversized buckets for us to fill. The guy told us where the ripest berries were located and we headed off in that direction.

The first thing Iris did when we set our buckets down was pick a huge strawberry and eat it.

"I just love strawberries, don't you?" she said.

"Are you planning to tell Asa that you ate that berry? It's stealing if you don't, you know."

Iris laughed. "It's not stealing. It's expected. They

wouldn't want anyone out here picking their berries who didn't just have to have a few."

I set to the task of filling my bucket. It was a bit daunting to realize that a half hour later the bottom of the bucket was barely full. Of course, I still had more in mine than Iris had in hers, though it was likely that she wouldn't be needing lunch.

"Don't they have machines that normally pick these things?" I said.

"Yes, a special kind of machine called a migrant worker."

"They use those in Connecticut?"

"Did you think they hired college kids at twelve dollars an hour?"

"I can honestly say I've never thought about it at all."

Iris looked down into my basket and said, "You're way ahead of me. I'm going to have to work faster." She started pulling berries off the vines with increased efficiency until she accidentally picked a rotten fruit, which bled all over her hand. I looked over at her and laughed, and she looked at her hand, confused for a moment over what to do – until she decided to clean herself on my shirt.

For an instant, this act stunned me. Iris had never done anything like this to me before. She thought it was very funny and she probably thought it was especially funny that I reacted the way I did. I remembered her doing this kind of thing with Chase several times: electric blue paint in his hair, snow melting inside the seat of his pants, cotton candy suctioned to his five o'clock shadow. As much as I always thought of her as the more serious and cerebral of the two, my memories of her were dotted with these acts of complete silliness and of Chase responding in kind.

I searched the bushes for another overripe berry but couldn't find one. I decided to do the next best thing, crushing a fruit between my hands and then moving to wipe them on her bare arms. She wriggled away from me and ran off, but I caught her from behind and smudged the juice into her shoulders.

"Not fair, I'm all sticky," she said.

"And I have a huge red stain on my sleeve."

"But you're not sticky – yet." Seemingly from nowhere, she produced another strawberry and drove it into my cheek. She ran away again and I ran after her. But when I realized that I wasn't sure what I would do if I caught her, I slowed down, feigning exhaustion and calling, "Truce."

She turned back and approached me tentatively. "Real truce?"

"Real truce."

"I can go back to picking berries without fear of retaliation?"

"At least for the rest of the day. I make no promises about the future."

She leaned over and kissed me on my spattered cheek.

"Mmm, delicious," she said, before returning to her bucket.

We stayed together until late in the evening. The entire time, Iris retained a girlish buoyancy that I hadn't seen from her – and only then on occasion – in a decade. Even when she fell asleep in the car on the way back, she seemed younger. It was such a marked contrast to how she appeared during her opening night and I wondered if in some ways it wasn't a response to it. Was she trying to show me that she could be as loose and carefree as she had been intense and world-weary after the show? Regardless, I was glad to have this Iris with me. I was glad that this Iris was still alive.

I woke her when we got back to her car. She sleepily apologized for leaving me alone on the ride back. Then she hugged me and held me tightly while she rested her head on my shoulder.

"This was fun," she said.

"It was. I'm glad you came down."

"When are you coming back to Lenox?"

"When do you want me?"

"Soon, okay?"

"Definitely soon. I'll call you after you get back."

She kissed me on the shoulder and got out of the car. "And clean up a little," she said. "You're a mess."

• • •

The next morning, I awoke ahead of the alarm. While I showered, I decided I'd take myself out to breakfast before going to the store. I thought about calling Iris to see if she wanted to join me, but I didn't want this visit to end with a brief coda and I certainly didn't want to take the chance that things would be different in any way from the day before.

When I got downstairs, I saw that my mother had already left for the day's errands. She seemed to be getting to these earlier and earlier. I drank a cup of coffee while I flipped through the *Advisor*, which of course took no more than a few minutes. On my way toward the door, I went into the den to say good-bye to my father. He was in his usual chair in front of the television, the sofa bed unmade with the blankets heaped near the bottom. I was accustomed to this morning scene at this point. Except this time, the television wasn't on. My father was staring at a dark screen.

"Hey, Dad," I said. "I'm gonna be heading off in a minute."

He lifted his arm to wave, but didn't turn his head.

"Everything okay in here?"

"Everything is fine," he said vacantly.

It was entirely possible that he was simply deep in thought or that he was practicing some kind of meditation technique to improve his condition. But this wasn't the impression I was getting and I didn't like the idea of leaving him this way.

"Do you want me to stay here until Mom gets back?"

He lifted his arm again, though this time he didn't wave. "I'm okay, thanks."

These were precisely the kinds of "conversations" we'd been having since he returned from the hospital and I could feel my concern shifting to aggravation. He was much too young to allow himself to become an invalid but he wouldn't even consider the most rudimentary forms of help. I shook my head and turned to go. If he didn't want anything from me, then it was ludicrous of me to offer anything.

I'm not sure what made me turn back toward the den. I'm even less sure of what made me think of the chess set that was sitting in a box on a bookshelf. But without saying anything more, I retrieved the box and set the game up on the card table.

I wasn't a chess player. I knew how the pieces

moved and I understood the basic rules, but that was all I'd really learned. My father would play regularly with Chase, though, with this set of ivory pieces on a leather board, or with a plastic set at the store that they would set up in the back room, alternating trips there from behind the counter to make their moves. I knew my father took this game seriously and could stay focused on it regardless of distractions. He was also very good at it. I was in the room the first time a fourteen-year-old Chase beat him and, as my brother pounced out of the room in exultation, my father sat quietly at the table regarding the final game board in admiration. Their matches became more hotly contested after that, and while the results were relatively evenly split, there was no mistaking Chase's pride that he could finally keep up with the old man or my father's pleasure in no longer needing to hold back.

I knew there was no chance that I could beat my father. I would consider it a moral victory, however, if I could even get him to make a move.

"Let's play," I said, sitting at the card table. If my father had been aware of my setting up the board, he gave no indication of it. When I spoke, he turned toward me, looked down at the table, and then looked back up in confusion.

"Let's play," I said again.

He looked at the board and then back at the blank television. "Not right now. Maybe later."

"Later when, Dad? I'm going to be very busy later and we'll never get to it."

"I thought you didn't know how to play chess."

"Which means you'll kick my ass. I would think

that would be an offer too good to pass up. And I do know a little."

He turned back toward the television and I thought for a moment that he was simply going to ignore me. But then he pulled himself up out of his chair and sat across from me, moving his pawn to King Four at the same time.

We didn't say much. In fact, I don't recall saying anything at all. But as my father regarded the board or reached to move a piece, I could see that the game engaged him. I played as conservatively as I possibly could given the modicum of knowledge I had. I didn't want to be too easy an opponent for him and I didn't want the game to end too soon, knowing that when it did he would return to his chair. I took extravagant amounts of time to consider my moves, though my understanding of strategy was minimal. And I steadfastly refused to resign, even when the outcome was inevitable. Still, after slightly more than twenty moves, he checkmated me.

I shrugged when the game was over, my acknowledgement to him that I'd tried my best.

"You know a little," he said.

"I should work on it."

He reached toward the board and put his rooks back in line. "You should," he said.

We got up at the same time, me to head toward the door, him to settle back in his chair.

"Have a good day, Dad," I said to him as I reached the door.

"Yeah," he said, offering a half wave.

CHAPTER TWELVE
Really Good Seats

The next time I went to Lenox, there was a huge up-surge in tourists and summer residents. Iris and I spent the afternoon wandering the burgeoning streets, dodging strollers while viewing sidewalk art displays, sipping milkshakes while listening to a pair of talented folk guitarists, and eavesdropping on cell phone conversations while browsing craft shops. Of course we spent some time at the CD store (I bought a German import of an Elvis Costello album) and then wandered over to Paperworks. The place continued to fascinate me. I would never have guessed that this level of creativity could be applied to a stationery store and I promised to direct the new owners of Amber Cards, Gifts, and Stationery here for inspiration. Assuming we ever made a deal with anyone.

Iris was in another great mood. She was more Lenox Ensemble Iris than High School Sweetheart Iris in that she didn't do anything silly or reckless, but she was utterly relaxed. As we walked, she slipped her arm around mine and we continued that way for much of the day. There was nothing romantic to the gesture and I didn't think of it that way. But the collegiality of the act, the physical acknowledgement that we were sharing this day together, was very satisfying to me.

Iris had gotten us tickets for Tanglewood that night and we picnicked on the lawn with a meal we purchased from a natural foods store in town (though we also stopped at a bakery for absurdly rich brownies and a liquor store for a sauvignon blanc).

"Nice blanket," I said, running my hands along the soft wool.

"It was my grandmother's."

"We're sitting on an heirloom on the grass?"

Iris laughed. "It was my grandmother's picnic blanket. She'd crack up if she heard you call it an heirloom."

"It feels so substantial."

"Oh, you know, things were 'built to last' back then. I think this is something like fifty years old."

"Which means if I drop some hummus on it, I'm a dead man, right?"

"I'd just warn you to stay away from my grandfather."

I poured more wine for both of us and leaned back on my elbows. Though it had been in the mid-eighties during the day, the evening air was much cooler, which meant it felt exactly the way nights like these were supposed to feel. Iris was completely prone on the blanket now, looking up at the sky.

"I don't do this enough," she said.

"Lie down?"

She smirked and propped herself up, gesturing around her. "This. Galleries, picnics, Tanglewood."

"Aren't you supposed to do this all the time if you

live here? Isn't it in that book of bylaws you keep in your office?"

"That kind of stuff drives people here, but it does-n't mean that those of us who actually do live here – especially those of us who live here year-round – get around to it much. We're taking care of business just like everybody else."

I thought about what she was saying and won-dered if I'd wind up treating Tucumcari the same way I'd treated Springfield. "Glad I could pull you away from the grind," I said.

She patted me on the leg. "I don't know what I'd do without you." She took her last bite of brownie and then finished her wine. The amphitheater was filling up. "Want to go to our seats?"

I took another sip. "Or we could stay here."

"I got us really good seats."

"*These* are really good seats."

She gave this some thought and then laid back down. "Maybe until intermission."

The concert itself was revelatory. While Tangle-wood was the summer home of the Boston Sym-phony Orchestra and the occasional popular performer did shows there, tonight six experimental musicians occupied the stage. I'd never heard of them and would never have chosen to attend, but Iris was very familiar with their work and very enthusiastic. There were long patches of minimalist music punc-tuated by short bursts of bebop and atonal vocals. For the first several minutes, I had a difficult time ad-justing my ears, but ultimately it became mesmeriz-ing. Every now and then, Iris would whisper a comment about a particular piece of the performance and her narrative added meaning to me. She made me aware of the subtle, intentional inconsistencies to the repetitive notes of the keyboards, to the way the saxophonist would insert a countermelody with varying levels of insistence during the loop. I would not have noticed these things and Iris' observations both impressed me and made the pieces considerably more enjoyable. Just before intermission, I said something about one of the percussionists and she nodded appreciatively. I was very pleased with myself.

We did in fact take our seats after intermission. The second half of the show was slightly more traditional, beginning and ending with two extended jazz pieces. The audience seemed more animated during these performances. When the concert ended around 10:30, the temperature was in the low sixties and, as the house lights came up, I rubbed my bare arms.

"You wish you'd borrowed that jacket now, don't you?" Iris said.

"No, I'm fine."

She gave my arm a quick, vigorous rub and said, "You brave the elements well. So what did you think of the show?"

"It was kind of amazing."

"Aren't they great?"

"Yeah. I wasn't sure what to expect, but yeah."

"You'd never heard any of their stuff before?"

"Nothing. How do you know them?"

She smiled. "Some of us just are just more in the loop than others."

We followed the crowd out toward the parking lot. No one seemed in a particular rush to leave. I wondered if this was because it was early in the season or if the music had somehow hypnotized everyone. As we exited the amphitheater, people were handing out flyers for a huge craft fair the next day.

"Wow, this sounds great," I said to Iris. "Are you going to this?"

She took the flyer from my hand. "Is this tomorrow? Yeah, it's great. They do it every year."

"I kinda wish I was going to be around for it."

She handed the flyer back to me and said, "So stay. I have a guest room."

"Really?"

"Yeah, of course. They can spare you at the store again tomorrow?"

"They can spare me at the store permanently. I think Tyler humors me while I'm there."

"Then stay. I have some stuff to do at the office in the morning, but I know I can get away in the afternoon. We'll go to the craft fair. It really is very good."

This felt like a very intimate act to me. Other than that unconscious New Year's, Iris and I had only spent the night under the same roof one time before. I recalled the tender sounds of her making love with my brother and I drew back inwardly, hopefully not showing her any of this. Certainly, this was something that good friends did with one another and, at the very least, I wanted Iris to be comfortable enough to ask me to stay over. And the nonchalance with which she suggested it told me that she was placing considerably less meaning on this gesture than I was.

"It won't be a hassle for you?" I said.

"Do you make loud noises when you sleep?"

"Not that I know of."

"Then it won't be a hassle."

"Okay, then." She smiled, took my arm, and we headed toward the car.

• • •

A couple of days later, my mother knocked on my bedroom door at 7:30 and handed me the phone.

"It's Jack Calley," she said.

"Who?"

"Jack Calley. He owns the bakery across the street from the store."

I asked her why he was calling me, but she simply handed me the phone. I never had my wits about me when I first woke up and I obviously sounded that way when I answered.

"Hugh, sorry to be bothering you at this time in the morning if this is a false alarm, but I was wondering if there was something wrong with the store."

The image of another water main break came to mind. This time the damage was so severe that Jack could see it from across the street. "Something wrong?" I asked.

"Well, you're usually open by 7:00 and the store is still closed."

It took me minute to remember that the woman who normally opened the store was taking the day off. Tab was covering for her. "No, there's nothing wrong, Jack. Thanks for letting me know."

I hung up and dug around for Tab's cell number. From the way she answered, it was clear that she had been asleep. When I reminded her that she was supposed to be in the store, she admitted that she'd "spaced it." She told me she could be there in an hour. If this was her idea of coming through in the clutch, I didn't need her. I told her to take the day off, threw on some clothes, and headed there myself.

When I arrived, there were a half dozen people standing outside the front door. Who stands outside waiting for a stationery store to open?

"Problem here today?" a middle-aged man asked me gruffly as I opened the door.

"Staff screwups. Sorry," I said. The man stood next to me while I cut the plastic bands off the bundles of the *New York Times* and the *Boston Globe*, grabbing one of each from the pile and palming his exact change onto the counter. Another guy walked purposefully to the magazine rack, grabbed a copy of *Barron's*, and waited impatiently for me to ring up his sale. A woman headed directly to the cards and, while I rang up her purchase, she muttered something about needing to be across town in ten minutes.

I was a little dumbfounded by this activity. To begin with, I'd been awake for less than twenty minutes and I never liked having to deal with a lot of action when I first got up. I also didn't take the time to get coffee or something to eat and now wondered if I was going to be hungry until 10:00 when Tyler showed up. But what baffled me the most was that there would be any activity in the store at this time of the morning, let alone fervid activity. Were any of these purchases essential? Couldn't these people have made them somewhere else? Did they possibly warrant waiting outside of a closed store as though tickets for a Led Zeppelin reunion were going on sale? As the fourth and fifth people who had been at the door to greet me completed their purchases, I shook my head and set about getting the newspapers on their rack.

A sixth person, an elderly man, had been waiting with the others, but patiently. He browsed a few magazines while I prepared the papers and then picked up a *Times*, a *Globe*, and a package of Reese's Peanut Butter Cups before coming to the counter.

"Where's Ellen this morning?" he said.

"She had some family thing."

"Did you think the store was supposed to open later?"

"It's my father's store and it's been opening at the same time for more than thirty years. It would be kind of hard for me to get it wrong." I said this curtly, expecting yet another complaint. "Someone else was supposed to be here."

The man nodded and handed me three singles. It became immediately obvious that he wasn't planning to bitch about my inconveniencing him and I felt a little guilty about speaking so stiffly.

"You're Richard's kid, huh?" he said. "You look a little like him. I heard about his problem. How's he doing?"

"He's all right. The doctors think he's going to be fine."

"That's good. He's a good man. Been here a long time, always nice to the customers."

I wondered if that wasn't a polite reproach for my tone of voice. I handed the man his change and he pocketed it while at the same time pulling out four dollar bills and putting them in his other pocket.

"Everything's okay with Ellen, right?" he said.

"She's fine. Just had something to do with her daughter this morning."

"That's good." He smiled at me. "We've become friends, you might say, over the last few years. I come see her every morning during the week. Get my papers and my candy and we catch up a little. Then I'll go over to the coffee shop and get my French Roast and my blueberry scone and sit there and read for a while. I guess you'd call it a ritual. Been doing it every day since my Dorothy passed nine years ago."

The man had been doing the same thing every day for nine years. I couldn't imagine how anyone could become so completely locked into the same habit. Did he mean that he'd been coming to the store and the coffee shop for all that time? Or did he really drink the same French Roast and eat the same blueberry scone every single day? Did he ever buy a Crunch bar or perhaps a Milky Way? I wondered if there was a story behind this ritual. I wondered if his wife used to come into town to get the papers before she died. Maybe she made him blueberry scones on Sunday mornings. Or maybe all of this was new, a way of showing that he'd been able to move on, at least a little, after she died.

I never considered that the small talk we exchanged with customers had any value, but now I thought about the kinds of conversations Ellen had with this man. Was there some role that she had in the ritual that I needed to fill? Had she told Tab about it (and if she had, would it have mattered, since Tab would almost certainly have "spaced it")? I'm not sure why, but I felt the need to entertain this guy for a couple of minutes. I asked him about his plans

for the day and told him about the fair I'd gone to in
Lenox. He told me about his garden and his youngest
daughter coming to visit him from Philadelphia and
about the books he loved to read. Finally, he pulled
the four dollars from his other pocket and told me
that it was time for him to get down to the coffee
shop. I wondered if they had his meal waiting and if
I'd screwed up his schedule by opening the store late.

"Tell your father that Mickey said hi and wishes
him the best with his recovery," he said as he headed
toward the door.

"Hang on a second," I said as I walked around the
counter. I took another package of peanut butter
cups and handed them to him. "If you've really been
buying these for the last nine years, it's about time
you got one on the house."

He smiled, patted me on the shoulder, and walked
out the door. On the way back around the counter,
I took another package of Reese's for myself. Breakfast.

• • •

The next morning I walked into the den with two
mugs of tea, set them on the game table, and set up
the chessboard. Without a word, my father turned
off the television and sat down at his place. I moved
a pawn to Queen Three and we started to play. I
wasn't any better this time out than I had been a few
days earlier, but if anything I was even more deliberate and conservative. Neither of us spoke for the
first several moves, though my father at one point
made eye contact with me as I established the most

rudimentary possible defense. There was the faintest bit of amusement in his expression.

I'd been thinking more and more lately about the women I'd been involved with over the years. They'd been something like the participants in the parade that takes place every Fourth of July on River Road. They'd stop in front of me for a moment or two, do whatever it was that they were planning to do and then move on to entertain someone else. And like a spectator at one of these parades, I would be amused for a moment and even tickled by the spectacle of it all, but I would eventually be left wondering why everyone got so worked up about these things.

As my father began to dismantle me slowly on the chessboard, my thoughts returned to these women yet again. My father took my queen's bishop and I offered him a wan smile. I considered the fact that he knew almost none of the women I'd been with.

"You liked Gillian, didn't you?" I said.

He narrowed his eyes for a moment and then looked back down at the board. I wondered if he thought I was trying to do something to distract him.

"Do you remember her?" I said.

"Short brown hair, green eyes, very pretty. Said 'well' a lot."

I nodded and moved my knight back to King Three, where it had been three moves earlier. My father glanced at me disapprovingly.

"I had the feeling that you liked her that time I came back here with her."

"She seemed very nice. It seemed that she liked you."

"I think she did. I think we were doing okay then."

He slid his Queen's Rook to Queen's Knight One. I had absolutely no idea why he did that.

"I never told you what happened between us," I said.

"No, you never did," he said flatly. I wasn't sure if he was being sarcastic or not. I never explained any of my relationships to him.

"The lease on my apartment came up for renewal."

"That kind of thing breaks up a lot of romances."

"It wasn't the apartment itself; it was what to do with the apartment. You know, do I renew for another year, do I look for something else, do we get something together? I was selling real estate then, so I had a lot of access. What I didn't have was a lot of inspiration. It was like the lease on my relationship with Gillian had come up for renewal as well. And I knew that I didn't really love her. She was so easy to like and she made me feel comfortable, but it was like sitting in a Barcalounger, you know? At some point, you have to get up because you can't sit there for the rest of your life. And on top of everything else, I hated selling real estate. So I told her I was moving on."

Other than raising an eyebrow, my father didn't react to this. We exchanged several more moves.

"It was very different with Emily," I said. "That whole thing in Atlanta was so strange. We met when I got that office managing job at Allied. She could never really understand that the suit-and-tie thing was a phase to me, like a costume change. She was so corporate and type A, and for a while that seemed very exciting and exotic. Do you know what finally killed us?"

"Your car needed an inspection?"

"Yeah, funny. What killed us was that this junior executive position opened up. Emily pushed me like crazy to go for it. I mean, she was relentless. She sent me memos. It would have been comical if it weren't infuriating. When someone else got the job, she started lecturing me about missed opportunities. I quit Allied two days later and got the hell out of town."

My father took a sip of his tea and then made another move. Since he barely spoke anymore, it was hard to tell whether his reticence now had to do with his condition or the topic. I hadn't intended to talk to him about any of this. But I thought that shaking things up a little might actually be beneficial to him. I thought if I told him a little more about what I'd been doing the last few years that it might cause him to reconnect with the world in some small way. And since this was what was on my mind, it seemed the natural way to do it. A part of me actually wondered what he thought. I'd never really gone to him for advice, even when I was living at home. I spoke this way with my mother a little, and it was so much easier to talk to Chase than to either of them. But for any number of reasons, I wouldn't have minded hearing my father's impressions now. Instead, he continued to build an attack that I'd never seen before and couldn't have parried even if I had.

I told him about how Kristina had called me "soulless" the night before I left Minneapolis. I told him how Susan just walked away. I even told him about a woman I met at a bookstore and how my interaction with her haunted me even though we never dated. All the while, he trapped and captured my pieces. As with our previous match, my defeat was inevitable, but I refused to surrender.

When he at last checkmated me (something that it seemed to me he could have done several moves before he actually did it), he took a final sip of his tea and handed me his mug. I expected him to return to the television, but he sat back at the game table instead.

"Do you know how many women I've slept with?" he said.

"You grew up in the sixties, Dad. I don't know, a hundred and twenty?"

He smirked. It was the most expression I'd seen on his face since he returned from the hospital. "Not everyone participated in free love. I've slept with exactly one woman in my life. Which hardly qualifies me as an authority regarding the ups and downs of relationships. But I dated quite a few women before your mother and you know what I learned? Love isn't hard work. It might be trying, but if it feels like hard work, it probably isn't love."

He raised himself up on his arms, walked over to his easy chair and reached for the remote control. I'm sure that little soliloquy exhausted him. I sat at the table for a few minutes thinking about his message. Was he endorsing the breakups I told him about? Was he telling me that I didn't know anything about love? Was he assuring me that I'd know it when the right thing came along? I had no idea, but the virtual outburst from him left me strangely reassured.

I put the chess set away and made a note to myself to get a book on the game before our next match.

confiding in Iris for months about her desire to have a baby and about the male gay friend she'd been conflicted about doing it with.

"Yeah, Burke. They just decided to make it happen. I'd been wondering why she hadn't been talking about it as much lately. She's six weeks. Burke is going to move in with her when the baby is born."

"Doesn't Melanie have a partner?"

"She does, but Shelly's okay with it. They're all going to live together and raise the kid as a team."

"That takes unbelievable guts."

"Well, you know Mel."

I had in fact gotten to know Melanie a bit from my visits to the office and much more from the way Iris talked about her. Certainly, if anyone were going to make a juggling act such as this work, it would be she. She was very centered and methodical and I'd never seen her get flustered. Still, I was sure that there would be times when the dynamic would get awkward between the three adults.

"That's great news, I guess."

"It is great news. It's a long way from *Ozzie and Harriet*, but we happen to *be* a long way from *Ozzie and Harriet*."

I nodded and decided that Iris was right that this was good news. The household might feel a little crowded from time to time, but the key was that the kid would be in a situation where all of his parents really wanted him. With that in his corner, he could deal with everything else.

The conversation settled for a moment and I felt an ache in my right shoulder that had been bothering me all day. I tried to stretch it a bit as I drove.

"I don't know what I did to my shoulder," I said to Iris. "I must have slept on it wrong or something last night."

Iris reached over and squeezed the shoulder a few times. "I remember the first clandestine night Chase and I had together," she said. "It was the first time we had actually slept – as in actually sleeping – together and he could barely lift his arm the next day because I had my head on it the entire night. He made some ridiculous excuse about it to your mother the next day."

She laughed, and I laughed with her, but the casual mention of her sleeping with Chase had caught me off guard. We'd been talking about him less lately and hadn't really talked about him in his role as Iris' boyfriend for a while.

I'm not sure why what Iris said now threw me off so much. Chase was always somewhere on my mind and certainly I never forgot how Iris and I had become friends in the first place. But we'd developed such a meaningful present that the past had become a little diffuse. I'd started to think of her as *my* friend and I realized what I was feeling at this moment was a form of jealousy. It was the first time that the mention of Chase's name had inspired that and I found I wasn't particularly interested in continuing this line of conversation. I don't know what Iris thought of my sudden silence or if she thought about it at all, but we didn't say anything the rest of the way back to her place.

"Some wine?" Iris asked when we got in the door.

"Yeah, wine would be great."

Iris continued into the kitchen. "I got some of that

Super-Tuscan you were telling me about."

The dog bounded up to me and I knelt to pet her. "It's delicious. You'll love it."

"I love it already. I had a glass last night."

I sat on the couch and looked around the room. There were no pictures of Chase here. A shot of her mother. One of her cousin. A very prominently placed photo of Iris with Sam Shepard taken during his visit to see the Ensemble's production of one of his plays. A number of photographs with no people in them at all.

As we drank the wine, we talked about our plans for the next day and even for the next week. Slowly, the discomfort from my bout of jealousy abated. I was in the present with my new best friend, Iris, and we were talking about the things we were going to do. As long as I looked at things from this perspective, I was totally fine and even relaxed.

A short while later, Iris went to bed and I went to the guest room. There was a quilt on the bed that hadn't been there the week before, Iris had put a decorative clay pot on the nightstand, and a handmade clock was now up on a wall. These touches warmed the room, made it feel less like a spare and more like a place where someone stayed. I assumed she did them for my benefit and this pleased me. I lay down on the new quilt and looked up at the ceiling. The paint was still chipped from a leak that had happened years before and I found this surprisingly reassuring.

I thought back to the casual way that Iris had mentioned making love to Chase earlier. She wasn't someone to say anything without thinking. Had she done this to make sure that I understood that what was developing between us was purely friendship? Or did she do it because she had no reason to think that I would react badly to it in any way?

It was becoming more and more obvious to me that Iris and I saw our relationship in entirely different terms – even as I understood that it would be more perilous if she didn't feel this way. I understood that the limitations, real or imagined, that Iris put between us allowed me my fanciful thoughts. If she had not exercised this level of caution, I almost certainly would have had to.

And there was the quilt, the pot, and the clock. There were the plans for tomorrow and the next week and, presumably, the week after that. If what was evolving here wasn't what I fantasized (more often than perhaps I should have), it was still the best the world had to offer me.

• • •

When I got up that Thursday morning, my parents were already off to see my father's cardiologist. I believe this was the third time my father had left the house since coming back from the hospital. I'm not sure what it was about being here when my parents weren't around, but I found myself exploring again. This time I headed toward the basement.

This level of the house was perpetually "semifinished." There was carpeting on half of it and my father, in a burst of productivity a couple of decades before, had nailed cedar paneling to the walls of that half. An old Fisher television was in one corner, along with the couch that once sat in the den. My parents still had the set plugged in and the rabbit ears were pointed in whatever direction had provided snowy reception the last time anyone turned on the TV. Chase and I had loved to come down to the basement to watch this set, though it was less for the quality of the picture than it was for the freedom to jump as hard as we wanted on the couch. I turned the set on, half expecting it to play *Scooby-Doo* or maybe *Sesame Street*. When a morning talk show appeared instead, I shut it off without changing channels. The set wasn't dusty and neither was the carpet or the couch, which meant that my mother still came down here to clean, even though no one had used this space in years.

I opened the door of the wall unit that held our games and toys. There was the copy of Operation that we would hunch over in the early morning, determined not to let the buzzing sound awaken our parents. There was the copy of Booby Trap, a game that caused Chase to guffaw every time it exploded (even when we were in our teens). There was the copy of Stratego that my father brought home for me for no reason at all, the only time I could ever remember him doing that. I never liked the game particularly much, but I would play it anyway because there was something special about it. I found the big red ball that Chase and I would play dodgeball with ("not against the paneling," my mother would say, calling down from the kitchen). Deflated, of course, but it looked like it would be ready for another match if an air pump were available. The same basket held my catcher's glove, some street hockey pucks, and a Nerf basketball. On "Olympics Days," Chase and I would pull the basket out and compete until we'd used every bit of equipment, keeping the "medals totals" on a tiny blackboard. I looked up to see some of my Star Wars action figures and Chase's boxing gloves. My Magic 8 Ball and *Baseball Encyclopedia* and his football helmet and remote control car.

I had forgotten how much time we spent in this basement, even through high school. While we decidedly had the run of the house, this part was truly our turf. Mom could come down to clean (as long as we weren't in the middle of something) and Dad was welcome to put up some more paneling if the inspiration ever struck (as long as he left us at least one wall to throw the ball against), but the basement was ours. We'd be down there at least an hour a day, sometimes much longer if the weather was bad. And even when we weren't together, one of us would often be down here.

Across from the television was a collection of boxes that hadn't been there when I lived at home. I opened the first to find Chase's schoolwork and report cards. I didn't need to look at these to remember that they were mostly As, the exception being the C he got from his tenth grade history teacher, "that maggot" Mr. Olafsson, and the Bs he would always get in Art because he thought it was "silly."

In the second box, I found a bunch of my papers, mostly high school stuff. It was difficult to place archival value on ancient trigonometry tests and a book report on *The Man Who Fell to Earth*, but I'm sure my mother didn't know which of these things would be meaningful to me and which wouldn't. There was my speech after I became sophomore class president. Did I really say things like "We can make the future ours" and "This school can only do for us what we let it do for us," or did I more effectively edit myself when I actually delivered it? I remember a lot of applause, so perhaps there was one further draft that didn't make it into this box.

Under a few more quizzes was my acceptance letter to Emerson. I'd applied to three other schools and gotten accepted to all of them, but this was the one I wanted. The letter came a full two weeks after the last of the others, but I refused to consider the option of Ann Arbor or College Park or Syracuse. Emerson was small, it was progressive, it had one of the best communications programs in the country, and it was in a city I loved. The day I received it, Chase talked some guy outside of a liquor store into buying a bottle of champagne for him to give me.

Right underneath the Emerson letter was one of my notebooks. Every time my father's store would stock a new kind of notebook (different binding, different color, different rule size), I would make him bring me one. I wouldn't use these for schoolwork, but rather for personal writing: schemes, white papers, opinion pieces, a bit of journaling, stream of consciousness stuff that should be forever stored in boxes. And my lists. There was a time when I attached great importance to itemizing the best of everything. The best rock songs (what ever made me put Sting's "Fortress around Your Heart" ahead of the Beatles' "Ticket to Ride?"). The best movies (a tie between *E.T.* and *Close Encounters of the Third Kind* for first place). The best novels, the best ice cream, the best cop shows, the best presidential speeches (student council not included), the best state governors, the best TV news anchors, and, of course, the best amusement park rides. I had notebooks filled with these and I would review and revise them on a regular basis.

I sat on the couch and flipped through the notebook for several minutes. I had to laugh when I thought about how important these lists once were to me and yet how I had almost entirely forgotten them. I wondered if I should start making lists again. Best Women Who Gave Me the Time of Day? Best Job Exits? Most Annoying Exchanges with a Customer? Or perhaps Best Days in Lenox? Best Music for the Drive Back?

Maybe Best Reasons Why Iris and I Should Remain Only Friends?

I closed the notebook and put it back in the box. I flipped through some more term papers and postcards before closing it up and putting Chase's back on top. I'd get to the other boxes at some point in the future.

I walked past the carpeting. I remember thinking when I was much younger that there was some kind of magic involved in crossing from the carpet to the concrete. That it was the dividing line to some other world. What it really was, of course, was the byproduct of some crisis in the store that required all of my father's attention for an extended period. Once the crisis was over, his desire to finish the basement had dissipated and the floor remained half naked.

The unfinished half served as both a repository for old things no longer useful (both of the discarded refrigerators, my mother's sewing machine, the console stereo) and as storage space for Christmas decorations, the aluminum folding table, the forty-cup coffeemaker, and other items utilized during the occasional festivity. And there, too, under a white sheet that had in fact gathered dust, was my woodworking equipment.

This was as close to Zen as I got when I was a kid. I could spend huge stretches (usually when Chase was engaged otherwise; he would be too distracting even if he was just watching TV) carving, sawing, sanding, and finishing. I created pieces that often served little function other than letting me transform them, but also lamps and bookends and even, once, a chair. A number of these were still in the house, but had folded so completely into my image of the place that I hadn't picked them out as my own inventions since I'd been back.

In the intervening years, one of my parents had drawn the equipment together and pulled it under this sheet, but it hadn't been touched otherwise. I took the sheet off entirely now and moved things out into an approximation of the workstation I'd used back then: workbench in front of me, belt sander to the left, lathe and band saw to the right. I still had a block of wood positioned in the lathe. It was long and thin and I couldn't remember what I'd planned for it. I picked up a file from the bench and ran my fingers over it, dislodging sawdust that had been in place for nearly a decade. I'd spent so many hours here building things and imagining building others.

I looked at my watch and saw that it was time for me to get going to the store. I put the file back down on the bench and gave one more glance at the block of wood in the lathe, telling myself that I would come back down here when I had more time.

• • •

Before my next chess match with my father, I went out to get a couple of whole-wheat bagels for us to have with our tea. My mother wasn't sure why I couldn't just make some toast, but she didn't object, either.

As I'd promised myself, I'd bought a book on chess strategy. I got it in the bookstore in Lenox the last time Iris and I were together. ("Will this make you a professional overnight?" she asked. I told her I was simply hoping to give my father a better game.) I'd read it carefully and practiced certain situations in my mind. The result was an opening I'd never used before and I could see from the expression on my father's face that he hadn't anticipated it. Six moves into the match, though, I was once again out of my depth.

"Did I ever tell you about the job I had in Columbus?" I said.

My father nodded "no," never taking his eyes off the board.

"I was the head sandwich guy at this huge deli near Ohio State."

He brought out his Queen's Knight and said, "Well, it's good to hear you were the head guy."

"All that education really paid off," I said. "The place was a sandwich factory. We'd make hundreds of them a day. I had three people working for me. I did things with smoked turkey that others could only dream of. In other words, it was a ridiculous bore."

"What made you think that it wouldn't be boring to you?"

"I didn't really think about it very much. I liked the town and I liked the vibe. And the guy who owned the deli was hilarious."

"All sturdy reasons for a career choice."

I moved a bishop to Queen Four as the book suggested I do. "You know, I actually did give some thought to my career when I went to work for Minnesota Public Radio. I had to bullshit my way into the job after all of the other things on my resume, but I connected there a little. The first month or so was entry-level production assistant stuff, but I got to know the station manager and after a while he let me do some programming. I was good at it, I think. Not as good as I was at making grilled jerk chicken on sourdough maybe, but pretty good. I used to have a cassette with some of the shows, but I can't seem to find it."

"So what was the problem this time?"

"Stuff got weird with Kristina and it sort of affected everything."

"Kristina was the woman you were seeing in Minneapolis?"

"Yeah. And when things started to go south for us, I found it a little hard to hang on. And at that point the radio thing started to be a little bit of a hassle."

My father returned his focus to the board.

"You know, I've never once been fired," I said.

"Congratulations."

"I'm not bragging, but I thought you might have been wondering. I've never left a place because of that. Though there were one or two times when I thought I could be fired if things kept going the way they were going."

My father made his move and then sat back in his chair. I glanced over the board carefully to see if he had somehow checkmated me while I wasn't paying attention.

"Do you know what Amber was like thirty-four years ago?" he said. "They weren't exactly selling out the inns for $250 a night. It was all very speculative back then. Some good years when the town seemed to be going somewhere and then a number of down years would follow.

"I leased the space on Russet Avenue during one of those down periods. We had a little bit of money and we'd had some encouraging conversations with the town planners. It seemed like a good idea. Obviously, it turned out to be a good idea, but those first few years were a bitch."

He breathed deeply and then exhaled. "I loved making that store work, though. I was always moving merchandise around to see what drew the customers' attention. I tried out different lines to see which ones worked best, I changed the colors of the walls, the kind of music we played, the volume of the music we played, and even the hours we were open. In those first few years, I was tinkering all the time."

We exchanged moves. I had never heard my father talk about the store this way before. He'd never told me about the work that had gone into making it what it was. For as long as I could remember, it had looked relatively the same.

"Of course, not long after we opened the store,

your mother became pregnant with you. There was so much going on back then. A couple of stores closed on Russet Avenue and I was worried that I was going to have to close mine too if things didn't pick up. I was in the store from opening to closing just about every day while your mother took care of you. I felt bad for leaving her alone like that, but I knew that my job was to put money in the bank. And then she got sick."

"Mom got sick?"

"Very sick. You never knew about this?"

"I'm pretty sure I would have remembered."

"A terrible stomach problem. She lost a lot of weight and needed to spend most of her time in bed. The doctors kept giving her different things to do about it, but none of it seemed to work. It was a rough stretch for both of us. I was worried that she was going to be like that forever – or that it could be even worse than that. I wanted to take care of her, but I couldn't give her all of my attention because of the other responsibilities. She didn't get better until a couple of months before she became pregnant with your brother. The doctors finally got it right, I guess, because she's been fine ever since – though you'll notice she stays away from spicy food."

I glanced toward the kitchen, even though I couldn't see it from where I sat. "I can't believe I never knew about that."

"It was in the past. And things turned around after that. Anna was feeling better and the store was treading water. And then that article about Amber came out in the *Times* and suddenly we were the next big thing. People moved in, tourists started coming, and business took off. By the time your brother was born, things were moving.

"I like to say that it was my marketing genius that made the store the success it's been. But in truth it was just a number of very good breaks."

It was fascinating to hear my father speak this way. Aside from the fact that he was speaking this much at all, he was telling me things I never knew before, adding a voice-over to the home movies I had in my mind.

My research into the game of chess didn't pay immediate dividends. The inevitable checkmate happened sooner than expected. Sooner than the last match, for that matter. My father hadn't even finished his bagel.

He looked at the clock on the far wall. "You've gotta get to the store, don't you?"

"I have a few minutes."

"Nah, you've gotta get to the store. There's a show I want to watch anyway."

CHAPTER FOURTEEN
Ingredients

I tried to call home from college every Wednesday around dinnertime. It was my father's early night at the store and he and my mother tended to be home. One particular night, though, I called and got Iris on the other end.

"Chase is in the shower and your mom and dad decided to go out on a date," she said. "Your mother left us a pot roast for dinner."

"A specialty of the house."

"So I've heard. Your mom's a pretty good cook."

"She likes doing it and we like eating it. It works."

A Suzanne Vega album was playing in the background. It had to be one of Iris', as it definitely wasn't Chase's kind of music.

"How's the semester going?" she asked.

"Great so far. I have a lunatic philosophy teacher who's sort of 'all Kant, all the time,' and I finally had to give in and take the physics class I've been avoiding since my freshman year. But my media classes are very good. I especially like the documentary video course."

"Do you make them or watch them?"

"Make them and watch them. The making part is the final."

"Let's see; you're going to do a video on John Belushi as the best suicidal comic of his generation."

"Actually, I was thinking of doing it on you and Chase as the best couple."

"Best couple of what?"

"Yet to be determined. I haven't finished my research."

"Can you hang on a second?" Perhaps a quarter of a minute passed and then Iris was on the line again. "God, I love that part. The rim shots toward the end of 'Luka' get me every time."

I found myself smiling broadly. "Are you coasting through the second half of your senior year?"

"Semicoasting. I actually have to work in my AP English and AP World History classes. I'm also involved in the school play. We're doing *Streetcar*."

"That's serious stuff for high schoolers."

"The director wanted to do *Judgment at Nuremberg*."

"Give me a break."

"I mean it. I think the PTA talked him out of it."

"Do you have a big role?"

"Decent role. I'm Stella."

"*You're* Stella?"

"Are you suggesting that you don't think I can handle the role?"

"You just don't seem to be the Stella type to me."

"I guess we all have our secrets."

"Stella, wow. I can't wait to see it."

"I'll save you two on the aisle."

"One on the aisle will be fine. Unless I'm taking Chase as my date."

"I think he'll be waiting in the wings for me. So when are you coming down again?"

I hadn't actually planned to come back to Amber anytime soon. I needed the weekend time in the studio and there was the woman at the record store. But when Iris asked, I realized that I really wanted to see more of her and Chase.

"I was thinking about coming down this weekend. Are you guys going to be around?"

"Well, I can't ever be sure what Chase is going to want to do. For all I know, he could be planning to go up to see you. But yeah, I think we're going to be around."

"Great, we'll hang out."

"Sounds good. Want me to see if Chase is out of the shower yet?"

"No, it's not necessary. I'll catch up with him on Friday. Just let him know I called."

• • •

The next time I went up to Lenox, Iris and I spent the afternoon on our usual walk through town. There was nothing redundant about this – there always seemed to be something new going on – and it had become a very pleasant ritual. On this particular trip, a farmers' market had opened and we browsed the local corn and zucchini, the wide array of herbs, and the handmade breads, pies, and fresh pastas.

"I'm making dinner for you tonight," I said as I reached for a summer squash.

"You cook?"

"I *have* cooked."

"Successfully?"

"Triumphantly at times. You obviously don't know about me and the sandwich shop in Columbus. And thanks for having so much faith in me, by the way. Yes, I have cooked successfully and I'm going to do so for you tonight."

Not entirely sure what I was planning, I wandered around the market gathering ingredients for the meal. Other than my stint at that deli, I'd never spent very much time in a kitchen, though I liked cooking and I especially liked the satisfaction of making a meal for someone else. I decided to keep it fairly simple, planning pasta with yellow squash, tomatoes, and basil, and a salad, accompanied by a baguette and a peach tart we purchased from the bakery.

When we got back to Iris' house, I set to work immediately, chopping vegetables and herbs, putting a pot of water on to boil. Iris opened a bottle of wine for us and sat at the kitchen table watching me. I accidentally put the squash into the pan before the oil and hastily removed it before it stuck.

"Were you searing?" Iris said playfully.

"I was screwing up."

"Is that part of the recipe?"

I smirked at her and she took a sip of her wine in an attempt to hide her grin.

"You know, the last time a man made dinner for me, I was sick for two days afterward."

"You hang around with the wrong men."

"So I've been told."

"It's unlikely that this meal will make you sick. It may make you lose your appetite, but it won't make you sick."

"I'll take my chances. You look good at a stove. Almost like a natural."

"Was that meant to be a compliment?"

"Absolutely. It smells good, by the way."

Twenty minutes later, dinner was on the table. Iris seemed tickled when I set the plate in front of her. The food turned out fine. Maybe even a little better than fine.

"Um, delicious," she said. "Will you be making all of our meals from now on?"

"Don't count on it."

"Even if I compliment you profusely?"

"Compliment me profusely and I'll think about it."

Iris twirled a forkful of linguine and said, "Nah, you'll just get a big head. We'll eat out."

We talked about little things while we ate: reviewing the day, anticipating the work challenges of the coming weekend, touching on items in the news. Though this was the first time we'd had dinner in a kitchen together, we fell into it like people who had been doing this kind of thing for years.

Iris insisted on cleaning up and I didn't argue with her. While she did, I dialed up the new Beck album on her iPod. When she was finished, Iris brought in the remainder of the wine and sat with me on the couch. Other than commenting on a couple of the songs, we didn't talk at all until the music ended.

"What should we do tonight," I said, looking over at the clock. It was just past 8:30. We'd still have time for a movie or we could wait a while and head to one of the clubs for some live music.

"I'm okay just staying here," Iris said.

Ever since I'd been coming to Lenox, we'd always

done things. The idea of simply staying in her house felt foreign, as though she had said she wanted to go line dancing or something. At the same time, it was very appealing to think of putting on some more music, finishing the wine, and either talking or not talking for the rest of the night.

"You don't mind?" I said.

"I'm actually feeling very settled tonight. Must have been the meal."

"You'll be closer to a bathroom this way."

"Yeah, I thought of that, too," she said, pushing my knee with a bare foot.

I settled back into the couch, not realizing until that moment that I'd been planning to get up. As we listened to a Tim Buckley album recorded before either of us were born, my thoughts wandered back to the kitchen.

I started thinking about what I would make the next time I cooked for Iris.

CHAPTER FIFTEEN
Rounding the Square

A few days later, I handed the contractor the final check for the repairs to the back of the store. He told me it was "good doing business with me." I told myself that I wished I could say the same.

Tyler and I surveyed the repairs. Certainly, I'd never seen this part of the store in better condition: fresh carpeting, damaged displays replaced, clean white walls. *Now let the damn thing sell*, I thought. We spent the next hour putting merchandise back up. My father had used this space mostly for paper goods and party supplies and it was nearly comical when a man walked up to buy some birthday napkins and winked at me, as though to say "glad you've got these in stock again." I glanced over at Tyler, who made an elaborate display of patting me on the shoulder.

Feeling as though we needed to mark the occasion in some way, I told Tyler I was taking him out to lunch. He'd stepped into the breach when the water main broke and on more than one occasion since, he'd allowed me to vent my frustrations over the ways in which the repairmen operated, and through it all, he'd been a real colleague, more of one than just about anyone I'd ever worked with. Lunch was the least I could do.

"What do you mean?" Tab said when I told her we were going out.

"We're going out to get some lunch," I said plainly.

"Both of you?"

"Together, in fact."

She looked around the store. There were perhaps a half dozen people there. "What about the customers?"

"We thought, if you didn't have anything else planned, that maybe you'd take care of them, since that's why you get a paycheck."

She scowled and I decided not to take the conversation further. Ever since she failed to open the store a few weeks back, I'd been finding it harder and harder to tolerate her. I nodded toward Tyler and we left.

"How go the adventures in the Big Apple?" I said as we settled in our seats.

"I'm making headway, I think. I went on a follow-up a couple of days ago with an interesting firm and I had a couple of other interviews while I was in the City."

"All of whom you impressed the pants off of, I assume."

"Yeah, maybe. I know this sounds strange, but I'm actually kind of enjoying the interviewing process. I feel challenged by it and I feel like I have good answers. I know some people hate them."

I raised my hand to indicate that I belonged in that group.

Tyler tabulated my vote and then added, "But I find it stimulating."

"Since you like it so much, you can take a page out of my book and change jobs every six months. This way you can keep interviewing your entire life."

We ordered and then Tyler leaned forward, putting his hands on the table. "You know what the best part of this trip was, though? I hung around that night and went to see Beam at the Bowery Ballroom. Do you know them?"

"Just that one song."

"They're incredible. It's like being under siege. They're relentless. I don't think I've ever been to a show this intense before."

I made a note to download some songs of theirs. Some of Tyler's tastes veered toward the sentimental, but other than that, he tended to do an excellent job of identifying the good stuff – and Beam certainly didn't sound sentimental to me.

"So what did you do this time on your midweek weekend?" he asked.

"Iris and I did one of our walking tours of Lenox and then I made her dinner. We drove up near the Vermont border the next day."

"What is it with you and this woman, anyway?"

"Just friends."

"You drive two hours to see her every week and you're just friends?"

"It's complicated."

"She's beautiful, by the way."

"I'm aware of that." I paused for a beat, wondering if I really wanted to talk to anyone about this. "She was my brother's girlfriend."

"Oh," Tyler said elaborately, as though I'd given him all the explanation necessary. I wondered if in fact I had.

"She's great. I always thought she was great. And I've always liked being with her. And there are times, you know, when it sort of feels like there should be more between us. And then there are other times – most of the times, I guess – when I feel like that would be like moving into the luggage compartment of a jumbo jet."

"In other words, it's complicated."

"I couldn't have said it better myself."

"And you've been doing this for the last ten years?"

"No, not at all. Until I came back to Amber this time, I hadn't seen her since Chase died."

"You and your brother were close, huh?"

"Really close."

"It's such a drag what happened to him. I've been thinking about that more ever since you came to town. I mean, it's not like I knew him, but knowing you and knowing your dad, he just flashes into my head sometimes."

"He has a way of doing that. I go from thinking about him constantly, to finding constant reminders about him, to having him on my mind a lot. It rarely dips below that level."

Tyler looked off into the distance, as though he was processing what I'd said. When he looked back at me, I just smiled and we switched topics.

When we got back to the store, there must have been ten people waiting in line at the register while Tab methodically tended to the one in front of her. She was moving even more languidly than usual and

I was certain that it had something to do with our going out and leaving her alone. I glanced over at Tyler and the two of us headed behind the counter to do triage. Within a few minutes, the rush had ended. Tab grabbed her pocketbook from under the counter and walked away.

"I'm going to lunch now," she said before leaving the store.

As she walked down the street, Tyler turned to me and said, "And she was *that close* to a huge raise."

• • •

The next morning, I checked in on my father (watching *The Today Show*, but with his head propped up on his right hand – a new position for him), checked in on my mother (paying bills at the kitchen table), grabbed the unopened box of Honey Nut Cheerios, and went down to the basement. My mother looked up at me as I opened the basement door, but then went back to her work.

I sat down at the workstation, running my hand over the block of wood mounted on the lathe again. I wished I could remember what I was planning to do with it, though it's entirely possible that I didn't even know back then. I would often simply turn the lathe on and start carving, allowing the piece to become something while I worked on it.

I didn't know how I could have so completely stopped thinking about this equipment. I'd spent so much time with it during my teens. I'd come down here to recharge while studying, or to decompress if Chase had pissed me off about something, or to

mollify myself if some girl brushed aside my affections. I'd come down here when I was feeling highly
creative and when I was feeling tapped out. And
often I'd come down here because I'd begun a project that had taken hold of me and I was driven by the
need to complete it. And yet, despite the passion I'd
expended on these tools, I had spent a couple of
months living under the same roof with them without
even wandering down for a visit.

I picked up a carving tool and wondered if I remembered what to do with it. I decided to find out. I
turned the lathe on and watched it whir, feeling a little thrill at hearing a sound I hadn't heard in a
decade. I put on my gloves and my goggles and I bent
toward the spinning block of wood. I touched it tentatively with the carving tool, finding reassurance in
the familiarity of the experience. But when I pressed
a little harder, the block splintered, a segment cata-
pulting against the wall across from me. I turned off
the lathe and looked at the damage. The wood had
obviously dried from being in the same position un-
treated for all these years.

I pulled the remaining shards from the lathe and
then retrieved the one that struck the wall. I held
them in my hands, unsure of what to do next. There
were a few more blocks available, but they would
certainly be in the same condition as the one that had
just cracked on me. I threw the shards in a trash basket, took off my gloves and goggles, and went back
up the stairs.

"Were you using your tools just now?" my mother
said while writing a check.

"Yeah. I'll be back in a little while."

She looked up at me at that point, but didn't say anything. I couldn't read her expression, which I actually considered progress since the expression I had been reading on her face the past few weeks was so disapproving.

I assumed that Wilson's Lumber Yard was still in the same place it had been when I lived in Amber. By the time I was in high school it had already been in the area for more than sixty years. I became something of a regular customer there, certainly not like the contractors who visited almost daily, but enough to trade small talk with members of the staff. Not that I was expecting any of them to remember me.

Wilson's was in fact right where I left it, though they'd painted the red cedar shakes cream, the parking lot featured a trio of sheds selling landscaping equipment, and there was a large sign near the front door inviting customers to visit their Web site. The lumber department itself, however, was refreshingly familiar. If they had made any changes to the layout or the merchandising in the past ten years, these escaped my notice. I browsed through the aisles of plywood, 2x4s, and studding materials in the same way I'd walked the aisles of the record store in Lenox my first day there. Names, smells, and textures came back to me. It was like a class reunion.

I'm sure this wasn't behavior that the staff was accustomed to seeing, and after a few minutes a guy came up to me to ask if he could help. I gave him my order and he was perhaps a little more efficient in delivering it to me than I would have liked. I piled the armload of wood into the trunk of my car and drove back to my parents' house.

By the time I had a new piece mounted on the lathe, I had to get to the store. Still, I felt the need to turn the machine on just for a moment. I put the gloves and goggles back on and I picked up the carving tool. With one smooth motion, more assured than I would have guessed, I began the process of rounding the square block.

I didn't have time for this and I knew if I went any further, I could be here for hours. I turned off the machine and looked at the piece that had now stopped spinning. It was going to take some work to turn this into anything, but I promised myself I'd get back to it tomorrow.

• • •

"So here's a little bit of news," Tyler said as we sat at the Cornwall. It had become something of a habit for us to go out for a drink after work on the nights we closed the store together and we'd decided to keep the date even though we'd been out to lunch only the day before. "I hadn't wanted to say anything to you because I'm a little superstitious about this kind of thing, but I've started seeing someone. Her name is Sarah."

"Great," I said. "When you say 'seeing someone,' does this mean you're getting involved with her or just going out on a few dates?"

"I think we're getting involved. It hasn't been that long – you'd probably say that it was only a few dates, in fact. But yeah, I think we might be getting involved. She gets to me, you know?"

"Yeah, I hear you. This is good news. How'd you meet her?"

"You're going to laugh, but I met her in the store."

"Please tell me you weren't reading the cards to her."

"Hmm, I'm gonna have to think about what it means that you thought that. No, nothing that ridiculous. She just came in a couple of times and we talked – I took care of every customer while we were doing so, boss – and we wound up deciding to go to a movie. It sorta grew from there."

"So the message here is that if I stick around long enough my dream woman might come through the door?"

"No, but if you stick around long enough *my* dream woman might come through the door. At least you'd get to say hi to her."

I raised my beer glass in an approximation of a toast. "This is good for you. I hope things go well with this."

"Thanks. It's actually feeling good. It's been a while, you know?"

It was nice to see Tyler's expression when he talked about this woman. It mirrored the one he wore when he talked about his career. I found his enthusiasms encouraging.

"Do you ever think about what you would do with the store if it were yours?" he said.

"If you're asking if I ever think about what's wrong with the store, then yes, all the time."

"But do you ever think about what you'd do with it? Don't get me wrong, I think your father has done a very good job with the place, but it isn't what I would do." He shrugged. "But what the hell do I know. I haven't been running it successfully for thirty years."

"The very first thing to go would be that radio station," I said. "I'd replace it with an iPod dock. We'd play soft stuff, but listenable stuff, you know? Lucy Kaplansky, Lucinda Williams, David Gray, Matt Nathanson. And I'd turn the volume up. Maybe all the way to '3'."

Tyler laughed. "You can do that now, you know. It's not like your father has the place monitored or anything."

"Except that one day he'll walk into the store, hear Mark Knopfler, and have another heart attack." The truth is, I didn't really think about how easy it would be to make that change. Since I'd been back in the store, I'd followed nearly every one of my father's hard-and-fast rules to the letter. I didn't even reorder the BlisterSnax after the first box sold out.

"I'd do something about the display cases in the front," Tyler said. "That white Formica finish might have looked fresh in the seventies, but now – it just looks like it came from the seventies."

"What about the *stuff* in the display cases? I think interest in those things faded about the same time as people stopped using the word 'trinkets.'"

"Amazingly, we actually sell some of that stuff."

"Which says everything that needs to be said about the people who come into this town. I'd bring in more handmade stuff. Import some things from Italy. Go to a craft show or two. Read a catalog that's been printed in the twenty-first century."

"Wackier toys."

"And cooler cards. Definitely cooler cards."

"The magazines could be merchandised better."

"The candy rack should be moved."

"Higher level paper goods. The people around here can afford it."

"And change the name."

Tyler put his beer down on the table. He'd been holding it close to his mouth but not drinking during this entire exchange. "What?" he said.

"You don't think 'Amber Cards, Gifts, and Stationery' is a bit on the ridiculously obvious side?"

"It tells people what the store is."

"In other words, it's pedestrian?"

"I mean if you change the name, you still need to make sure people know what's inside."

"I guess that leaves out calling it 'Graceland.'"

Tyler finally took a sip of his beer and I made eye contact with Phil the pirate.

"We could do this, you know," I said.

"You want to change the name of the store?"

"Not that. But some of these other things. Certainly the simple stuff like the music, the candy, and the magazines. But some of the other things, too. Bring in some new vendors. My dad's credit line is great."

"What about the sale?"

"What about it?"

"Doesn't screwing around with the store at this point throw things off a little?"

"I'm not sure that they can be thrown off any more than they already have been. It might even help. And if nothing else, it'll keep me entertained."

"Gutsy move."

"Desperate move. As long as I'm stuck here, I might as well do something with my time. And maybe we'll get lucky."

CHAPTER SIXTEEN
Anything Could Happen

I had been home for the spring break of my junior year for less than an hour when Chase sat on my bed and told me that he'd split up with Iris. I sat on the floor with my back propped up against the wall with my Eric Clapton poster and spent the next hour trying to get him to tell me how it had happened and why. Chase offered soliloquies and babbling, but no cogent reason other than to take full, regretful responsibility for it. Since he seemed so upset about it and since he seemed to think it was entirely his fault, I asked him why he didn't try to do something to patch things up between them. All he would say was that he'd ruined things and that the damage he'd done could never be repaired. I briefly considered the possibility that he was putting me on, but he wasn't kidding this time. Eventually he went into his room and played a Nirvana CD at a volume that suggested that he wanted Iris to hear his anguish all the way across town.

That night, he asked me if I wanted to go out with him and some of "his guys." Though I hadn't met any of them before, I recognized several from Jim Krieger's New Year's party – Chase's lacrosse teammates who had played their drinking game until they passed out. While I had done a great deal of drinking in college, I wasn't entirely sure I was a match for this group. My goal had always been to achieve a certain level of blissed-out-edness and then to carefully maintain this state throughout the evening, like steering a sailboat toward a fixed point. For this group, it was about racing a hydrofoil into as much turbulence as possible before flipping over and bailing out. By the time we'd left our first stop, a bois-terous joint across the river, everyone else had slammed a half dozen shots of tequila and a pitcher of beer apiece. It was intimidating in so many ways.

After Chase and his friends took turns pissing into the river not a few hundred feet from where we'd had our first long conversation about Iris, we headed up the highway to a club I'd never visited before. There this group met up with their flannel-shirted brethren to mosh to alt-rock covers played by an incensed band sporting Kurt Cobain haircuts. I got within five feet of the edge of the mosh pit, but couldn't convince myself to go farther. It wasn't as much that I was frightened as that the angst and pseudo-angst re-pelled me. Eventually I retired to the second level of the club while I waited for Chase and his guys to emerge from the mass of furious boys. At one point, I saw him carried atop the pit, pumping his fists and screaming the lyrics to some Chris Cornell tune. When the pit swallowed him back up, I didn't see any of the group again for nearly an hour.

Though it would have been unsportsmanlike for me to say so, I was ready to go home at this point. But there were other stops to make. The first involved an all-night diner where the group ate huge stacks of pancakes and bacon while heckling the waiter, hurling insults at each other at the tops of their lungs, and annoying the other patrons. I was certain the manager was going to throw us out, and I think if it had been earlier in the evening and the diner was fuller, he might have. I was surprised that Chase participated in some of this, but I wrote it off to his being upset over Iris.

By this time, it was 2:30. I was working on only a couple of hours of sleep because I'd had a paper to turn in before heading from Boston and I was starting to wear down. But we weren't quite finished. First, we had to go to an alley between a sporting goods store and a bar on River Road where Chase and his guys participated in one of the most distasteful competitions I've ever witnessed: the vomit-off. Chase seemed a little disappointed that I chose not to join in, but for once, he was not going to cajole me into doing something stupid. Standing at the "starting line," they gagged themselves, awarding points for distance and "style." I nearly got sick to my stomach witnessing this and turned my back while they argued over who "won."

I didn't get up until nearly two o'clock the next day. My father was at the store and my mother was with her sister. Chase was shooting baskets on the driveway. He smiled when he saw me, clapped me on the shoulder, and then handed me the ball. I took a couple of shots and any lingering fog from the night before began to dissipate. Eventually we settled into a game of H-O-R-S-E, which I won, and then a game of one-on-one, which Chase took easily. Afterward, we sat on grass that snow had covered only a week and a half earlier. Chase asked me if I wanted a beer and I cast him a disparaging glance. He just laughed and leaned back to look up at the sun.

We sat there for a long time. Talk about baseball and new music quickly evolved into a lengthy conversation about Iris. Chase told me about things they'd done over the past weeks, speaking as though nothing had happened to interrupt their time together. At the end of this, he told me that it had been three days since he'd last seen her and his expression darkened. Again, I tried to get him to tell me what happened and again I failed. I couldn't be sure whether shame or confusion prevented him from talking to me about this, but he seemed utterly incapable. He went off on a long stream of consciousness disposition about love and about what it meant to him before, during, and after Iris. He talked about missing her and wondering what she was doing, but never once would he entertain my suggestion that he call her. I'd never seen Chase indecisive and he wasn't being indecisive now. In fact he was adamant in his belief that whatever had transpired between them was final, even though it caused him more pain than he'd ever felt before. We talked until my mother pulled up to the driveway, after which Chase patted me on the knee and approached her, wrapping an arm around her shoulder.

By Wednesday of that week, after a few more conversations of this type, I thought about calling Iris myself. Partially, I wanted to do this to see if I could get any sense from her of whether she'd be willing to talk to Chase. But I was also partially wondering how she was doing. I'd come down from Boston the weekend before anticipating seeing both of them. By this point, I no longer considered her to be simply one of Chase's accessories. If Chase was hurting this much from the breakup, then there was a very real chance that she was hurting as well. And that meant something to me. I'd even nearly convinced myself that she would be expecting me to check in on her, that our relationship had developed to the point where she would want me to make sure that she was okay.

In the end, I couldn't do it. What held me back was the fear that I wouldn't know what to say once I got her on the phone or perhaps that she might even be hostile toward me, seeing me as an agent for "the enemy" and railing at me.

But there was something that overrode this concern: the glimmer of recognition that my intentions in making this call might not be entirely honorable. That in fact a part of me wanted to hear from Iris that things were irreconcilable between her and my brother. That she was available. Once that thought entered my mind, and once I found that I couldn't easily shoo it away, I knew I couldn't speak to her.

By Sunday afternoon, it didn't matter. While my mother prepared an early supper and I got ready to drive back to Boston, Chase surmounted whatever obstacles he'd placed in the way of reaching out to Iris. He bounded into my room, threw himself on my bed, and told me that he'd just finished talking on the phone with her for an hour and a half and that they were seeing each other that night. I could swear I even saw his eyes glisten for a moment when he said how relieved he was that he hadn't completely lost her. I hugged him when I heard the news and gave him a playful punch in the stomach to lighten the moment.

He never did tell me what came between them and I never asked again.

• • •

Since Iris was coming to Amber to visit her mother, I didn't drive up to Lenox the next week. However, we did keep our Wednesday "date." I picked her up midmorning and we went to the beach at Beacon Lake. In that summer ten years earlier, Chase, Iris, and I spent a fair amount of time on this beach, splashing in the water, burying each other in the sand, and drinking illicit margaritas from a thermos. I hadn't been back since Chase died and couldn't get there now without directions.

Iris was considerably more organized this time around than we had been a decade before, packing lunch in a cooler (no margaritas as far as I could tell) and bringing a huge beach blanket (not an heirloom) from her mother's house along with an umbrella. She set this up methodically while I watched, certain that any attempt to help would make a negative contribution. When she pulled off her T-shirt and shorts to reveal the royal blue bikini underneath, I remembered another convention of those summer days past: the forays Chase and Iris would take into the woods to make love while I lay in the sun. Iris' skin was lightly tanned and her body was as lithe as I remembered it from all those years ago. I'd seen her this undressed several times before on this very beach, but was somehow a little unprepared for it this time. She sat down on the blanket and I felt a moment's self-consciousness about removing my own shirt and shorts before sitting next to her.

There were a few dozen other people on the beach with us. A child poured buckets of water onto his mother's feet. A group of kids kicked a red rubber ball around in the sand. A man in a dress shirt and pants talked on a cell phone. Two teenagers lay very close together, kissing. A few swimmers bounced around in the lake.

"Are you still a madman in the water?" Iris said. "I'd just like to know before I decide whether or not to go in with you."

"I was never a madman. Chase was the madman and he coerced me into acting like him."

"That's not what he told me. The first time we all came here together, if I remember correctly, you were out of control. Afterward, Chase said those exact words to me: 'my brother's a madman in the water.'"

I recalled the time clearly. It was after Iris and I had our first "moment" together and I was still feeling awkward about it. Seeing her nearly naked on the beach that day was a little more than I could handle and I remember being more animated than usual in an attempt to cover this up. Chase and I had always wrestled in the water and I took this to an extreme this time, relentlessly attempting to dunk his head.

"It's a bad rap. He brought out the lunatic in me. Trust me, you're safe."

Iris knocked her knee against mine. "Too bad," she said.

She lay back on the blanket and, after a short while, I did the same.

"He loved doing that stuff with you," she said. "At first it seemed kind of sophomoric to me in that dumbass male-bonding-jock kind of way. But then I figured out that there was something very intimate about this physical stuff between the two of you. Intimate and necessary."

"That's an interesting way of looking at it. I always thought he was just proving that he was stronger than me."

Iris turned her face in my direction. "I think he was actually buzzed about the fact that you were nearly as strong as he was. He didn't get a lot of that kind of competition."

"I assumed he was just going easy on me. I mean, he had a thirty pound advantage."

"'Thirty pounds of muscle,' let's remember," she said, quoting one of Chase's favorite proclamations.

"How could I forget?"

"You were the better singer, though."

"Something that has served me well in my later life."

She propped herself up on one arm. "No, really. Do you remember that time the two of you serenaded me by the campfire to 'Hey Jude'? He was only okay, but you were really, really good."

"I think your memory is playing tricks on you."

"Yeah, right. My memory is absolutely photographic from that time. You should sing more often."

"I sing all the time."

"I mean without the stereo blasting."

"Yeah, maybe for my next career."

"Don't mock." She lay back down on the blanket. "That was a great summer, wasn't it?"

"Most of it, anyway."

"Yeah, most of it."

Lying here on this beach brought Chase very much onto the blanket with us. I'm not sure what Iris' intentions were in suggesting we come here, if she had any at all, but we hadn't made a habit of visiting old haunts. The effect on both of us was obvious. This was and would always be Chase's place.

And now that I'd redirected the conversation, however inadvertently, toward the part of that summer that wasn't "great," I felt that I needed to say more. I'd told a grand total of two people about the role I'd played the night Chase died. One was the therapist I'd seen very briefly a few years ago. The other was Gillian at the point at which I thought we were becoming serious. Since Iris and I had begun our new relationship, I'd wondered on and off whether I should tell her. The thoughts had receded lately, but now that we were here and now that the subject was out there, it seemed essential.

I sat up and glanced from the teenaged lovers to two boys splashing each other in the lake.

"There's a good chance you're going to hate me more for this," I said. I could hear Iris turning on the blanket, but I didn't look at her. "I could have saved Chase."

"What are you talking about?"

"I was with him that night. I met him at Shanahan's after he'd already been there awhile. He was in a weird mood – weirdest I'd ever seen him in. And he got me pissed off and we argued. It was just another one of those arguments we sometimes had, but he was really wasted and I should have been paying more attention."

Iris was sitting up next to me now. "I don't understand."

"He was wrecked. I should have known that it wouldn't be safe for him to drive, that he was in real danger. I should have just told him to shut up and gotten him into my car. But what I did instead was just yell at him and walk out. I should have known that he was in no condition."

I looked over at her. I knew I was going to start crying if I said anything else, so I just stopped. She put a hand on my shoulder and I could see that she seemed ready to cry as well. I found her touch reassuring. When I'd started, I'd half expected her to pack up her things and walk out on me.

"Do you want to know why he was so drunk?" she asked.

I just kept looking at her. The question didn't seem to need a response. She pulled her legs up and wrapped her arms around them.

"That afternoon, I'd told Chase that I was pregnant. He freaked. I think it just stunned him that he could have done something that wrong. It was as though he didn't understand that there was always some level of risk."

She released her legs and dug a hole with her toe in the sand. I was having a little trouble breathing.

"Things got a lot worse when I told him that I wanted to keep the baby."

"How could you do that?"

"You mean between being eighteen and going to

Holyoke in the fall and all of that? He wondered the same thing. At least I assume he was wondering those things while he was screaming them at me. I just knew I could do it and I knew that he could do it with me. Do you really think your brother would have botched it if he put his mind to it?"

"I'm not sure he was ever tested at that level."

"Of course he wasn't. But there's no chance he couldn't have pulled it off. If he wanted to. I knew that nearly as much as I knew that I couldn't go through with an abortion and I certainly couldn't have the baby and then give it up. I've always known what I was doing, Hugh. This wasn't impetuousness on my part. I knew I could handle it, even if it meant transferring to MCS."

"Chase obviously didn't agree."

"It was the worst argument we ever had. He wasn't just upset. He was furious. As though my pregnancy was an affront to him. He couldn't sit down and the muscles in his neck were bulging. I'd never seen him like that before. I think he thought that if he got angry enough he could make me change my mind or make the whole thing go away or something. But I wouldn't give in. I wouldn't even say that I was willing to consider it. When he left the house that day, I wasn't sure what he was going to do. Obviously, he decided to drink it away."

She hugged her legs again and rested her chin on her knees.

"He wouldn't have been in the condition you saw him in if I hadn't made him get that way in the first place. The irony is that I had a miscarriage in September. That was one hell of a first semester at school."

I had no idea what to say. I was stunned and saddened and confounded all at the same time. I put my hand on her shoulder and she turned from me and lay down on her stomach. As though to reassure me that she wasn't moving away from me, she reached her hand out for mine. I held it, though I didn't lie down next to her.

"I'm sorry," I said.

She squeezed my hand. "You couldn't have known what was going to happen to him. He'd driven drunk any number of times before. He was good at it."

"He was very drunk."

"He'd been very drunk before. There was no way you could have anticipated it."

"I'm not sure. It seems so inevitable to me now."

"I know what you're saying. Don't you think I've told myself ten thousand times that I should have handled that last conversation with him differently? The way he looked when he left, I should have known that anything could happen. I should have run out after him and told him that we both needed to take a little time with it. It could have changed everything. It *would* have changed everything."

"It was your baby."

"It was *our* baby."

I lay down on my back. "My God, Chase was going to be a father," I said. I looked toward Iris. Our faces were perhaps a foot apart from each other. I was close enough to see the tears forming in her eyes and the first one roll across the bridge of her nose. I reached out and touched her calf with my foot and she touched her forehead against mine.

"Now you know more about me than you ever wanted to know," she said.

"Not possible," I said. But even though I said it, I wondered if it was true. Even up to the point when I started speaking, I wasn't sure that I would ever tell Iris about my involvement with Chase on that night. And yet she had responded by sharing a secret that was so much more revealing. And now that we'd done this, it seemed inconceivable to me that we could possibly go back to being "running buddies" again. And I simply didn't know if I was ready for that.

"I'm gonna go take a dip in the water," I said. "Want to join me?"

"Go ahead. Maybe I'll come in a couple of minutes."

Eventually she did and we spent the next couple of hours pretending that everything was as it had been.

I know Iris knew that it wasn't, and I knew that she understood me well enough to know that I knew it as well.

• • •

I spent much of the next morning down in the basement putting my latent woodworking skills to practical use. After my drinks conversation with Tyler and after discussing it with my father (the only time I'd brought up the subject of the store with him during his convalescence), I'd decided to make some of the changes we discussed. Among them was replacing the chipped white Formica display cases in the front of the store. In a flash of inspiration, I started to build the new ones myself. I'd made a couple of false starts before some of the old techniques came back to me and this morning I was cutting, sanding, planing, and hammering fluidly.

All the while thinking about Iris and the conversation we'd had the day before. She'd been pregnant with my brother's child. This revelation led me, however foolishly, to think a little differently about her romance with Chase. I'm not sure why. Was it that it made the sex between them more serious? That certainly couldn't be the case since the pregnancy was accidental, not to mention that the notion of some sex being more serious than other sex among committed couples was somewhat silly in the first place. Was it that the accidental pregnancy suggested a level of urgency to their passion – I need to have you right now regardless of the consequences – that elevated their physical connection? Maybe. Was it that Iris' determination to keep the baby was confirmation of her desire to have a permanent relationship with Chase? In some sense, I'd known that all along.

Regardless, what Iris and Chase had between them seemed more intimate to me after that conversation. It was as though what she'd revealed wasn't just a physical reality, but an emotional one as well. And it left me utterly off stride. I'd vaguely considered the notion of becoming her brother-in-law. But becoming an uncle had so many additional implications and reverberated so much stronger ten years later.

I lay the top of the case on the workbench and pulled out a carving tool. I didn't want to do anything elaborate with these displays, but I thought a few etchings would improve them. I set to work carving three subtly curved lines on each side. This was the first time I'd used this tool in ten years and I needed to exercise great care. The concentration allowed me a few minutes' diversion.

But then there was the other thing to think about from the day before – the argument between Chase and Iris when she'd told him that she was pregnant and the way he'd walked out on her that day. For the past ten years, Iris had been carrying around the belief that this argument had led in some way to the accident that night. It was so easy for me to dismiss it, especially given my much closer proximity to Chase – and my much greater opportunity to save him – in the time before he took his fatal drive. But was I dismissing it too easily? Chase surely got as drunk as he did that night because he was upset about the way his future was redefining itself. Could Iris have handled the conversation differently? Should she have allowed the fact of the pregnancy to sink in before she confronted him with her conviction to keep the child? Was Iris right in carrying this guilt with her a decade hence?

I pulled back and noticed that I'd angled one of the curved lines incorrectly. This was going to take some work to fix. And perhaps today wasn't the best time to do it.

I put the tools aside and shut down the workshop for the day. I spent a few minutes bouncing a ball against the concrete wall before heading upstairs. They weren't expecting me in the store, but I decided to go there anyway.

CHAPTER SEVENTEEN
The First Coat of Varnish

"You're playing like a drone," my father said as we sat across from each other during our next chess match. "Your moves are totally predictable."

"If they're so predictable, why are you having so much trouble countering them?"

"I have to do something to keep myself entertained."

A comment like this would have stung a few weeks earlier. But I knew that the books I'd read and the practice games I'd played online were making me better. There was still no chance that I could beat my father, but I was putting up more resistance. Hence the "trash talk" from him. I think this was his way of letting me know that I was becoming a worthier opponent.

I sat back and took a bite from my bagel. Whole wheat, which would never be my first choice. My favorites were salt bagels, but eating one in front of my father seemed cruel. He moved his Queen's Bishop to King Five. I quickly countered.

"I saw that one coming," I said. "Speaking of predictable."

He scowled. "I'm baiting you and you don't even realize it."

"How do you know that *I'm* not baiting *you*?"

He glanced up at me as though he was giving my question a moment's consideration and then looked back down at the board. Consideration over.

It turned out to be the longest match we'd played to date. I'd been keeping track of the number of moves it took until checkmate for several weeks now.

When we were finished, I reached into a bag that I'd gotten from the bagel store and pulled out a glazed chocolate doughnut. I broke the doughnut in two and reached out with a piece to my father.

"Whoa," he said. "This is not exactly on my approved diet."

"I gave you the smaller piece."

He took the doughnut from me. "Have you decided that since you can't beat me you're going to kill me?"

"You saw right through that one, huh?"

He looked at the doughnut for nearly a minute before taking a bite. After he did, he took another one quickly and then closed his eyes, as though this would allow him to heighten the sensation of the taste. When he opened his eyes, his expression was sadder than I would have expected and he put the unfinished piece down on his plate.

"I feel like my life is over," he said.

In many ways, I'd been expecting this conversation from the very first time I set up the chessboard.

"Baby steps, Dad," I said.

"I'm not taking any steps at all."

"You *are* taking some. You're kicking my ass in chess. That requires at least a little effort, right?"

"Not much."

"But it's something. And you can take more. The doctor says you can, doesn't he?"

"The doctor doesn't live inside of me."

"Do you feel like something is happening? Do you feel weak? Do you feel like something is coming on?"

"I just feel wrong."

He pulled his robe close around him and, for the first time in a week, tied the sash. He got up and moved tentatively to his chair.

"You've never gone through anything like this before," I said.

"I've gone through *something* like this before," he said sharply.

"I meant you've never gone through anything like this physically."

"What's your point?"

"That maybe you're supposed to feel wrong because your body is making adjustments."

"Or maybe I feel wrong because my heart is about fail on me at any minute."

"So from your perspective it's better to petrify than to die, huh?" This came out more critical than I'd intended and I thought about saying something else to soften it. But when my father looked at me, he didn't seem angry or hurt, but rather a little baffled.

He settled back in his chair and reached for the remote control. "Let's leave this for now," he said, turning on the television. "You played a good match today."

I kissed him on the forehead and walked away. Before I left the room, I took the rest of his doughnut.

• • •

Iris and I usually spoke on the phone at least once every couple of days, but in the five days since we'd been on the beach, I hadn't called her and she hadn't called me. I knew this was sending her a message. I just wasn't sure whether I wanted to send it or not and, regardless, I didn't know what else to do. Eventually it didn't matter anymore when my mother woke me out of a sound sleep with the phone in her hand.

"It's Iris," she said, turning to go back to her room before I could even apologize for waking her.

"I wasn't expecting to get your mother," Iris said. "Why don't you answer the phone?"

"It's not my house. Why didn't you call my cell?"

"It went straight to voice mail. Do you think your mother's angry with me?"

"I think she's probably asleep again already."

We fell silent. I sat back against the headboard.

"You haven't called," she said.

"I know."

"I've kinda gotten used to you calling."

"I know. I'm sorry, I should have called."

"That was a little weird on the beach last Wednesday, wasn't it?"

I slid down to lay my head on the pillow. "I don't know what it was last Wednesday. I guess I have been feeling a little weird about it."

"I shouldn't have told you about the pregnancy."

"Of course you should have told me about the pregnancy. We're supposed to be able to talk to each other like that, aren't we?"

"Are we?"

I thought for a minute. "Yeah, of course we are."

"But it still made you feel weird."

"I didn't say that there would never be a time when we would feel uncomfortable."

"What are you uncomfortable about?"

"I'm currently uncomfortable with feeling uncomfortable, so this might not be the best time to ask me that question."

"I don't want you to lose respect for me."

"The very last thing you ever have to be concerned about is my losing respect for you."

"Are you sure?"

"Very sure. Whatever I'm feeling has nothing to do with that. You being pregnant with Chase's kid was a bombshell. We haven't talked about anything at that level before. And going back to the day that Chase died brought up a lot of stuff. It's not a big thing."

"It's a big thing to me that you haven't called."

"I was planning on calling. You haven't called me, either."

"But I *did* just call. As your mother, currently tossing and turning because I woke her up, will attest."

"You're right; I was wrong."

The air between us was still for several seconds. "I felt a little weird, too," Iris said.

"Why?"

"I don't know. Telling you that stuff, I guess. Hearing what you had to say about that night with Chase. I was feeling pretty naked out there."

"I know."

Things fell silent again. I was glad to have her here. Glad to know that she'd reached out to me. If we were together, it wouldn't have seemed so strange that we weren't saying anything.

"What have you been doing?" she said.

"The usual stuff with the store, working on display cases down in the basement, losing to my father, reading Updike. I special ordered a couple of books about New Mexico and they came in yesterday, so I've been reading those. I'm starting to have second thoughts about Tucumcari."

"Specifically Tucumcari or about New Mexico in general?"

"No, specifically Tucumcari. Some other towns sound more interesting. That's assuming, of course, that the store ever sells and I get sprung."

"It'll sell. You'll get the chance to make your getaway soon enough."

"I should be so lucky."

There was another pause.

"Listen, Hugh, I know I'm supposed to play along with this and tell you to keep your chin up and that you'll be free soon, but I wouldn't be honest if I did that. I don't want to lose you. I feel like over the last few days that I've lost you a little and I don't like that. Your friendship has become much too important to me. New Mexico is very far away."

I wasn't sure how to feel about this. I'd been missing Iris over the past five days, missing how she energized and expanded me. Even if Chase's ghost had his arm draped permanently around her shoulders, I felt diminished being away from her. And even though I had no idea what it meant to her that my friendship had become so important, it meant a great deal to me to hear her say it.

"You're not going to lose me," I said. "I promise you that."

"That's why I had to call you."

"I'm glad you called. And I think I hear my mother snoring in her bedroom."

"Then everything works out."

"Yeah, everything."

"Are you coming up on Wednesday?"

"Of course. If you want me to."

"Didn't we just have this conversation?"

"I'll be there."

"You should get back to sleep now."

"Thanks. And thanks for waking me up."

• • •

The cases I'd been building weren't ready yet, but some of the other changes were already in place. The iPod dock I'd bought played Lucy Kaplansky's "Ten Year Night" album. The music wasn't loud, but I didn't set the player on "1," either. We'd repositioned the candy rack and I'd not only ordered more Blister-Snax, but I'd added several other renegade confections as well. The vendor seemed nervous about this at first, but then brought in samples from his car to hook me further.

We'd remerchandised the magazine rack, organizing it by interest category and putting some hotter titles in prime locations. We'd received a shipment of mildly subversive stuffed animals and put them up front, were expecting a shipment of hand-painted tiles from Mexico early next week, and handmade coffee mugs from Northern California a few days after that. I'd ordered dozens of new catalogs on the Web and had made tentative plans to go to a craft show in Norwalk a couple of weeks hence in search of writing supplies.

I'd contacted the greeting card guy who lived down the street from Iris and ordered an assortment of his home-printed work. This shipment had just arrived and Tyler and I struck a four-foot display to put them up. The order consisted of two vastly different styles of work. One was on glossy white stock with pen-and-ink drawings on the front in black and red. Lots of sharp lines and bold images. The other was on marbled paper with brushstrokes in metallic ink and calligraphic writing. Many of both sets of cards were blank inside, which was what I liked. Those that did have sentiments were crisp and clever in the former case and understated in the latter.

"These are fabulous," Tyler said, reading one before putting it on display.

"Here, listen to this," I said as I opened a card. "This one reads, 'I think you pressed my reset button.'"

"Hey, I know what he means."

"Or this: 'I'm not celebrating this birthday. I'm celebrating all of your birthdays. Thanks for being alive.'" I picked up a marbled card and read, "'I love you because of the spaces.' If I were going to buy cards with writing in them, these are the kinds I would buy."

"But you wouldn't."

"Wouldn't what?"

"Wouldn't buy cards with writing in them."

"Anything's possible."

I opened another package, peered inside the top card, and put it on the rack. The title cut from the

Lucy Kaplansky album came on, an achingly romantic song about a couple's tenth anniversary.

"I love her," Tyler said.

"Sarah?"

Tyler laughed. "Maybe her, too. But I was talking about Lucy Kaplansky."

"Yeah, she's great. And this is a great song. You love Sarah?"

"I think I might," he said, smiling. "I think there's a very real chance that I might. We have a lot of range. I mean, it hasn't been that long, but we have all of these modes and all of them seem to be in good working order."

"Could be love."

"Could be."

It was that easy for him. A woman comes into the store, they start talking, they go out, discover how much range they have, and fall in love. And while there might be complications there that Tyler wasn't telling me about (or maybe wasn't even aware of), the opportunity was available. I wondered if Tyler realized how lucky he was to be in this place. I guessed that he probably did.

Brian, the guy handling the register up front, walked over to let me know that his shift was supposed to be over fifteen minutes ago. I'd lost track of time. The ever reliable Tab was scheduled to take over. I asked him if he could hang on for her arrival and he rolled his eyes and returned to the counter.

Tyler and I finished putting up the new cards and then stood back to admire them. This little four-foot section of the store seemed transformed by them, though the cards looked a bit incongruous

juxtaposed against the others in the section. In an effort to announce their arrival, Tyler and I arranged a
few cards against easels on the front counter, moving a spinner rack of costume jewelry that had been
there since before Tyler was born. As we were doing
so, Tab arrived.

"More new stuff," she said as she walked through
the door. I turned to see her looking at the display in-
differently and a surprising spurt of anger shot
through my system.

"Is that code for, 'God, I'm so sorry that I'm late
and that I've forced Brian to stay here after his shift
is over?'"

She shrugged. "I'm not that late." She nodded and
smiled at Brian. "And Brian could probably use the
extra cash, right?"

I looked at my watch. "You were supposed to be
here forty minutes ago," I said.

"It's okay, Hugh," she said. "I'm here now." She
started to walk behind the counter and I realized that
I'd been harboring some form of grudge against her
from nearly the moment I met her.

"Go," I said. Obviously, Tab thought I was talking
to Brian, because she didn't react to this.

"Tab," I said, "go."

She had been putting her purse under the counter
and she looked up at me. "What?"

"You don't work here anymore. Go."

"You're firing me because I came in a little late?"

"I'm firing you because you think forty minutes
is a little late. To name one of several hundred
reasons."

She stood up, switching her weight to her right

leg. "I don't think you can do that. Don't you have to talk to your father or something first?"

"It's done, Tab. Leave. I'll mail you your last check."

She looked to Tyler and then to Brian. She seemed surprised and a little flustered, truly the most emotion I'd seen from her the entire time I'd known her. Then she simply took her purse from under the counter and walked out.

"That was the right thing to do, right?" I asked Tyler after she left.

"That was the right thing to do six months ago."

I told Brian he could leave and Tyler and I walked behind the counter.

"Steve and Chris, too," I said. "I'm gonna get rid of all the people who are barely conscious around here."

"Wow," Tyler said. "The Terminator."

"Yeah, the Terminator." I went toward the office to get Steve and Chris' phone numbers. "Do you have any idea how to go about hiring people?"

• • •

I was varnishing the first of the display cases that night when my mother came down to the basement. We hadn't spoken all that much lately, though she'd begun to show a certain amount of interest in the chess matches I was having with my father.

"Looks nice," she said, running a hand along a dry side of the case. "This is for the store?"

"I'm replacing the Formica display in the front. I talked to Dad about it."

"He told me. Are you enjoying doing this stuff again?" She looked over at the woodworking station.

"I am, actually. It's coming back to me."

She sat down on the rotating chair. "I remember when we bought this equipment from Ben Truesdale down the street when he got new things. He asked your father what kind of work he was planning to do with it. When your father told him that this was for you, Ben said, 'these are not toys, Rich.' I think he was seriously considering giving your father his money back and selling this equipment to someone else. Your father took great pleasure in inviting him over to look at that lamp you made for us."

She'd never told me that story before. "Ben was kind of a lump, wasn't he?" I said.

"A nice man, but definitely a lump. And it was a very beautiful lamp."

"Thanks." I turned back to my work.

"You always loved building things. Even when you were a little kid. I think your first major project was a robot – at least you said it was a robot – that you made out of Play-Doh and Popsicle sticks for your brother right after he was born. When Chase was about one, he thought that robot was the greatest thing in the world. He'd carry it all around with him. One day he was running and he dropped it and it broke into dozens of pieces. He cried for twenty minutes."

I had no memory of this at all. I wished in some ways that I could remember what the world felt like when Chase arrived. It's a funny thing that the birth of a sibling is such a huge event in someone's life, yet many of us are too young when it happens to have any recollection of the event.

"Play-Doh and Popsicle sticks. I should have considered that medium for this display. Maybe the next one." I concentrated on finishing a side panel while my mother sat there quietly watching.

"Your father says you're doing some other things to spruce up the store."

"A few things, yeah. It needed the sprucing."

"I'm sure that's true. It would be hard for us to see that after all this time."

"I know; it always is. Hopefully it'll help increase buyer interest in the store."

"That hasn't gone well at all, has it?"

"That's a kind way of putting it." I finished the first coat on the first side and moved toward the back. "Was there a reason why you came down here?"

"No reason, really. I was just curious that you'd taken to doing this again and I thought I'd come down to see what you were working on. You never let me sit here like this when you were a teenager."

I remember thinking of her visits back then as invasions. The last thing that most teenaged boys want is their mothers peering over their shoulders while they work at a hobby. "I'm easier about that kind of stuff now," I said.

"I appreciate it."

She continued to sit there while I put the first coat of varnish on the rest of the case. I would apply another coat tomorrow night and a third the night after that. When I was finished, I cleaned the brush and went back to the workbench where she was sitting to get started on another piece. When I did, she got up from the chair and kissed me on the cheek.

"I know you'll be gone again soon, Hugh," she said. "But it's good to have you here with us now."

She kissed me one more time and then went back upstairs.

CHAPTER EIGHTEEN
A Bit of Temporary Abandon

It was the first unseasonably warm afternoon of the early spring. The kind of weather made for irrational behavior. As had become a habit in recent months, since I had no classes on Fridays, I came down from Emerson for the long weekend. I'd only realized a few weeks earlier that I was doing this to spend more time with Iris and Chase. And particularly to spend more time with Iris. I was no longer kidding myself that I was fascinated with her. That bit of self-delusion had ended on the drive back to Boston after Chase told me that their weeklong breakup had ended. I'd finally admitted to myself that, during that entire week, I had been intrigued with the notion that Iris was a free agent, even as I counseled my brother on trying to get her back. Still, I was aware of the boundaries and I never intended to cross them. I could never have done that to Chase, no matter how much Iris filled my thoughts.

On this particular Friday, Chase came back from school, grabbed a beer with me while we caught up on the week, and then left the house again. He told me that Iris would be by soon and asked me to entertain her until he returned. He'd been doing this with increasing frequency and it didn't feel like an imposition. I'd even begun looking forward to it. I would get Iris something to drink and sit with her on the couch exchanging clever thoughts about school, politics, and her boyfriend until he returned. When Iris and I were together like this, I could almost imagine that she had come to see me. I even began to sense that she liked having a little time with me before Chase swept her back into his world.

On this day, though, whether it was because of the air, or my increased consciousness of my attraction to her (exacerbated by the tank top and short skirt she was wearing to celebrate the warm weather), or the fact that Chase didn't come back for a very long time, things were different between us. I found myself nervous around her, more aware of what I was saying and what I looked like. My eyes kept traveling furtively to her knees, and even when I wasn't looking at them, I envisioned the curve of her calves. And I thought I sensed, though I was sure I was imagining it, that she seemed a little more nervous around me, that she was aware that something was passing between us that hadn't been there before. I had absolutely no idea what to do with these feelings and wondered if I needed to prepare better for them in the future.

"Where did he say he was going?" Iris said after an uncertain silence.

"Chase tells you where he's going?"

"I guess that was a silly question." She looked at me thoughtfully. "The two of you are so different."

"You've noticed. Of course there is no one in the

world like the singular entity known as Chase Penders."

"You're right about that," she said amusedly. She offered me another meaningful glance, though perhaps at this point, I would have considered any glance from her to be meaningful. "You do okay, though."

"Hey, everybody needs a straight man."

She leaned slightly in my direction and her expression softened. I'd seen her look at Chase this way when she was trying to convince him to take something seriously and I always thought that I would have taken anything seriously if she looked at me that way.

"You don't really think that's all you are, do you?"

"Did I say it like it was a bad thing?" We had never talked about me in this way and I wasn't entirely sure how to handle the attention given everything else running through my mind.

"Yes, you did," she said, smiling. "And if you're just doing the modest thing, that's cool. But I sometimes think you really don't get it."

"What am I missing?"

"The caring, the sensitivity, the intelligence, the wavy brown hair. Hugh, you're a great package."

"You mean like Doritos?"

She laughed. "I mean like a really interesting guy that lots of people would want to know and some people would want to know really well."

Hearing this from Iris when I was feeling the way I was feeling was all too intoxicating. I stood up and walked around the room.

"Okay, this is getting a little more intense than I can handle," I said.

She smiled at me and leaned forward.

"Do you really not like to talk about yourself that much?"

"I'm fine with talking about myself. I just think that talking about myself – like this – with you is a little tough."

"Why?" She tilted her head and I could swear that her eyes got a slightly deeper shade of blue.

"Let's talk about something else."

"No," Iris said with a cajoling laugh. "What did you mean by that? Really."

At that moment, I realized I'd been waiting for this opportunity. I had fantasized situations where I told Iris how I felt about her. In every one of those fantasies, Chase was not a factor. Perhaps the only time in my life when that was the case. If I thought of him at all, I imagined that he had moved on from Iris, in fact condoned what I was doing.

I was all nervous energy at this point. I'm not sure I even realized right away that I had moved to sit next to her or that our knees were touching.

"Because – I can't believe I'm telling you this – I think about you a lot. More than I should, frankly. And when you say things like you're saying about me, it makes me think things that I really shouldn't be thinking."

Her smile softened and the look of amusement left her eyes. But that other look was still there.

"I know what you're thinking," she said quietly.

"I really don't think you do."

"Yeah, I do. Hugh. I think about you, too. It's weird for me because I'm so in love with Chase, but I do think about you. It's impossible for me to be around you as much as I am and not think about you." She paused for several seconds. "Can I tell you something?"

"I'm gonna have to reserve judgment on that."

"When Chase and I split up a couple of months ago – for reasons I still don't understand – I was feeling really awful. I just completely didn't understand what happened. But in the middle of it, I realized that one of the things I was feeling awful about was that I missed you. Not being with Chase meant that I wasn't going to see you anymore and that shook me up. I seriously thought about calling you, but I thought you might think I was calling for a different reason."

"I almost called you," I said, my throat a little dry.

"I wish you had. It would have meant a lot to me. I needed you."

I didn't want to wrap my mind around what she was saying. I didn't want to consider the implications. Any of them. At that moment, all I wanted to do was kiss her. I leaned toward her and she moved toward me at the same time. Our lips met tenderly and we kissed in slow motion for a long time. It was the moment in my life when I realized that it mattered who you were kissing when you kissed like this. My hand found its way to the bare knee I'd been admiring since she walked in the door and I pulled her closer. Everything was unhurried. From my perspective, I just wanted to live in this space and I didn't care what came next. But there's no chance at all that we would have stopped there if we hadn't heard Chase's car pulling up the driveway.

The sound jarred us, as though a stage hypnotist

had snapped his fingers. As we sat back on the couch, Iris looked at me with an expression that spoke of both embarrassment and regret. She didn't need to tell me that she didn't know what came over her, just as she didn't need to tell me that we couldn't allow it to happen again. To her, she had only surrendered to a bit of temporary abandon, nothing more.

I don't think that I ever felt emptier than I did at that moment.

• • •

It was cool for early July. As I got out of my car for my midtrip stop (I didn't really need a break on the drive to Lenox, but I liked that diner I'd found in Enfield and the woman who always helped me there – it had become part of the process for me), I wondered if I should have brought a sweatshirt along. Iris and I were planning to see an outdoor performance of *A Midsummer Night's Dream* that night and it would be considerably cooler in the Berkshires. As it turns out, it didn't matter.

Neither of us was pretending that we hadn't had that middle-of-the-night phone conversation. Iris held me just a little bit longer than she usually did when I kissed her hello and as we walked and drove through the afternoon, we each mentioned numerous times how much we enjoyed this weekly foray. For my part, I wanted to make sure that Iris understood that she was important to me and that, regardless of any awkwardness from our talk on the beach, I still considered her a critical part of my life. I'm assuming that she felt somewhat the same way, because she was more openly affectionate with me than she'd been in the past, touching my arm while we spoke, at one point grabbing me around the shoulders and at another gently bumping me while we walked.

She made dinner for me that night, keeping it simple because we had to be at the theater by 7:30. One of the rituals that had evolved between us was that we didn't debrief each other on the events of the week until dinner on our first night, turning our first afternoons into a running set of observations about whatever we might be doing. While we ate, I told her about firing Tab and the others and about the progress I'd made on the display cases. She talked about the beginning of rehearsals for the Ensemble's September production and about a mildly traumatic trip to the veterinarian. I'd come to appreciate these conversations because they indicated how much we had drawn ourselves into the fabric of each other's lives. She could tell me that Tab was taking up space without ever having met her and I could anticipate her dog's response to an unnecessarily aggressive vet.

Toward the end of the meal, Iris became quiet and seemed more focused on her wine.

"You know what I've been thinking a lot about lately?" she said. She smiled, eyes downcast, almost bashful. "That time when we kissed on the couch."

"You've been thinking about that?" I asked tentatively. We had never once talked about this.

"I have. I mean it's not like I haven't thought about it before. It's just that it's been on my mind a lot the last few days."

I took a sip of my wine, thinking that not responding might be the only appropriate response.

"That kiss had a lot in it, didn't it?" she said. "It was illicit. It was innocent. It was warm. It was intense."

"It was over much too soon," I said, surprising myself that I would be this candid.

She looked up at me. "It was?"

"For me it was."

"Chase came back."

"I know. I was never less happy to see him."

She began to inscribe lines in the condensation on her wineglass. "That was a strange day," she said. "Chase noticed that I was a little preoccupied, but I pretended I didn't know what he was talking about. I think that was the most dishonest thing I ever did to him."

I nodded. I wrestled with myself over telling her how much that kiss meant to me, how much it redefined kissing for me. But I wasn't sure why she'd brought this subject up and I felt like I needed to wait to find out.

"I'd imagined kissing you before then," she said.

"You had?"

She shook her head. "A few times. It would just come into my head. I really liked you, Hugh. I always did. I liked talking to you, especially on those afternoons when you would babysit me for Chase."

"I loved that time."

"You know what I thought about after that day? And I thought about it a lot. I thought about what we were going to be like over the course of our lives together after that kiss. I really believed that Chase and I were going to get married. I imagined you and me dancing at my wedding. I imagined you coming for dinner while Chase was away on business and the two of us taking the kids for ice cream. I imagined the four of us – me and Chase and you and your wife – at some lakefront resort when we were in our fifties.

"And in all of these cases, I imagined that we'd have a little thing that passed between us that acknowledged that kiss without ever saying a word. Didn't quite work out that way, huh?"

I was feeling a true loss of equilibrium. I had believed in the moments after we kissed that Iris had made every effort to erase it from her memory. And even after what we'd begun here – whatever it was that we'd begun here – I was still convinced that she would have preferred it if that kiss had never happened.

"I obsessed over it," I said.

"You did?"

"Truly obsessed over it. The first couple of weeks after, I could hardly think of anything else. It was just so confusing."

"Why?"

I paused for several seconds, looking down at my dinner plate, looking up into her eyes. "Because I was crazy about you. And the kiss brought so many things into focus. It confirmed so many things I was feeling. And none of it really mattered because you had Chase – and I had Chase – and I just had to live with that. I was actually angry with him for a few days before I came to my senses enough to realize how irrational that was."

She reached out and squeezed my hand. She left a

tiny patch of moisture from where her index finger had been playing with her glass.

"Our kiss this spring was different in a lot of ways," she said. "At first I had to ask myself if I'd done it because you were Chase's brother and I was trying to reach out to him a little. I convinced myself that wasn't it. But that left me with something that was a lot scarier."

"By stopping the way you did, you probably saved me the anguish of having to go through that myself."

"I guess I did. Though I'd be lying if I said I was doing it with you in mind."

"And I'd be lying if I said I understood it at the time. It took me a little while to catch up to you."

She tightened her lips and then took another sip of wine. I felt like I'd said the wrong thing to her, but I couldn't understand what I'd done.

"Needless to say, I've thought about that one a lot, too. Especially since we see each other every week now."

For a moment, I thought she was going to tell me that it was too hard to keep seeing me this way and I felt a wave of sadness. I knew if she said this that I would have to fight desperately to change her mind.

"We have a good thing here," I said.

She smiled at me. "It's a very good thing. A very good thing. I've kinda come to depend on it."

I think in that moment I realized that I would never be living in Tucumcari or anywhere else in New Mexico. I had no idea where I was going to wind up next, but it had to be somewhere within driving distance of Iris.

"Me too," I said.

Again, she reached out for my hand and this time she held it. After a few beats, she looked at her watch. "I'm not really in the mood for Shakespeare," she said.

Instead, we refilled our wineglasses and moved to her living room to watch her DVD copy of *The Graduate*. About twenty minutes into the movie, she leaned against the opposite side of the couch and put her feet up on my leg. I massaged them for a while and then just held them for the rest of the film.

When I went to bed that night, I tape-looped our dinner conversation. In the past few hours, I'd seen two new faces from Iris: first, the tentative one as she drew her finger along the wineglass, and then the contented one as she lay on the couch and I rubbed her feet. Both were of course beautiful, but both suggested that there was so much more of her to see than I'd seen already. I wanted to know all of her expressions. I wanted her to continue to surprise me with her observations of the past. But more than anything, I wanted her to share a future with me. That future might be nothing more than DVDs and walks through farmers' markets, but I needed it.

Since I was playing all of this in my head, I wasn't asleep when Iris came into my room a couple of hours later. She opened the door and I propped myself up on one arm.

"Is everything okay?" I said.

I sat up and she sat down next to me on the bed, reaching a hand up to touch me gently on the face. She ran her fingers slowly down my cheek and let them rest on my lips.

"I need to kiss you again," she said.

I kissed her fingers and then she pulled me toward her. She kissed me hungrily, as she had that night in Amber. Unlike that time, though, I was eminently aware of how much I wanted her, how much these kisses – and her desire to give me these kisses – meant to me. Without moving away from her, I pulled myself out from under the sheets and we were lying together, our bare legs intertwined, my hand rubbing her T-shirted back while her fingernails played over my naked shoulders. She moved both hands to cup my face and she dotted me with quick, deep kisses.

I was nearly senseless with desire, but at the same time, these kisses – their urgency and their tenderness – held me fast. The sensation of her lips mesmerized me, as did the look in her eyes in the moonlight as she pulled back from me and then kissed me again. It was the first time I'd really noticed her eyes while we were kissing and it was perhaps the proximity of our eyes together that was the most dizzying feeling of all.

Eventually, I reached under her shirt to run my fingers up her spine, to massage the small of her back and then to reach under her panties to gently squeeze her closer to me. She drew up against me, our eyelashes practically touching. I kissed her nose and cheekbones softly. I wanted to say something, but was afraid that anything I might say would be overwhelming to her. Instead, I pulled her tighter and kissed her face and the nape of her neck.

I could feel Iris' body go slack as she put her forehead down on my shoulder. Knowing immediately that she didn't want me to continue, I pulled my hand above the waistband of her panties and rested it on her hip, tilting my head to nestle hers.

"Do you think you could just hold me?" she said.

I moved my face down to meet hers. She wore yet another new expression, one that I couldn't entirely interpret at that moment.

"Anytime you want," I said.

She touched my face again and then rested her forehead against mine. Without saying another word, she pulled the sheets on top of us and we settled onto a pillow.

"Can you sleep like this?" she asked.

"It might take me a few minutes," I said, smiling, "but, yeah."

She kissed me one more time softly and then said, "Thanks." We repositioned ourselves so that her head was resting on my chest. Surprisingly, I fell asleep almost immediately.

I awoke in the morning when Iris moved off me. She was getting out of bed when she noticed me stirring. She leaned back and kissed me on the cheek.

"Did you sleep okay?" she asked.

"Extremely well, actually."

"I'm glad I didn't keep you up. I'm insanely hungry for some reason. I think I'm going to make waffles. Sound okay to you?"

"Waffles would be great," I said.

She smiled and turned to get off the bed before turning back to me. "Last night meant a lot to me," she said. "All of it. Is it okay if we give this some time?"

"Of course it is," I said.

She reached over and squeezed my hand before leaving the room. In that simple gesture, I understood that this wasn't going to be like the last two times.

And yes, we both needed to wait a bit to understand where we were going to go from here.

CHAPTER NINETEEN
This Isn't a Job Interview

When Howard Crest called to tell me that he had a
potential buyer coming in to see the store, he provided all the inspiration I needed to finish the display
cases and to install and merchandise them. It required staying up most of the night, but it was likely
I was going to be doing that anyway. I'd grown somewhat accustomed to having something to think about
after seeing Iris and I certainly had an entire sleepless
night's worth of thinking in store after our last visit.
That I could make productive use of the time was a
side benefit. That all of the thinking wasn't going to
provide me with any kind of resolution was a given.
I felt simultaneously more and less in control of my
fate with Iris. More, because she seemed to be inviting me into the process. Less, because her doing so
gave Chase a more prominent place in the room in
my mind.

The cases, on the other hand, looked great. Simply
removing the white Formica and replacing it with
oak would have been dramatic enough. But I was
genuinely pleased with the work I'd done. After a
few false starts, this long-abandoned skill had come
back to me readily. And while I hadn't been doing

anything like this, I'd been doing enough with my hands over the past decade that the extra ten years of experience seemed to make me smarter and more efficient in the workshop. Jenna, one of the three new people I'd hired, helped me stock the shelves. We started with the new merchandise I'd ordered, which had been sitting in the back room awaiting the cases. But even some of the dusty old items my father had been selling (or not selling) for years looked better in this new setting.

"Big improvement," Jenna said when we stepped back to look at what we'd done. Since she had only started a few days before, she was speaking specifically about the displays. But I wanted to believe that she was talking about the entire minor renovation I'd given the store. Face Melters on the candy shelves. Financial and Men's Health sections in the magazine rack. A four-foot section of Dave Kringer cards. HuggaGhouls. Mexican tiles. Handmade coffee mugs. Jon McLaughlin on the iPod. Improvement indeed, at least in my eyes, though I wasn't sure what my father would think of it.

The previous week had been the largest nonholiday week in the store's history. I'd actually needed to call in backup staff on Saturday. I wanted to believe that the work I'd done had contributed to that, though it could very well have been because of the great tourist summer Amber was having. Regardless, as I looked around, I was pleased.

Howard came in with his client about an hour later. Pat Maple owned several stationery stores in Westchester County. He seemed to be a couple of years younger than my father, but he was decidedly more entrepreneurial. Within the first ten minutes of our meeting, he'd explained to me why he'd chosen each of his six locations and who his target customers were.

"I've got great spots," he said. "Scarsdale, Larchmont, Rye. People with lots of money who don't mind spending four bucks for a three-subject spiral bound. We don't have as much – " he glanced around him " – different stuff as you have here. I tend to think you stick to the basics: school supplies, cards, candy, newspapers. But I guess this is a different kind of neighborhood, huh?"

"People seem to like the other stuff around here," I said.

"Yeah, well from what Howard's told me, your old man has done okay with this place, so I guess he knew what he was doing. Sorry to hear about his heart attack, by the way."

"Thanks."

We walked around the store and Pat asked me a number of intelligent questions. I'd prepared so many details about the store over the past few months in expectation of a debriefing that hadn't come. It was refreshing to talk to someone who wanted this information, even if I got the impression that he was sneering at the carving on my display cases.

"We're not exactly around the corner from Scarsdale up here," I said. "What made you come to Amber?"

"The daughter. She's twenty-four and she's been out of school for a few years and still doesn't know what she wants to do with her life. She likes it around here. I figure I can install her in this area if I find a store I like. I guess she'll want to come look at this herself. She'll probably like all the things you have in here. She's like that. Tell me about the water problem."

"It's not a problem. Some pipes gave way long before they were supposed to. We did extensive work on it. Extensive. I have all the documentation."

"I'm sure you do. You been running this place for your old man long?"

"Just a few months."

"You seem to know your way around."

"Grew up with it."

"Ah," he said, laughing. "It's in the blood. I wish my daughter was more like that. What're you gonna do after the place sells."

"I really haven't decided yet."

"Well if you wanna come down to Westchester, I might have a store for you to run." He laughed again, though it wasn't clear what he was laughing at. "But this isn't a job interview. Let's go look at the books."

We spent another forty-five minutes together. There was little question that Pat Maple knew his business and when he saw that some of the toy and gift merchandise sold especially well, I could almost see him recalibrating. Maybe the Mexican tiles would survive after all.

As we walked out of the office, he said, "Can Patrice come to take a look tomorrow?"

"Yeah, of course."

He nodded and pulled out a cell phone to call his daughter. Howard Crest smiled at me and I tilted my head in his direction. While it certainly seemed that Pat liked the store and that this was the kind of playpen he'd been looking for, I wasn't about to get overly excited until we had an offer on the table.

That afternoon, Tyler walked into the store carrying a bag of truffles from the chocolate shop.

"You have to stop coming in here on your off days," I said when I saw him.

"Just a quick stop, I promise. You said you were going to put the displays in today and I wanted to come by to take a look at them and to give you these." He handed me the truffles. "Congratulations."

"Thanks," I said, touched by the gesture. "The cases look pretty good, huh?"

"They look terrific. You're good at this. Maybe the next profession?"

"I'll add it to the list. Hey, a guy came in to look at the store today. He seemed kind of interested."

"Great. Time to go west, young man."

"Well, I'm not so sure about that anymore, but that's a story for another day."

"Sounds like we'll be having an extra drink tomorrow night." He looked around the store and I could see a mix of emotions on his face. Pride. Satisfaction. Maybe a hint of nostalgia, though I might have been imagining that one. Then he flipped his eyes back to me and pointed to the bag. "Those are champagne truffles."

I opened the bag and tilted it in his direction. "Want one?"

"Actually, the truffle part is for you. The champagne part is for me."

"Meaning?"

"I got a job in the City."

I pulled the bag back and threw an arm around his

shoulders. "That's great. That place you really wanted?"

"They were still trying to make a decision as of this morning. And then out of nowhere I got a call from one of the guys I saw that first trip after graduation. The guy at that independent marketing firm? Something opened up and he'd been holding my resume on his desk since I went in to talk to him. I'm starting in three weeks."

"That's fantastic. I'm really happy for you." I paused and threw him a semifacetious look of disappointment. "Even though you're abandoning me."

Tyler laughed, though his eyes traveled down to the floor as he did so. "I'm not abandoning you. That guy who came in today is going to make a great offer and soon both of us will be on to new conquests."

I put my arm around him again and walked him toward the back of the store. "Yeah, you're still abandoning me, but I'll pretend that what you just said makes me feel better. Let's go eat some chocolate and you can tell me all about it and then I can tell you how you're going to hire your own replacement."

I closed the door to the back office and we talked for nearly a half hour while Jenna guarded the store up front. I was very happy for Tyler and I had certainly known that this moment was in the offing, but I couldn't help feeling a little saddened by the fact that he was leaving. It wasn't about losing him as an employee. The store didn't need anyone nearly as competent as he was in order to run effectively. It was about losing his presence, especially on closing nights. For as long as I stayed in Amber after he left, it was going to be emptier without him.

While we talked, Howard called. Even before having his daughter come to see the store, Pat Maple was making an offer. It was a lowball and not one that Howard was asking me to take to my father, but he was certain that Maple was serious. We discussed strategy for a short while – it was the first time I'd been impressed with the way Howard's mind worked – and then he hung up to call Maple back.

When I got off the phone, I told Tyler what was happening.

"Looks like you'd better start packing, Hugh," he said.

That certainly seemed to be the case. The clock was ticking down on my days in this town. That meant that all notions about where to go next would need to stop being fanciful ones.

It was daunting and it was stimulating.

CHAPTER TWENTY
Planning Ahead

The distance from which I saw Iris' expression after our very first kiss ten years ago was no more than twelve inches. It might as well have been twenty miles. Throughout the spring, though, that distance continued to expand. I had never been entirely sure whether this was a product of my imagination or if Iris was in fact as reluctant to face me as I now was to face her. I felt a combination of guilt, validation, and frustration over the events of that afternoon. Much as I tried to convince myself that I hadn't betrayed Chase in any way, this was by far the most significant thing I'd ever done to him behind his back. Before this, the most selfish act I'd performed to his detriment was giving myself the largest slice of pizza in the box. But at the same time, I took some consolation from the fact that Iris had at least felt enough of the things about me that I was feeling about her to allow the kiss to happen. This spoke to me on a number of levels: I hadn't imposed myself upon her, she'd told me that I meant something to her, and kissing her had been even more thrilling than I'd expected it to be. But this was more disconcerting than the fantasies that preceded it. Kissing Iris was so over-whelmingly powerful, so soul satisfying, that it would forever change the meaning of the act or the interaction that led to the act. Kissing Iris felt the way it did because it was Iris. And yet Iris was inextricably linked with the only person in the world who meant more to me than she did. As a result, I was compelled to come down less often on weekends and to spend less time with the two of them when I was in Amber. Everything was easier that way.

At the wedding of my mother's goddaughter, however, I had little choice but to be with them for an entire evening. I actually considered begging off with the excuse of a term paper (I'd used the one about my "independent studies" too often already), but Lisa's family and ours had been close since before I was born and at the time it seemed ridiculous to change all of my plans because of my brother and his girlfriend. So the three of us drove together in my car and I made as little eye contact with Iris as possible without being obvious.

That doesn't mean that I didn't look at her. I found myself taking every opportunity to glance over at her in the reception hall while I was engaged in other conversation. Iris was wearing a strapless navy dress that ended just below the knee and she looked spectacular. Though she didn't know many people at the wedding, she carried herself gracefully through conversations with relative strangers on the occasions when Chase was playing with someone else. Admiring her, I found it impossible not to think about how we had been together or the conversation that had led up to it. Just as it was impossible for me to fool myself into thinking that what I was feeling for her wasn't real desire.

If Chase noticed any of this, he didn't acknowledge it. On the drive over, he asked why I wasn't coming down from Boston as much. But he never suggested that he saw any change in the way I acted around Iris. And yet I couldn't help wondering how I was going to approach this as time went on. Making my feelings go away didn't seem to be a viable option. Bringing the issue out into the open seemed counterproductive. And competing with Chase for Iris' affections seemed disloyal and plainly absurd.

Halfway through the evening, Chase and I found ourselves thrown together in the middle of the dance floor during one of those group dances that were obligatory at weddings. As a precursor to my "madman in the water" episode later in the summer, I took this opportunity to act out of character and behave even more outrageously than my brother, dancing comically, suggestively, and utterly out of control. At one point Chase, never one to surrender the stage to another easily, stepped back and folded his arms in front of him to watch my exploits. I'm sure most of the people in the room thought I was drunk, which was fine with me, though I in fact found myself uninterested in drinking at all. Eventually, Chase rejoined me and as the song ended, we threw each other on the floor, rolling around and laughing.

Afterward, I went to the bar to get another Coke, dabbing perspiration from my face. Iris was there. It would have been impossible (not to mention ridiculous) to avoid her, though it was the first time we'd been together without Chase since "the moment."

"You should have come out on the dance floor with us," I said, quickly breaking eye contact to get the bartender's attention.

"I didn't want to get injured."

I took my drink and turned back to her. "I guess we looked pretty stupid, huh?"

"You were funny." It seemed for a moment that she was going to reach up to move some hair from my forehead, but then she put her hand back at her side. "Chase loves playing with you."

I nodded. "It'll probably look pathetic when we're in our sixties, but I suppose we can get away with it now."

"I'll still think it's funny when you're in your sixties."

"Then it'll be worth it," I said, immediately regretting having done so. This kind of comment would have seemed entirely innocent a few months before, but now it seemed charged with innuendo. Iris brought her drink to her mouth to cover whatever reaction I might have seen and then looked off behind me. A moment later, Chase came up to us, punched me on the shoulder, and threw an arm around Iris, kissing her on the neck. I excused myself and went off to find someone else I knew.

A short while later, I was talking to Lisa's sister Mia near the edge of the dance floor when the band began to play "The Way You Look Tonight." Chase and Iris were slowly spinning in time with the music and she was laughing and saying something to him that I couldn't hear. He pulled her close and they moved together, Iris' head on Chase's shoulder, his eyes closed as he rested his face against her hair. Iris

pulled back from him for a moment and Chase regarded her with a look of contentment I'd never seen
on his face before. Then they folded together again,
barely moving as couples danced nearby.

I tried to continue my conversation with Mia, but
this vision of the two of them transfixed me. While
I'd been obsessing over one moment of abandon with
Iris, they were becoming more and more completely
enmeshed. Never before had it seemed so obvious to
me how absolutely in love they were. I knew then
that it was time to stop playing with my illusions.

I'd been unconsciously turning my body away
from Mia and toward the dance floor as I watched.

"Do you want to go out there?" Mia asked.

It took a beat for her question to register. "Nah," I
said. "Not my kind of thing."

• • •

For the first time since I'd known Iris, I was feeling nervous as I approached her house. I was certain
that it had to do with the charged atmosphere the last
time we saw each other and the easy intimacy of the
phone conversations we'd had since. I'd left for
Lenox that morning with a huge sense of anticipation and I was sure this was what led to the bubbling
in my stomach as I turned up her street. If I believed
in intuition, I would have interpreted the sensation
differently.

I'd learned via one of the dozens of e-mail newslet-
ters I received that Richard Shindell was playing in
a club in Stockbridge a couple of weeks hence. Shindell's sometimes bleak, always passionate songs had

been favorites of mine for the past several years and he was one of the first artists I'd introduced Iris to when we reconnected. I'd only seen him in concert once and knew the experience would be a richer one with another fan by my side. I bought tickets for the show online and planned to surprise Iris with this news when I saw her.

Iris offered me a quick kiss on the lips when she opened the door and then hugged me tightly. When she pulled back, she smiled up at me and then turned to let me into the house.

"Good trip?" she asked.

"Yeah, very good."

"Doughnut or muffin?" She was referring to the pastry that accompanied my mid-drive coffee break.

"Neither actually. I think it's finally gotten through to me that the combination of caffeine and sugar isn't necessary for the last hour of the drive. I also think I've put on a few pounds."

"I'd noticed," she said teasingly. "I'm glad you brought it up before I had to."

She walked over to the couch and sat against one side with her arms wrapped around her legs. I sat on the other end and faced her. We smiled at each other.

"Stop," she said, laughing.

"Stop what?"

"Let's just . . . ." She made a flitting motion with her right hand.

"Let's just be natural?"

"Yes."

"You and I might interpret the term 'natural' differently."

"Let's just be us."

"Whatever that means."

"You know what I mean. We don't need to be weird." She chuckled, offering a glimpse of her girlish side and then turned to me with the most stunning grin I'd ever seen on a human being. "What are we going to do today?"

"I'm not sure what we're going to do today, but I can tell you what we're going to do on August second."

"What? Planning ahead? From you?"

"Only in this case. Richard Shindell is playing in Stockbridge and I got us tickets."

"Really?" she said, reaching over and squeezing my leg. "That's so great. The second, you said? Let me go write that down."

She stood up to go into the kitchen where a calendar hung from the refrigerator. While she did, I put Shindell's newest album on her iPod, thinking it would be nice to sit together on the couch and listen to it before we headed off for the day.

Iris was in the kitchen for considerably longer than it would take to mark the date. When she came back, she offered me a compressed smile and then sat next to me on the couch. The smile didn't say, "Let's get cozy." It seemed to say, "Let's not talk for a while," though I had no idea why. I put my arm around her shoulders, she leaned into me a little, and we sat that way through the entire album. Shindell's complex, brooding melodies seemed appropriate for the situation, though I couldn't have possibly said what the situation was or how the air in the room had so completely altered in such a short time while seemingly nothing happened. A few minutes in, I asked Iris if she was all right and she nodded. She'd gone from buoyant to contemplative in the time it took to walk back and forth from the kitchen and she clearly wasn't ready to discuss it. I wondered if this wasn't in some way her response to what the last week had been like for us and to the presumptiveness of my planning ahead.

When the music finished, we sat on the couch for several minutes more. Then Iris patted me on the leg and said, "Let's go for a drive."

We headed up Route 7, past Pittsfield, the iPod going the entire time (Green Day's "21st Century Breakdown" album, Iris' choice). Eventually, we stopped at a deli for sandwiches and ate them sitting on the grass at a nearby park. The connection between us had recalibrated again, back to what it was like just after Memorial Day. We were talking easily about surface-level things. I'd expected that this day might have some awkward moments. I'd even braced myself for the possibility that Iris was going to tell me that she didn't want our relationship to go deeper. I was completely unprepared for what came next, though.

As we finished lunch, Iris lapsed into silence again, her eyes focused on the distance. I put my hand on her shoulder and she leaned her head into it for a moment before looking back out.

Without turning to me, she said, "I had to flip the calendar to August. The first thing I saw was the tenth."

The tenth was the anniversary of Chase's accident.

"It's not like I didn't know it was coming. But having it announce itself to me like that when I turned the page was a real shot to the stomach. Especially since I'd gone in there all excited about the concert."

She looked at me with an expression that mixed sadness and something more unsettling. It seemed like defeat.

"I always have a hard time with that date, Hugh. An extremely hard time. It can sometimes take me days to get past it. You won't want to be anywhere near me."

"I'll be near you," I said. "We'll do it together. We *should* do it together."

She looked back out toward the horizon and leaned her head away from me.

"I don't know that I'm ever going to be able to look at you without seeing him, Hugh."

For months now, I'd believed that to be true. In many ways, it was true for me as well. But it didn't matter – it wasn't real – until Iris said it herself. And in doing so, she'd defined our future. We could continue with the fits and starts. But we would never get past this absolute. Every relationship comes to its insurmountable place. Ours happened to be the foothills, in fact the very ground itself.

I took her hand and stood up. "Come on, let's head back."

"We don't have to. It's a nice day out. Maybe we could go for a walk.

"No, I think we both really want to get back to Lenox."

I didn't stay that night. In fact, I didn't stay for more than forty-five minutes after we returned to her house. I told Iris that I thought it might be a good idea for me to leave and she only made the slightest attempt to disagree. She was sitting on the couch when I kissed her forehead and said good-bye.

Ten years ago, I'd considered it a cruel act of destiny that the first woman to ever inspire me was committed to the person I loved more than anyone in the world. But this was exponentially harder to deal with. I knew more now. I'd been through more now. And I knew Iris better and she captivated me even more. For the first time in my life, I truly wanted someone and I was ready to make a life with her. I was willing to climb whatever mountains I needed to climb, including the several considerable ones I'd already scaled.

But I wasn't willing to cause Iris pain. And what had become heartbreakingly clear to me that afternoon was that loving me was simply going to be too hard for her. If she were ever going to have a romance that stood the test of time, it was going to have to be with a person who could finally walk her beyond the events of August tenth ten years ago.

In other words, it could never be me.

• • •

I wasn't supposed to be at the store the next day, but since I'd come back from Lenox earlier than I'd planned, I went in anyway. Ironically, I'd even made contingency plans in case I wound up staying an extra night with Iris if things moved forward as they seemed they might.

When I walked in the door, Tyler looked at me quizzically and I simply said, "You don't want to know." He didn't push it, the store was busy, and we

didn't get back to it. But still, I found Tyler's presence comforting. He wouldn't be around much
longer and I wasn't anxious to see him go. And even
though I couldn't confide in him on this day, the very
fact that he was around seemed to help.

When I returned to my parents' house that night, my
mother was in the kitchen and my father was on his
usual perch. I called in to him and he waved back. I
went to sit with my mother while she prepared dinner.

My mother was an earnest cook. Her meals neither
offended nor dazzled the palate, but they were rich
with intentions. She'd always seemed to enjoy cooking for us and I think she found a considerable
amount of satisfaction in our responses. Chase had
of course been the most vocal respondent, regularly
suggesting she put a dish in "heavy rotation" or, occasionally, "drop it off the playlist." I'm not sure how
she was finding the inspiration to put in the effort
these days. I only ate with them three times a week
and my father's most enthusiastic reaction to any
meal might be, "Good, Anna," while he focused on
the television. Still, she refused to descend to a level
of preparation that would have been more appropriate to my father's ennui. Tonight, she was putting together a salad with arugula, red leaf lettuce, walnuts,
mangoes, and grilled chicken.

I kissed her on the cheek and reached around her
for a piece of mango. She slapped me on the wrist
playfully.

"I assumed you'd be home for dinner," she said,
"though you didn't tell me you would. A less thoughtful mother would have you eating peanut butter and
jelly tonight."

"And don't think I don't appreciate it, Mom."

"Why are you here, anyway?"

"Things came up with Iris."

While still chopping, she looked up at me briefly, looking back down at the mango when I didn't say anything more.

"How are things at the store?"

"Really busy again today."

"Anything new from that guy from Westchester?"

"He's asked for a bunch more information. I guess now that we didn't agree to just give the store away to him, he wants to make an informed bid. His daughter seemed to like the place, though."

"I suppose that's progress. And it's very good news that the store continues to be busy."

"Certainly makes the hours go faster."

She looked up again to offer a faint smile and then began putting together a vinaigrette for the salad. As she was doing this, my father appeared in the doorway. As always, he was wearing his robe, but he'd cinched the sash snugly around his waist.

"Richard," my mother said when she saw him.

"I thought we'd have dinner in the dining room tonight."

"That would be good," my mother said, whisking her dressing briskly. "We'll be ready in a few minutes. Hugh, would you set the table?"

There was an unusual level of conversation at dinner that night. My father talked about the day's news events. My mother talked about things going on in and around town, information she'd gleaned from her hours out. I told them about the customer who'd bought two Mexican tiles and one of the handmade mugs I'd purchased. My father even suggested an outing for him and my mother the next afternoon and my mother graciously agreed without asking where this was coming from.

It had been nearly a year since we'd last shared a meal together like this. Back then, it was hard to imagine that I'd ever consider something as casual as this to be momentous. But at the same time, I was only partially aware of what was going on. I couldn't help but think that I wasn't supposed to be here tonight or that the reason I was here to witness this watershed event was because of another that had happened the night before.

I certainly didn't intend to talk to my parents about this. But then there was a lull in the conversation and I found it unnecessary to retreat into my own thoughts.

"Listen," I said, "you know that I've been spending a lot of time with Iris lately, right?"

My mother nodded. My father looked at me as though it was the first time he'd heard Iris' name in a decade.

"We've become really good friends. You know, we were friendly when she was with Chase and all, but in the last couple of months, we've been doing a lot of things together and having a good time."

"Is something happening there?" My mother asked me this the way she might ask how a critically ill person was doing.

"Something happened. For me at least. For her, too, I think. I fell in love with her. Even with all of the reasons why I knew I shouldn't, even with all of the weird stuff going through my head about it, I did. I just find her incredible."

"But something went wrong," my father said.

"Something went wrong. She just can't do it. As I said, I'm fairly sure that she feels a lot of the same things that I'm feeling, but it isn't enough for her. She can't overcome the fact that I remind her of Chase, and she can't be with me what she was with him. And on top of everything else, I'm wondering how I can possibly get past this when she can't. Does it mean that Chase meant less to me? That I wasn't as destroyed by his death as she was?"

My father took a deep breath and looked at my mother. Then the two of them turned to me.

"Chase died ten years ago, Hugh," my father said. "We all lost him and none of us will ever fully recover from losing him. But it was ten years ago. We've been waiting a long time to hear you feel about anything the way you feel about Iris."

I looked down at my plate. "Not that it matters, as it turns out."

"Of course it matters," my mother said sharply. "Don't be stupid. It might not get you Iris and it might not even be right for the two of you to be together anyway, but it definitely matters. You have to get on with your life sometime, Hugh. God knows, we know what we're talking about."

I looked over at my father. He let out a small chuckle.

"Yes, I heard that, too," he said. "Your mother knows what she's saying. Usually does. I hope it works out with you and Iris. You don't like doing anything the easy way, do you? I always liked her. She might just need to come around to this in stages. And none of us are as clear about this kind of thing at this time of year as we are at others. I hate August."

My father looked out the window, and for a moment, I thought he was going to stare out there indefinitely again. But then he inched forward and set his elbows on the table. "And if it doesn't work out with her, think about what's happening right now. Think about how you're feeling. Don't think about this as a defeat or as an excuse to go backward."

I looked down at my plate again. Nearly all of the food was gone and I didn't remember eating any of it. I took a last bite of chicken before looking up at them again. I wasn't sure how to tell them that I would try to keep what they said in mind, so I simply made eye contact with each of them. This seemed to be enough.

"Do we have dessert?" my father asked.

The next afternoon I got a call from Iris begging off from our plans for the next Wednesday. She said something about the Ensemble, but the only real question was who was going to make that call first. Still, I found the conversation deflating and was ready to end it moments after it began. But at least a bit of what my father said had gotten through to me.

"Maybe the Wednesday after next?" Iris said. I was certain she was doing it to make the separation easier.

"Let's not set up anything formal," I said. "I'm here. If you want to talk, just call me. If you want me to come up, I'm there. And it's okay if none of it happens."

   She didn't say anything and I wasn't sure if she was upset, confused, or relieved. I said good-bye to her and hung up the phone.

CHAPTER TWENTY-ONE
A Certain Balletic Grace

There were thousands of tourists in town and it seemed that at least half of them were coming into the store. Late July/early August was always the peak of the summer for us, and the great weather (and, I wanted to believe, the improvements to the store) meant that we were busy all the time.

During this particular rush, the temporary "A" team was in place. Tyler, two shifts from the end of his tour of duty, manned the cash register. Jenna, who'd become his ostensible replacement, bagged and wrapped. I prepped the next customer in the line. Jeff, a new stock clerk, worked in the back, putting up a display of marbled paper.

I'd often complained about the limited space for the staff behind the counter, but we were making the most of it now. Jenna and I would twirl around each other to perform various functions, gesturing with our heads to announce movement in a certain direction and never once getting in each other's way. Meanwhile, Tyler was all arm motion, pulling the goods from the counter, ringing up the sale, receiving money, giving change. Perhaps Bruce Hornsby's piano arpeggios on the iPod suggested this to me, but we seemed to have a certain balletic grace to the way we approached this challenge. It was unlikely, though, that we'd be performing at Jacob's Pillow any time soon.

"Tell me the truth," I said to Tyler, "you're going to miss this."

"I already told you I was going to miss this."

"But you're really going to miss this. That marketing firm is going to seem sedate by comparison. Lots of sitting around drinking coffee and talking about where you can get the best sushi in the neighborhood."

"Twenty minutes from now, you'll send Jeff to Bean There, Done That and we'll stand around talking about baked goods."

"You're missing the point."

"I got the point. Go help a customer."

There were still a dozen people in line when a man cut in front. "Can someone help me with the kaleidoscopes?"

"I've got it," Jeff said, coming from out of our line of sight to take the customer over to the display.

Tyler looked at me and offered an arched eyebrow.

"Who needs you?" I said.

When things slowed down in the store, I went on the coffee run myself, feeling like it was wrong to assign the task to Jeff after he'd shown himself to have greater value. The line at Bean There was huge, which I found a slight bit humbling.

Walking back to the store afterward, I stopped for a moment to look down the street. This really wasn't the Amber of my mind anymore. Many of the merchants had changed hands over the past few years and their replacements were for the most part more sophisticated and knowledgeable about their products. The guy selling silver jewelry designed much of it himself. The new boutique had hand-painted scarves created by an artist in South Salem, NY, and handmade leather purses from a woman in Portsmouth, NH. The deli had a menu of original sandwiches that had become customer favorites, along with a chalkboard listing "this week's creations." Even the visitors seemed different to me. Fewer BMW'd couples getting their annual fix of "quaint" and more families who actually touched each other and pointed ahead to the next shop they wanted to see. I could appreciate why people would want to visit this town, and I realized that when I returned for a visit to Amber from wherever my next destination might be, there were shops on Russet Avenue that I'd want to drop in on.

I got back to the store and Jenna was handling the cash register while Tyler helped someone choose a mug. When he was finished, we drank our coffee and the conversation almost surrealistically drifted to a comparison between Bean There's cinnamon rolls and the ones sold at the bakery across the street.

A short while later, I received a call from Howard Crest telling me that Pat Maple had made an "excellent" new offer.

"It's still not what my father is asking," I said to him.

"That's true, but it's very respectable. He's obviously serious."

"But it's not what we're asking. My father based those numbers on real multiples. We didn't just pull them out of the air. I'm sure Maple's calculator works the same way ours does."

"You're right, Hugh, but I think we're very close and I want to be able to tell Maple that we're getting there."

"We're getting there, Howard. But I'm not even going to talk to my father about this until Maple comes up another twenty-five percent."

Howard was quiet for a moment. "That's going to be tough. He's not going to want to bid against himself like that. And we don't have anyone else who's even close to being interested."

"Well maybe we need to find someone. Have you been in the store lately? Did you look at the numbers for last week's sales that I sent over?"

"I looked at them. They're very impressive. Everyone on the street is having a great summer. But we've been through what the market is like for a store like this."

"I'm serious, Howard. I'm not going to take a bid to my father until it comes up by twenty-five percent."

"That could kill the deal, Hugh."

I closed my eyes and forced myself to relax. "It isn't going to kill the deal."

• • •

The next night was Tyler's last in the store. As though the community wanted to give us some time to ourselves, there was virtually no business during the last hour. We stood behind the counter sampling the new candy and reading to each other from *New York Magazine*.

Tyler and I had planned to go out for a drink as we always did on closing nights, but I couldn't leave it at that. Once I locked the front door, while Tyler counted the register, I opened the back door to let the rest of the staff in – including my father and mother, who were making their first trip to the store since his heart attacks. When Tyler came back to the office, the surprise stunned him. But when he saw my father, his eyes rimmed with tears and they held each other for nearly a minute.

"I was going to come by before I headed off," Tyler said to him.

"You can still come by. But I wasn't going to miss this."

We drank champagne and ate flourless chocolate cake and strawberries while Tyler detailed his plans for taking on Manhattan. He outlined what he hoped to accomplish in his first eighteen months at work, the sights he planned to see with Sarah, and the various clubs and concert halls he intended to visit. It was an ambitious agenda, and from anyone else I would have simply rolled my eyes. But I'd come to expect that Tyler was capable of accomplishing what he set out to do. It was unlikely that these tasks would be any more daunting to him than any previous ones.

About a half hour after everyone got there, my father told me that he wanted to "see what you've done with the place." We left Tyler to entertain the rest of the staff and walked out of the office. My father

stopped almost as soon as we set foot on the new carpet, examining the repair work.

"They did a good job back here," he said.

"Eventually, yes."

"You used Cullins, right?"

"That was who you had listed in your book."

"His people always do a good job."

"I'm glad you like it. The repairmen almost earned
residency status while they were doing it."

We moved from station to station so I could show
him the new merchandise, the display cases, the ad-
justed racks. The iPod wasn't on and I decided not to
bring up the subject. He wrinkled his nose at the
HuggaGhouls, but ran his fingers over the leather di-
aries.

He stood by the front door and looked out at the entire store. His eyes landed on the display of cards at
the front counter and he picked one up to examine it.

"Remade this place in your own image," he said.

"Not really. Just a few touches. Helped pass the
time."

He put the card down and appraised me. "I should
have done some of this stuff years ago."

"You put a lot of thought into this store."

"The goal is to keep thinking. I'm not surprised
that business has picked up."

I realized at that point that I'd been expecting him
to like the changes. I hadn't made any of them with
the notion that I might offend his sensibilities (except, perhaps, with the music) or that I was altering
the spirit of the store. I was simply expanding on his
original vision. Still, I was pleased that it pleased him.
I was pleased that he didn't feel I'd corrupted the

place. I was pleased that he was even standing here.

"Come on," he said, patting me on the shoulder, "let's get back to the party."

People were making plans to go out together when we returned. The three people I'd recently hired, who obviously had much less of a connection to Tyler, left for a bar a few minutes later. The others stuck around a little longer and then left in groups. I was surprised when Carl, the quiet stock boy who I'd barely spoken with in the past few months, hugged Tyler and made him promise to stay in touch. He then shook my father's hand and told him how much he'd missed him and how glad he was that he was beginning to feel better. These were literally more words than I'd heard him say the entire time I'd known him.

A short while later, my father patted my mother on the leg and said, "What do you think, Anna, a quick drink at the Cornwall before we head home?"

"You aren't supposed to drink," she said lightly.

"But that doesn't mean I can't get you drunk," he said with a grin I'd never seen on his face before. They stood up and Tyler came over and squeezed both of them, saying that he'd stop by in the morning before he left.

When they were gone, I poured the rest of the champagne for us.

"He liked it?" Tyler said, motioning toward the front of the store.

"I think so."

"That's gotta make you feel good."

"Yeah, it does." I clinked glasses with him and took a drink.

"I'm glad he appreciates it. You have really made some serious improvements."

"Thanks."

"Ever think you should change your mind about selling?"

I looked out toward the store and then back down at my glass. "No, not really. It's still this place, you know?"

Tyler nodded. "Yeah, I think I get it." He took another drink and we sat quietly for a little while. "My last night here," he said. "I sorta figured it would get to me, but I'm having a little trouble with the idea of actually leaving."

"You've been here a long time. You've invested yourself. That's so impressive to me. But keep in mind that this was a way station for you. Monday you head off on the real journey."

"I guess." He smiled. "Hope I don't lose my luggage." He looked around the room again. It was hard to believe that he was getting nostalgic about this back office, but it certainly seemed that way.

"You think that guy is going to come up with the offer you're looking for?" he said.

"Howard is skittish, which is like saying Howard *is*, but I have a feeling he will."

"And then?"

"Then?"

"Where do you go for *your* real journey?"

I shrugged. "Someplace."

"You thinking about New Mexico again?"

"New Mexico. New Guinea. Someplace new."

"You really think it's over with you and Iris?"

"Over as in we'll never see each other again? No.

I think it'll be weird for a little while and then once things are finished over here, we'll have some version of a friendship long-distance."

"You can send her a card every now and then."

"I'll have to remember to stock up before I leave."

Tyler finished his champagne, reached for the bottle, saw it was empty, and sat back.

"It really isn't 'better to have loved and lost,' huh?" he said.

"Sure doesn't seem that way."

A few more minutes passed silently. This was processing time, something we'd used effectively on drink nights in the past. I wondered if there would be any more of these in our future and I realized how unfortunate it would be if this were truly the last.

Tyler stood up and looked around one more time, sticking his head out into the store, though the lights were now off. "I should probably get going. Sarah's brother is coming with his truck at eight tomorrow."

I got up with him and we left through the back door. I threw my arm around his shoulders and walked him to his car.

"I'm gonna miss you, you know?"

"Hey, I've got a few feet of floor space in a studio closet over on Eleventh Avenue whenever you need it."

"I'll take you up on that."

"I'm counting on it."

When we got to his car, I looked back at the store and then reached out to shake his hand. "Thanks a lot," I said. "You made this a lot easier."

"You made it easier yourself," he said, hugging me before he opened his door. He got in and rolled down his window, reaching out his hand one more time. "I'll give you a call next week and let you know how my master plan is going. Call me before then if anything happens with the store."

I nodded and he drove off.

I got in my car and thought for a moment about seeing if my parents were still at the Cornwall. I started the engine and decided to head back to the house instead.

CHAPTER TWENTY-TWO

That's Really All That's Important, Isn't It?

A few days later, I turned the store's date book to August. Since the book showed only a week per spread, I wasn't recreating the act that brought my relationship with Iris to a head, but of course that was the first thing that came to mind. Soon, Chase would have been dead for exactly a decade. I'd long ago stopped expecting to hear his voice when I walked into the house, but I knew I would never stop hearing his voice in my mind. There was something very arbitrary about noting a landmark anniversary. It was, of course, just another day along the line. Still, I knew that the next few weeks were likely to bring a wide range of emotional storms from which I had only a modicum of protection.

I hadn't heard from Iris since before Tyler's party. I had no idea what the rhythm of our friendship would be going forward, but I had a strong conviction that I needed to let her make that determination. I didn't want to force myself upon her by calling. The only way I could show her that I meant what I said the last time we spoke was by allowing her to make the first gesture toward whatever future we would have.

At the same time, I wondered how she would handle the melancholy that would surely come in the next few days. She had handled the other anniversaries without me, though by her own admission not particularly well. And that was before we had returned to each other's lives. Of the four people who were most affected by Chase's death, three of them would be together to nurse each other through the memories. But I suspected that the fourth would choose to deal with it alone. This saddened me not only for what she was losing, but for what I was losing as well.

I was in the back office paying some bills when there was a knock on the door. A guy in his early twenties poked his head in.

"I was looking for Richard Penders and the girl up front told me to come back here."

"Richard's not here. I'm his son. Can I help you?"

"You were Chase Penders's brother?"

"Yeah, I'm Chase's brother. Who are you?"

"I'm with the *Amber Advisor* and I'm doing a piece about his death ten years ago."

I turned my chair around to face the man, shaking my head at the same time. "You guys really don't have enough to write about, do you?"

The reporter held up his hands. He clutched a notebook in one of them. I was sure that real reporters were using a more high-tech method for note taking by now but, as I was well aware, real reporters didn't work for the *Amber Advisor*.

"It isn't the Middle East Summit, I know, but as

far as local stories go, this one definitely deserves a follow-up. Your father is a prominent area merchant. Your brother was something of a local celebrity. And this kind of suicide doesn't exactly happen in our sleepy little town every day."

I edged forward in my seat. "What did you say?"

"I don't mean to be flip. It's just that this was an unusual event in Amber."

"Why did you say 'suicide'?"

The reporter's face blanked. "I'm sorry; this must still be difficult for you."

"Suicide? My brother's car drove off the Pine River Bridge. He was drunk, if you're looking for an angle. But he sure as hell didn't kill himself."

The reporter took a step backward and seemed uncomfortable now. He clearly hadn't been doing this for very long. "I don't know; maybe I jumped to conclusions here. It's just that there were always those questions in the paper and then when I talked to someone in the police department, he told me that there was no way that someone could have driven off the Pine River Bridge without planning to do so – even if they were very drunk."

"There were questions in the paper?" I'd of course never read the coverage of the accident. "That flyer you work for actually asked questions about my brother's intent? You mean the *Advisor* led our neighbors in this 'sleepy little town' to speculate over their morning coffee about the death of the son of one of their 'prominent merchants?' And you want to bring this speculation back to the surface after all this time?"

I had raised my voice and I could tell that the

reporter was concerned about the fact that he'd closed the door behind him when he entered.

"If you see it a different way, I'll be happy to include your thoughts in the piece," he said.

While my mind reeled, I had enough composure to realize that I had come to a crossroads. I could leap out of my chair, physically accost a person for the first time in my life, and toss his fourth-rate newspaper out on the street after him. Or I could realize that this guy probably had no idea what he was getting into when he walked through the door.

I sat back, turned the chair around, and said, "Get out of here."

"Is there a good time for me to reach Richard Penders?"

I nearly turned around then, but willed myself to keep my composure. "Trust me, there's no good time to talk to my father about this."

The reporter left without another word and I tried to force our encounter out of my mind. I paid some bills, went up front to help Jenna with a rush, and talked to Carl about what I wanted in the back-to-school display. But it was ludicrous to think that I could operate as though nothing had happened after that reporter attacked my brother's memory in such a way.

I thought about going to my aunt's house to read the articles written in the *Advisor* about Chase's death. Did they openly speculate about him killing himself? Or did they simply make a few allusions to allow their readers to speculate for themselves? The entire thing seemed so utterly absurd to me. There was no chance that the Chase I knew would ever commit suicide, no matter what might have been going on in his life. That anyone could even suggest it was so deeply unsettling that I wanted to lash out.

As the afternoon stretched on, I found myself returning to the reporter's mention of a conversation with someone in the police department. I'd never read the police report on the accident, either. Now it seemed like it was essential that I do so, if for no other reason than to prove to myself that the reporter had led the cop he interviewed to his theory about what happened that night. I left the store a few minutes later.

An hour and a half after that, I sat with the same man the reporter had spoken to, a copy of the police report between us. The report essentially listed details: approximate time of the accident, angle of impact, recovery efforts. Any speculation on the page seemed to be limited to estimating the speed of Chase's car when it hit the curb, took off the top portion of the concrete embankment, and went into the river.

"I'm obviously not a professional at reading these things," I said, "but I'm having a tough time understanding how this information leads you to the absolute conclusion that my brother intended to kill himself."

"I never said 'absolute,' and that reporter is lying if he said I did. What I said was that the information in the report suggested that it was probable."

I pointed down to the paper. "What are you seeing that I'm not seeing?"

The officer turned the page toward him for a moment and then turned it back to me, pointing to several places. "How fast he was going and the way the skid marks veer off so sharply toward the lowest part of the embankment."

"He was drunk."

"That's in the report also. But this trajectory is not consistent with someone losing control of his vehicle. It's not even consistent with someone veering out of the way of a potential collision. He was going very, very fast and then suddenly made a direct line across the opposing lanes and off the bridge."

I glanced down at the paper and then trained my eyes on the officer. "So you're saying my brother committed suicide."

"I didn't know your brother, Mr. Penders."

"*I* knew my brother. There is no chance he would have killed himself."

"If you believe that, then that's really all that's important, isn't it?"

But of course, it wasn't. For ten years I'd been living with my grief, living with the loss of the Chase that was still to be, living with my sense of culpability in the accident. And now someone was attempting to alter the vision for me, to tell me that not only my perspective on this event, but the very understanding I had of my brother, was skewed. I had no idea what to do with this. My body physically rejected this new information. But as it was doing so, I found myself making subtle adjustments, allowing this speculation to present itself as a possibility.

And in so doing turn my world upside down.

I needed to talk to someone about this and it certainly couldn't be my parents. I got in the car and headed for Lenox.

CHAPTER TWENTY-THREE

Louder and Clearer All the Time

"Bro, it is all a pack of shit," Chase said when he saw me walk into the bar.

Shanahan's was on the other side of the bridge, frequented primarily by underage drinkers. I drove past it during my first trip back to Amber, a little more than a year after Chase died. By then, someone had converted it into a day spa after the cops finally busted the bar's owners. But on this night, it was concussive music, unsmiling patrons, and a young man sitting at a table by himself, wielding his beer bottle like a gavel.

"What's a pack of shit?" I said as I approached.

"It *all* is," Chase said, slamming his bottle down and causing an eruption of beer to spatter the tabletop.

This was clearly not his first drink. Perhaps not even his first bar. The only obvious indication one ever had that Chase was drunk was the intensity in his eyes. While the expressions of most people glazed over as they became inebriated, Chase's became fiercer, more laserlike. And his gaze was burning hotter tonight than I'd ever seen it before.

He'd called me an hour before and told me to meet him here. Shanahan's meant that Iris wouldn't be there and I assumed that at least a couple of his lacrosse teammates would be around.

"Why are you sitting here by yourself?" I said.

He pointed to a redheaded woman sitting at the bar. "Because Ms. Proud Nipples wouldn't come to join me, if you can believe that."

I looked over at the woman talking to the bartender and then cast a sideways glance at Chase. "Where are the Upchuck Brothers?"

"Last time I saw them they were drooling on each other and learning to count to three."

"You're done with your lacrosse posse?"

"I'm done with my posse. I'm done with lacrosse. Done."

"It'll be different in college."

"Whatever you say, Bro. What are you drinking?"

I went to the bar to get a beer for me and another one for Chase. When I turned back toward our table, he was scanning the crowd and laughing, though I couldn't see what he was laughing at. He took a huge pull from the bottle when I handed it to him.

"They're infants," he said.

"Who are?"

"The Upchuck Brothers, as you so aptly named them."

"I could have told you that."

"Mewling little babies."

"Coulda told you that, too."

He put his beer down and leaned toward me. "I guess some of us take longer to catch up, huh?" There was even more wattage in his stare tonight than usual when he was wasted. I'd been noticing some changes since the late winter, but tonight seemed to mark a quantum jump.

"Vance couldn't make it tonight."

"Who's Vance?"

"A really good friend of mine."

"A really good friend who I've never met?"

"Your specific densities don't match, Bro."

"Am I heavier or lighter?"

"Not the point." He looked off toward the crowd again and started bobbing his head to the omnipresent Nirvana song. I took a drink from my beer and watched the redhead hug and kiss a man who she'd obviously been waiting for.

"Where's Iris tonight?" I asked.

His gaze snapped back toward me and he finished his beer before speaking. "Playing with her Barbie dolls, I think."

"You mean she wasn't up for an evening of sophisticated entertainment such as this?"

"Whatever. Get me another beer."

"Your legs aren't working?"

He threw both palms on the table and stood up, walking away, saying, "Asshole." He took a few steps toward the bar and then turned back to me. "She isn't everything you think she is, you know," he said, leaning down toward me.

"What are you talking about?"

"You fucking idolize her. You think I don't know that? She's become the standard by which all women must be measured in your eyes."

This observation stunned me and I tried to deflect it. "I think the woman you love is great. I highly approve. Most brothers would see that as a good thing."

He sat back down without getting his drink. "It would be a good thing if it were anywhere near the truth."

"Maybe we should talk about this some other time."

"This is a good time to talk about it."

"What are we talking about? I'm a little lost on that point."

"I want to shatter your illusions, Bro. Illusions are always a bad thing. Iris is about as far from perfection as a leper is from being a supermodel."

"That explains why you've been dating her for nearly a year."

"*Was* dating her for nearly a year."

"You broke up with her again?"

He pulled back from his chair and moved quickly toward the bar. He came back with a beer for both of us, though the one I'd been drinking was less than half empty.

"She doesn't know it yet."

"Are you trying it out on me first?"

He laughed. "Yeah, that's what I'm doing."

"Do you want my advice?"

He took a long drink. "I don't think so."

"Sleep it off, Chase. Sleep it off for a couple of days if you have to. Sleep it off in a rubber room if you have to. You don't want to split up with Iris."

"Who are you, fucking Cupid? Iris is no different from everyone and everything on this planet, Bro. She's weak, she's deluded, and she's seriously screwed up. This is the way the machine works. When we're young, we think we're going somewhere, but we're really on a huge conveyor belt being fed into the machine. It grinds us up and molds us into McPeople – except for the ones who just get exiled to Zombieville."

"Do you hear anything that you're saying?"

"Loud and clear, Bro. Louder and clearer all the time."

He got up to go back to the bar, even though his own bottle still had beer in it. Something in his movements suggested to me for the first time that there might be something other than beer running through his system. I knew that Chase had played with drugs before. We'd even smoked pot together a couple of times. Now I wondered if he was experimenting with something new. I told myself to talk to him about it in the morning (or the afternoon, assuming he was going to need a little extra time to recover from this evening).

"She cheats," he said behind me as he returned. I turned toward him quickly, but he continued to his seat.

"She cheated on you?"

"She cheats," he said definitively.

"Are you telling me that she's gotten involved with someone else?"

"I'm telling you that she cheats at the game."

"What game?"

Chase leaned toward me. I now knew definitively that there was something in his eyes other than alcohol. "The game of life, Bro."

"What did you do, listen to too many Jim Morrison

records today? Are you saying that Iris has another boyfriend?"

"Who the fuck knows? I'm done."

"You're just gonna walk away from Iris."

"I've already walked away."

"This makes sense to you?"

"Welcome to the machine, Bro."

"What the hell is with you lately? Slurred rants, paranoid speeches, irrational accusations. Where have you gone?"

"I'm right here, Bro."

"I don't think so. Why'd you even call me to meet you here?"

"I thought we'd party like it's 1999."

"Well, I'm having a great time so far."

"Then leave if you don't like it." He finished the beer in one of his bottles and slammed it on the table. "I don't need you, either."

I stood up to go. I wanted to hit him. "I hope you're gonna get over whatever this shit is that you're doing in the near future."

He took a long drink on the next bottle and said to me, "I'm working on it."

"Work faster," I said as I turned away.

"Knew I could count on you, Bro," he said, calling out into the thrashing guitars. I nearly turned heel and grabbed him by the shoulders, reminding him that he had always been able to count on me, that there had never been a single day when I wouldn't have given him everything I had, and that I would never accept his trivializing this. But then I reminded myself how wasted he was and how disturbed he'd made me, and I knew nothing good would come of it.

On the drive home, I replayed the conversation in my head a dozen times, trying to figure out if there was substance in anything he'd said. It wasn't the first time he'd been this obtuse, but it was the first time I hadn't been able to smack him out of it. I rehearsed the talk I'd have with him the next afternoon, when I'd let him know that he'd gone too far.

That, too, had always worked in the past.

• • •

It was something like playing a game of telephone with myself. For two hours, I reran, in sequence, my conversation with the reporter, my conversation with the police officer, and the final one I had with Chase. Each time I did so, the dialogue would change subtly, filling in a line that I'd forgotten or chose now subconsciously to add to offer a better explanation.

No music, no muffins, and no coffee. Just two hours of insistent memory.

Why was I suddenly so willing to consider the possibility that Chase had killed himself? If it made any sense at all, why couldn't I have at least conceived the thought before today? Did this explain everything or simply allow me to deflect some of my own sense of culpability?

And if it was in any way conceivable that Chase could have intended to kill himself that night, *how* was it conceivable? How could he possibly have been so close to a decision like that without my having any notion? And why would he ever think that a decision like that made sense when he could have gotten his frustrations out in any number of ways with me?

It was late afternoon when I arrived in Lenox. I drove directly to the Ensemble and offered no more than an impolite wave to the guy at the front desk and a half smile to Iris' friend Melanie as I walked to Iris' office. There were three people in there with her when I arrived. She looked up and her expression offered a combination of surprise and disappointment. I can only imagine what my own expression suggested.

"I have to talk to you," I said.

"I'll need a few minutes," she said, nodding toward the others in the office.

"It would be really good if we could do this now."

Her brow furrowed and, for a moment, I thought she was going to ask me to leave. But then she rose up from her desk and excused herself, telling the others to continue the meeting without her. She walked up to me and then past me and we went outside.

"There was actually some important stuff going on in there," she said as we walked the grounds toward the theater.

"Did you ever think about the possibility that Chase might have killed himself?" I said abruptly.

She stopped and turned toward me, her face folding in on itself. "Tell me you're not doing this."

"Somebody came into the store today."

"Tell me you're not revising history in an effort to turn me around."

"Somebody came into the store today."

"Who came into the store today?"

"A reporter for the *Advisor*. He was looking for my father. He was doing a follow-up story on the tenth anniversary of Chase's suicide."

"That's just ridiculous. Why would you take somebody like that seriously for even a second?"

"I didn't take him seriously at all. Until he mentioned something about the police report. I went down to the station myself and talked to a cop about it. There are things in the report that are inconsistent with an accident."

"That's bullshit," she said as she walked away from me and toward the barn.

"It's speculation."

"Which is just another word for bullshit. Some guy comes by and whispers the word 'suicide' and you're willing to completely change everything you know about the most alive person I've ever met?"

"I screamed at the guy. I threw him out of the store. I was borderline disrespectful to the cop. But I couldn't stop thinking back to that last night and wondering if I was just too close to see the signs. They say that kind of thing happens all the time."

"There were no signs," Iris said as she threw open one of the barn doors and walked backstage. She found a chair, swung it around, and straddled it. "Is this really how you react when you're backed into a corner, Hugh?"

"What are you talking about?" I said, finding another chair and facing her.

"You think you're losing me so you concoct some speculation to blacken my memory."

"You think I'm making this up?"

"I think you're using it. Give me a break, Hugh. We would have known."

"How would we have known? You're not willing to

allow for one second that we might have been so caught up in what we believed Chase to be that we couldn't see what he was becoming?"

"I considered it, I rejected it. Instantaneously, because it is beneath serious consideration. Why the hell can't you do the same?"

Iris' facial muscles were taut and her body language was obscene. As it turned out, I didn't want to see every one of her expressions. I considered the very real possibility that this could be our last conversation.

"What do you remember about Chase's eyes?"

Iris' shoulders relaxed slightly. For the first time since we started speaking, she didn't respond immediately.

"His eyes were the most beautiful part of him. The only vulnerable part."

"Did they seem different toward the end?"

"I have no idea what you're talking about."

"You told me yourself that you had a huge argument with him that day. What were his eyes like?"

She closed her eyes and shook her head. "Chase could always get angry. You know that."

"But did you see something in his eyes that day? Maybe something you'd been seeing more frequently over the preceding months?"

"I don't think so."

I leaned forward in my chair. "What kinds of drugs was Chase taking?"

Iris' gaze flicked up at me. "Other than alcohol, none that I know of."

"Well even I know he was doing more than that. I

know he smoked some pot, but I'm thinking there might have been something that would have made him edgier. Coke?"

"Why?"

"Do you think it's possible?"

"Anything is possible. But why?"

"If he tried it, he would have liked it. You have to admit, it would be the kind of drug that Chase could get excited about."

Iris put her forehead on the back of the chair. "He was snapping more and it was taking him longer to recover from it." She lifted her head up and, for the first time that afternoon, she didn't seem furious at me. "I was afraid to tell him about the baby. I didn't mention this to you earlier, but it actually took me three days to get up the nerve to break the news to him."

I didn't say anything right away. When I did, my voice was weak. "What was the last thing he said to you that afternoon?"

Iris put her head back down on the chair for maybe a half a minute before she finally looked up at me again. "Just before he got in the car, he said, 'this isn't the way this is gonna go.' Then he just backed out of the driveway. He shouted something else to me, but I couldn't make it out."

Again, I didn't say anything. I wanted to give Iris time to process this conversation. I needed some time myself.

"Did you know he failed the lacrosse tryouts at Dartmouth?" she said.

"He didn't tell me that."

"He found out a few days before he died. I can't believe he didn't say anything to you. It was probably the first time in his life he didn't get what he wanted."

"It might have been."

She shook her head sharply. "No one kills himself because he didn't make the lacrosse team, Hugh."

"Or because his girlfriend tells him that she's pregnant and wants to keep the baby. Or because his brother refuses to sympathize with his suddenly paranoid worldview. Or because he started using way more of a recreational drug than he should be using."

"You don't really believe that Chase committed suicide, do you?"

I looked into Iris' eyes. I saw her the way he must have seen her hundreds of times over their year together. And in that moment, the vision of the brother I'd always known reflected back to me.

"It wasn't Chase," I said.

Iris reached out for my hand, placed it on the back on the chair, and laid her forehead down on it. We stayed that way for several minutes.

"I have no interest in going back into that meeting," she said.

"I'll make you dinner."

"I'm not sure I have any interest in eating, either."

"Let's go to the farmers' market. We'll shop for dinner, even if we don't eat dinner. It'll give us something to do."

She leaned her cheek against my hand. "I'm incredibly tired all of a sudden." She half smiled. "I was actually getting a lot done before you showed up."

We sleepwalked through the farmers' market, buying much too much to eat, even if we had the appetite to eat at all. It was the first time in more than a month that Iris and I made our way through this market without her arm at some point looping around mine. It was hard to know what this meant. Both of us had had Chase's death foisted upon us again today. And in some ways, it was like it was happening for the first time. Regardless of what we believed happened that night, we were forced to rethink it, to see Chase differently if only to try on the possibility that he might have been someone other than who we believed him to be.

In the end, we ate little and talked less. We drank a bottle of wine and opened a second all the while keeping the conversation to such a cursory level that an observer might consider us casual companions or a couple that had been together too long and had already said everything they were going to say. This was the second time in a row that Iris and I had been like this together and my first thought was that the reasons for it were vastly different on the two occasions. But then I realized that of course they weren't at all, that perhaps the only thing that could put silence between us had done so in a definitive way. Though the wine had relaxed me, for the first time all day, the sense of relaxation in itself made me feel uncomfortable. At the point at which the only reasonable thing to do was to move in some direction, the simple act of staying still was upsetting.

We'd moved to the couch. Iris had her feet tucked up under her legs and she leaned against the arm opposite from me. We drank more wine and talked idly. Finally, I decided that I needed to break away from this.

"I should get going," I said, standing.

"You're not staying?" she said, her voice cracking slightly.

I was surprised that she asked. "I hadn't thought about it."

"You've had a lot to drink. It's late for you to be driving back to Amber. Stay."

"Are you sure? I can handle the drive back."

"It's okay." She held me with her eyes. She was the only person I'd ever known who could do that. Not even Chase could do that. "I want you to."

I nodded. "I think I'm going to go to bed, then. It's been a full day."

She pulled her feet out from under her and stretched out on the couch. "I'm going to stay up a little longer and finish this glass. I'll see you in the morning."

"Good night," I said and turned toward the room I'd come to think of as mine but never would again.

"Anything's possible, Hugh," she said as I walked away. I turned back to her. "Anything's possible," she said again.

"Is it?"

"I think it might be."

I wasn't sure what else to say. I wasn't sure there was anything I could say. Something told me that she wasn't expecting a response. I turned and went to bed.

I didn't think I'd fall asleep as easily as I did. And I have no idea how long I'd been asleep when Iris slid into bed beside me. I turned to her and she kissed my forehead.

"Just hold me, okay?" she said.

I moved my arms around her and she nuzzled her head under my chin.

"Is this all right for you?" she asked.

"Of course it is." She moved her head a little further down my chest and stayed that way until I fell asleep.

When I awoke, the morning light had just begun to filter into the room. Iris was facing away from me, but my arms were still around her. Her profile in sleep was as soft and undisturbed as any I'd ever seen and I wished for the power to will it that way for all time. No matter what Iris had gone to sleep thinking, she had found something during the night to give her spirit some rest.

I didn't want to awaken her, though I knew, regardless of the hour, that I wouldn't be getting back to sleep myself. I placed a delicate kiss on her T-shirted shoulder and moved my arm out from under her. As I did, she stirred and reached her arm out to touch my leg. I put my hand over hers and she brought it back to her lips to kiss it and then wrap it back around herself. I thought she wanted me to go back to sleep with her and I settled my body next to hers. But when I did, she turned to me, our faces no more than an inch apart. Her eyes were wide open, but dreamy, and I wasn't entirely sure she was actually awake until she pulled my head toward her and kissed me deeply. She pulled back ever so slightly and kissed me again.

Nothing else mattered at this point – not anything or anyone between us. I knew right at that moment that it was impossible for me not to respond to her. That there would never be a time in my life when I wouldn't want her instantly if she showed any sign of wanting me.

My head was swimming. Desire on so many different levels filled me to the point where I felt I could drown the entire room with my longing. And when Iris propped herself up on one arm, caressed my face, and looked at me as though she was seeing me for the very first time, I lost all sense of control.

I had never before abandoned myself so completely. My senses expanded into a previously unmarked range as every touch, every sound, every sight impressed itself upon me with a bracing newness. And with every moment that passed – every moment in which this didn't end – I found myself surrendering more and more completely to the wonder of it. I'd imagined making love to Iris on numerous occasions, but I didn't have the sensual vocabulary to envision it this way. In every fantasy I'd ever had of us, she had gifted me with herself. I'd never conceived of what it could be like if she was actually giving herself to me, until now.

For a long time afterward – it might have been hours – we lay in bed kissing, stroking each other's hair. I certainly wasn't anxious to let her go, to let this moment go, though for the very first time when I was with her in any way, I didn't worry that this was a temporary thing. In the moments before we started making love, I saw that I wasn't going to have to think that way again.

"Can you stay?" she asked.

"I can definitely stay."

"What about the store?"

"There's an excellent chance it'll be there when I get back. What about the Ensemble?"

"They rely on me too much. They'll have to take care of themselves for the day."

She smiled and kissed me on the nose, then pulled me closer and kissed me softly on the neck.

"It doesn't matter how this started. Right, Hugh?"

"I think it might. But the thing that really matters is that it started at all."

She lay her face down on my chest. "I'm never going to forget him, you know."

"I wouldn't let you. I couldn't let you."

She pulled back to look at my face, studying it, imprinting it. "It's us now," she said.

"It's us."

CHAPTER TWENTY-FOUR
A Test of Some Sort

The next day I drove directly from Lenox to the store, not wanting to leave Iris a second earlier than I had to. She made me a thermos of coffee even though she knew I was going to go to see my "girl-friend" at the diner in Enfield along the way. As I drove, I listened to the new Marc Cohn album, a classic James Taylor record, and then a playlist I'd made of some of my favorite acoustic artists. It was a singer/songwriter kind of morning.

Jenna had already arrived for her shift when I got to the store.

"You made it," she said when she saw me.

"Was there some question about that?"

"You sounded like you weren't sure you were going to be in today when I spoke to you yesterday."

"I did? I think I said I would unquestionably be in today."

"Yeah, but you didn't sound like it." She smiled at me. To the best of my knowledge, she had no idea where I had been the past two days or why, but she seemed to have concluded that it had something to do with my personal satisfaction.

"Everything go okay here?" I asked.

"Yeah, of course. Monster day yesterday. But we just bore up."

"I owe you one."

"What you owe me is time and a half. I'm going to have a ton of overtime this week. But I'll forget about it if you tell me why you look like you're in such a good mood."

I laughed. "Overtime is fine."

"Too bad. Howard Crest called a few minutes ago. Asked that you call him when you got in."

I went to the back room and called Howard's office.

"Pat Maple has come through," he said when he came to the phone.

"Come through with another counteroffer?"

"Come through with your precise asking price. He went for the whole thing. I guess his daughter liked Amber very much and, while he was a little dubious about the last month's sales figures, he was also very impressed."

I felt slightly disoriented by this news. I'd begun to believe over the past few weeks that Maple would in fact ultimately make an acceptable offer, but I'd also come to understand that negotiating was a sport to him, one he played with the avidity of a semipro golfer. I expected that we'd get to the point where we were arguing hundreds of dollars before he finally forced me to concede. Of course, the first thought that crossed my mind was that we'd underpriced the store, though I knew that wasn't the case at all. If anything, Maple was willing to pay slightly above market value.

"What do we do now?" I asked.

"We make a deal. I assume this is where you need to turn it over to your father. I'd like to set up some time to talk to him and your mother this afternoon. Should I give him a call?"

"No, I'd like to do it. He's gonna be thrilled. I think. I mean, I think he'll probably be a little sad that this is the beginning of the end, but he's going to be happy with the deal we got."

"It's a great deal, Hugh."

"I know it is. Thanks."

"You had a lot to do with it. Between what you put into the store and how you held out for the best price. You did a great job for Richard and I'm sure he appreciates it."

I guessed that he did appreciate it, though I had no real way of knowing. We'd hardly talked about the process of the sale, even when he came into the store to see the changes I'd made.

"You'll set something up for this afternoon, then?" Howard asked.

"Yeah, I'll set it up. I'll call you back. Thanks again, Howard."

"You're welcome. I'm glad I could do it for Richard."

I hung up the phone and then started to dial home. I stopped, realizing that this was news I should deliver in person. I walked to the front of the store. Jenna was ringing up a sale and I helped the next customer in line and another after that.

"I have to head out again," I said when there was no one left at the counter.

"Is this a test of some sort?"

"It is, and you're doing fabulously," I said as I walked away.

The sidewalks of Russet Avenue were already active even though it was before noon. A small child weaved around pedestrians while his mother struggled to keep up. A gaggle of teenagers gathered outside of Bean There, Done That listening to hip-hop and pretending to be "street," a gesture that would have seemed humorously incongruous if I hadn't known it to be enacted in some form by every generation of homegrowns to come before them. A tourist couple in their late forties held hands and swung arms while moving from shop to shop. I'd been back in Amber for more than four months and had seen all of these things before. But for so many reasons I saw them with new eyes today. I saw the interconnectedness and the continuity and, even though I once believed that I would never use the term in association with the town I grew up in, I saw the evolution.

I looked back at the store. Continuity and evolution. Would Pat Maple continue to call the place Amber Cards, Gifts, and Stationery or would he change it to something more clever?

By the time I got to the car, I'd already made up my mind. In all likelihood, I'd made it up weeks ago without realizing it.

When I arrived at the house, my parents were sitting on the back deck with my Aunt Rita. I'd only seen her a few times since my Memorial Day meltdown and every instance had been very uncomfortable. Today, though, I walked directly over to her and kissed her on the cheek before saying to my parents, "I need you for a minute." We sat at the dining room table and my mother asked me if I wanted coffee, which I'd had more than enough of at that point.

"The buyer has come up to our number," I said.

My father took a deep breath and nodded slowly. My mother said, "That's great" wanly.

"I don't want you to take it." Both of them turned to look at me. I shut my eyes and gave myself a moment before continuing. "I want it. I'm here now and, completely without intending to, I've kind of gotten attached to the place. It's supposed to stay in the family."

My mother reached out and took my hand. My father took another deep breath.

"Howard Crest wants to meet with you this afternoon to finalize the deal. I'd like to call him and tell him that we're taking it off the market if that's okay with you. There's enough money in the store for all of us."

My father looked at me carefully. I imagined that he was recalibrating, though it's entirely possible he was gauging my sincerity.

"You're the boss," he said. "If you think this is the right decision, tell him."

I called Howard, who seemed relatively unsurprised and only mildly peeved at having lost the commission, and then, after my parents had gone back out to the deck with Rita, I called Iris to give her the news.

"You're doing the right thing," she said.

"God, I hope so. Do you realize what I just committed to doing?"

"You know you're doing the right thing. You don't have to wonder."

"You're right. I do know it. Jeez, a shopkeeper. Can you believe that's what I've turned out to be?"

"As long as you don't develop a paunch and start wearing an apron, I think you'll be okay. Hey, come on up tonight. We should celebrate in person."

"This commute is going to kill me."

She hesitated for a beat and then said, "Yeah, we'll have to think about that."

I sighed. I cradled the phone between my head and my shoulders, imagining that I was nuzzling Iris' face instead. "I think the last couple of days officially qualify as a whirlwind."

"I suppose they do."

"I can't wait to see you tonight."

"Come up now. I'll make some excuse."

"I think Jenna would hunt me down and kill me if I did that to her again."

"I'll wait then."

"I love you," I said quickly, not even understanding how right it felt to say until after the words came out of my mouth.

"I love you, too, Hugh," Iris said without any noticeable hesitation. "I love you, too."

That I was able to go back to the store at all after hearing her say that was the clearest indication yet that I had found my place.

CHAPTER TWENTY-FIVE

Two Locals Pretending to Be Visitors

I decided to find a place to live just over the bridge from Amber in Milton. I needed to be at least that far from settling down in my hometown. Iris came along with me as a realtor showed us a variety of apartments. For the first time in my life, I didn't simply take the first decent place that came along, and by the end of the morning I had three reasonable candidates to consider. Iris and I had lunch at a clam bar overlooking the water as we discussed my options.

"You really want my opinion, right?" she said.

"Of course I want your opinion."

"Take the duplex. It was a good space and I can definitely imagine spending time there. Nice bathtub."

"It did have a nice bathtub. Though realistically, you probably aren't going to be there very often. We're still going to want to have most of our time together in Lenox, right? I mean, Lenox is still exponentially cooler than it is around here, no matter how many handmade mugs I sell at the store."

"That brings me to the other thing I've been

planning to tell you today. Have you ever heard of the Spring Street Theatre Company?"

"I can't say that I have."

"You really didn't get out much when you were here, did you? Spring Street is an experimental theater group that puts on shows about ten minutes away from here. They've been around – getting great notices if you were paying any attention at all – for the past six years. For the past three, they've been trying to convince me to come on board."

"'Come on board' as in leave the Ensemble?"

"It would be a little tough to do both. Anyway, I always told them that I didn't have any interest in coming back to this area – until I agreed to meet with them tomorrow afternoon."

"Do you think you'll get it?"

She tilted her head. "I *know* I'll get it. Did you hear the part about them coming after me for three years?"

I actually felt my eyes tearing. "So you'd be right here."

"That's the idea."

"All the time."

"Tell me you aren't going to get hung up about that."

I tilted my head. "Did you hear the part about my dreaming about you for the past eleven years?"

"I deserved that."

Armed with this new information, we went to look at the duplex a second time. This time, as we walked through the rooms, I imagined how we would use each one. The bathtub took on new meaning. I signed the lease that afternoon.

That night we stayed at an inn just off Russet Avenue. Two locals pretending to be visitors for one more night before coming home. After dinner, we took a long walk and found ourselves at the base of the Pine River Bridge. We walked out onto it and leaned against the wall, looking upon the water.

It was August ninth, the day before the anniversary of Chase's death. I wondered briefly if there would be a piece about it in the *Amber Advisor* tomorrow and then let it go. I wasn't about to start reading that paper now. I'd get my community news elsewhere.

I reached an arm around Iris' shoulders and she leaned her head against mine. Numerous cars passed us by, shuttling between Amber and Milton. I could hear a boat somewhere off in the distance. Down on the beach, a hit song played on the radio and teenagers laughed. But the water was remarkably calm, barely lapping in the August stillness.

Iris turned her head and kissed me on the cheek. I pulled her closer.

Eventually, and without a word, we walked arm in arm back over the bridge.

ABOUT THE AUTHOR

I grew up in the New York area and I've lived there my entire life. I worked in retail and taught high school English before I got my first book contract. I have gotten several additional book contracts since then, which is fortunate because I didn't have the patience to work in retail and, while I quite enjoyed teaching, my approach was a bit too unconventional for most school systems. One school administrator told me that, "there are more important things than being a dynamic teacher." Since I couldn't name any of those things (at least in the context of school), I figured I didn't have a long-term future in the profession. Hence, I became a writer, where I believe people appreciate a certain level of dynamism.

My first several book deals were for nonfiction books. Though I started with nonfiction, I have always loved fiction and I have always wanted to write it. I've always had a particular affection for love stories. In fact, the very first book-length thing I ever wrote, when I was thirteen, was a love story. Mind you, it was the kind of love story that a thirteen-year-old boy would write, but it was a love story nonetheless. I have a deep passion for writing about relationships – family relationships, working relationships, friendships, and, of course, romantic relationships – and I can only truly explore this by writing fiction. My novels have given me a way to voice the millions of things running through my head.

My wife and kids are the center of my life. My wife is the inspiration for all of my love stories and my children enthrall me, challenge me, and keep me moving. One of the primary reasons I wrote my first novel, *When You Went Away* was that I wanted to write about being a father. Aside from my family, I have a few other burning passions. I'm a pop culture junkie with an especially strong interest in music, I love fine food (as well as any restaurant shaped like a hot dog), and I read far too many sports blogs for my own good.

"Michael Baron" is a pseudonym. This isn't because I'm in the Witness Protection Program, or anything of that sort. I'm writing these novels "undercover" because they're not entirely compatible with the nonfiction books I write and I didn't want to confuse readers. We're all different people sometimes, right? I just decided to give my alter ego another name.

My next novel is called *The Journey Home*. It's a love story, too, naturally. It follows three people going through three different types of emotional battles.

Joseph, a man in his late thirties, awakens disoriented and uneasy in a place he doesn't recognize. Several people are near him when he opens his eyes, all strangers. All of them seem perfectly friendly, but none of them can explain to him where he is or how he got there. They offer him a delicious meal and pleasant conversation in a beautifully decorated room. This would be a very nice experience if not for one thing: Joseph doesn't know where he is, and he has no way to contact his wife, who he is sure is worried sick over him. Thanking the people for their hospitality, he leaves to make his way back home. The only problem is that whatever happened to him has stripped him of most of his memories. He knows he needs to get back to his wife, but he doesn't know how to find her. He sets out on a journey to find his home with no sense of where he's going and only the precious, indelible vision of the woman he loves to guide him.

Antoinette is an elderly woman in an assisted living facility. She's spent the last six years there since her husband died, and most of those years have been happy. She enjoys the company of others in her situation, and her son comes to visit often. But in recent months, she's had a tougher and tougher time leaving her room. Her friends seem different to her and the world seems increasingly confusing. She spends an escalating amount of time in her head. There, her body and mind haven't betrayed her. There, she's a young newlywed with a husband who dotes on her and an entire life of dreams to live. There, she is truly home.

Warren, Antoinette's son, is a man in his early forties going through the toughest year of his life. His marriage ended, he lost his job, and in the past few months, his mother has gone from hale to increasingly hazy. Having trouble finding work, he spends more and more time by his mother's bedside. But her lack of lucidity both frustrates and frightens him. With far too much time on his hands, he decides to try to recreate his memories of home by attempting to cook his mother's greatest dishes using the rudimentary appliances available in her room. He finds the challenge surprisingly rewarding, especially because the only time he feels his mother is truly with him anymore is when she is eating the meals he prepares for her.

Joseph, Antoinette, and Warren are three people on different searches for home. How they find it, and how they connect with one another at this critical stage in each of their lives, is the heart of the story I tell in *The Journey Home*.

The novel goes on sale May 11, 2010. Check www.michaelbaronbooks.com in the early spring for a preview of it.